A BLACKGUARDS ANTHOLOGY

BRIGANDS

BRIGANDS: A Blackguards Anthology
Outland Entertainment | www.outlandentertainment.com
Founder/Creative Director: Jeremy D. Mohler
Editor-in-Chief: Alana Joli Abbott
Publisher: Melanie R. Meadors
Senior Editor: Gwendolyn Nix

Stories originally published in *Blackguards*, edited by J.M. Martin, Ragnarok Publications, 2015.
New edition curated and edited by Melanie R. Meadors.

Published by Outland Entertainment
5601 NW 25th Street
Topeka KS, 66618

Paperback: 978-1-9476-5939-1
EPUB: 978-1-947659-55-1
MOBI: 978-1-947659-59-9
PDF-Merchant: 978-1-947659-41-4
Worldwide Rights
Created in the United States of America

Editor: Melanie R. Meadors
Cover Illustration: Daniel Rempel
Interior Illustrations: Oksana Dmitrienko, Orion Zangara, & David Alvarez
Cover Design & Interior Layout: STK•Kreations

CONTENTS

IRINDAI

Bradley P. Beaulieu

CEDA FOUND BRAMA by the river.

She watched from within a stand of cattails, where she was hunkered low, cool river water lapping at her ankles.

Brama was playing in the water with a dozen other gutter wrens—playing!—apparently without a care in the world after he'd nicked her purse. She felt the anger roiling inside her like a pot boiling over. He'd probably come straight here to brag to his friends, show them what he'd done and challenge them to do the same, then demand tribute like some paltry lord of mud and fleas.

The lot of them were playing skipjack along the Haddah's muddy banks. One by one, boys and girls would run to the lip of the bank and leap onto a grimy piece of canvas pulled taut as a skin drum by seven or eight of the older children, who would then launch them into the air. They would flail their arms and legs mid-flight, screaming or yelling, before splashing like stones into the Haddah, water spraying like diamonds in the dry, desert air.

Her lips curling in disgust, Çeda watched as Brama was launched in turn. He barked like a jackal and flew through the air to crash into the water, arms and legs spread wide. After, he waded back to the canvas and relieved one of the others so they could make a run of their own—the same pattern he'd followed every other time he'd jumped into the river.

When he reaches dry ground, Çeda told herself.

Moving with a pace that would keep her position concealed, Çeda pulled out a locket on a silver chain from inside her dress. She pried the locket open, its two halves spreading like wings to reveal a dried white petal with a tip of palest blue. After taking the petal out, she clipped the locket closed and placed the fragile petal beneath her tongue. Spit filled her mouth. A shiver ran down her frame as the flavor of spices filled her. Mace and rosemary and a hint of jasmine and other things she didn't have words for.

The petal had been stolen from the adichara, a forbidden tree that bloomed only once every six weeks under the light of the twin moons. When gathered on such nights, they were imbued with breathtaking power. Part of her hated to use even one of the petals on Brama, but her anger over what he'd done was more than strong enough to smother any distaste.

As the effects of the petal spread, granting a barely contained verve to her limbs, she stuffed the locket back inside her dress and scanned the river. Colors were sharper now. She could *hear* more as well, not just the children in the river but the very breath and rattle of the city. It took effort in the early moments of imbibing the petals to concentrate, but she was used to doing so, and she focused her attention on those near and around Brama. A clutch of children were playing downriver, some trying to spear fish, others wading and laughing or splashing one another. Most likely they wouldn't interfere. There was one who gave her pause, though, a dark-skinned Kundhunese boy with bright blue eyes. He stood apart from the others, and seemed to be watching Brama and the children with almost as much interest as Çeda. She would swear she'd seen him before, but just then she couldn't remember where or when it might have been.

She worked at the memory, scratching at it, but like a stubborn sliver it only sank deeper in her mind, and soon Brama was handing over his section of the canvas to a girl with a lopsided grin.

The moment Brama gained the bank, Çeda parted the cattails and marched forward. "Brama!"

He turned, staring at her with a frown. Her identity was still hidden by her white turban and veil, so he wouldn't know who she was, but she could see in his eyes that he recognized the flowing blue dress she'd been wearing early that morning.

He scanned the area to see if anyone else was with her. "What do you want?"

"There's something you stole from me," she called, "and I mean to have it back." Çeda didn't know Brama well. He was a boy who liked to traipse about Sharakhai's west end, bullying some, shying away from others. He was an opportunist, and a right good lock-slip if rumor was true. She might have gone all her days and never thought twice about Brama but that morning he'd stolen something from her: a purse she was meant to deliver for Osman—a shade, as it was known in Sharakhai. It was as simple a task as Osman had ever given her—hardly more than a prance across the city—and she'd bungled it, but she'd be damned by Bakhi's bright hammer before she'd let a boy like Brama get away with it.

Brama's eyes flicked to the children in the river. They were watching, not yet approaching, but it wouldn't take long before they came to back him up. The moment his eyes were off her, Çeda drew her shinai, her curved wooden practice sword, from its holder at her belt. She didn't like walking around Sharakhai with a real sword—girls of fifteen, even tall as she was, attracted notice bearing steel—but few enough spent more than a passing glance at a girl wearing a shinai, especially in the west end where children practicing the dance of blades could be found on any street, alley, or open space one cared to look.

Brama's eyes were only for Çeda now. He looked her up and down, perhaps truly noticing her frame for the first time. She was tall. She had more muscle than he might have noticed earlier. She was holding a sword with a cozy grip—a *lover's* grip, the bladewrights called it, the kind that revealed just how intimate a sword and its master were with one another—and with the magic of the petal now running through her veins, Çeda was itching to use it.

Brama's friends were stepping out of the water now, and it seemed to lend him some confidence, for he swelled, not unlike like a man who'd had one too many glasses of araq might do, or the dirt dogs in the pits often did when they knew they were outmatched. He stuffed one hand down his still-dripping pants and pulled out a short but well-edged knife. "I've got nothing of yours"—he smiled as the other children fanned around and behind Çeda—"so why don't you run off before that pretty dress of yours is stained red?"

Brama had muscle as well, but it was the rangy sort, the kind that felt good to thump with the edge of a wooden sword. "You stole a purse, cut from my belt as I strode through the spice market."

"A thousand and one gutter wrens wander that market day and night. Any one of them might have stolen your purse."

"Ah, but it *wasn't* any one of them." She lifted the point of her shinai and thrust it toward Brama's chest. "The nick from your little knife wasn't nearly as clean as you thought, Brama Junayd'ava. I saw you running like a whipped dog down the aisles, and I *know* you heard me calling."

She thought he might be put off by the use of his familial name, but instead he squinted, as if he recognized her voice and was trying to place it. "I don't know who it might have been, but you're a fool if you think it was me."

The circle around her was closing in now, some with river stones clutched in their scrawny hands.

Çeda took a half-step closer to Brama and dropped into a fighting stance. "This is your last warning, Brama."

Brama merely smiled. "You should have run while you had the chance."

Çeda didn't wait any longer. She charged.

She brought her sword swiftly down against his hastily raised defenses. The wooden blade cracked against his forearms, then his rib cage, then his knee, not enough to break bones—though she could easily have done so—but certainly more than enough to send him crumpling to the ground.

Other children rushed in, but if her time in the pits had taught her anything it was how to maintain distance with the enemy, even many at once. She rushed past Brama's fallen form, twisting and striking a girl every bit as tall as Brama across the face. Another came barreling after, but Çeda dropped and snapped her leg out, catching the girl and sending her tumbling off the bank and into the river.

The ones with the stones loosed them at Çeda as two more boys braved the range of her sword. One stone struck a glancing blow against her shoulder, another squarely against her ribs, but the effects of the petal deadened the pain. Four quick strokes of her shinai and the boys were howling away, shaking pain from their knuckles and wrists.

She was alone now. None would come near. Even the boy with a rock the size of a lemon held in each hand remained still as a statue, the fear plain on his face.

Brama lay at her feet, cringing.

"Where's the purse?" she asked him.

His face grew hard, his teeth gritting away the pain. "I don't have it."

"That wasn't what I asked you, Brama." She grabbed a hunk of his hair—"I said, *where is it?*"—and slammed his head onto the ground. *"I don't have it!"*

Somehow, his refusal made her go calm as the night's cool winds. She let go of Brama's hair and stood, staring down at him with her shinai still held easily in her right hand. "When are you going to learn, Brama?" She raised her sword, ready to give him something to think about before asking him the question again, but she stopped when she heard a piercing whistle from somewhere along the riverbank. She turned, but not before laying the tip of her sword over Brama's kidney, a warning for him to lay still.

A man with broad shoulders wearing laced sandals and a striped kaftan was standing near the edge of the river, staring at her. The sun glinted brightly off the lapping waves behind him, so she didn't at first recognize him—and why by the gods' sweet breath would he be here in any case?—but soon she *did* recognize him.

Osman.

The very man she should have delivered the purse to this morning. But she'd failed to, because of fucking Brama.

She was half-tempted to bring the sword down across Brama's thieving little face. He flinched, perhaps sensing the brewing sandstorm within her, and that made her want to strike him even more, but she stayed her hand when Osman shouted, "Enough!" in that clipped tone of his. And then she saw what he was holding in his right hand, dangling like a fish.

The purse. *Her* purse, a small, red leather affair, the very one he'd asked her to pick up and bring to him at the pits.

"Come," he said, and turned to walk along the dusty bank of the Haddah.

Çeda had no difficulty understanding the command was meant for her, so she left, but not before kicking dirt over Brama's quivering form. As she walked toward Osman, she realized the Kundhunese boy with the blue eyes was watching her intently.

Not Osman. Just her.

"Hurry up," Osman said.

She refused to run, but she quickened her pace until they were walking side by side. She glanced back only once, and found that the Kundhunese boy had vanished. She scanned the river, curious, but she was so intrigued by Osman's sudden possession of the purse that she gave up after too long. How by the hot desert winds could Osman have learned not only that the purse had been stolen but that Brama had been the one to do it? And after learning it, how could he have found it so quickly?

The answer came to her in little time, but before she could say anything about it, Osman said, "Why confront him?"

"What?"

"Why challenge Brama while he's playing with his friends along the Haddah?"

Çeda shrugged. "Because I had to know where the purse was."

"You knew where the purse was."

"No, I didn't."

"Yes, you did. I saw you watching him as he hid his clothes and other things in the cattails. You could have taken it while they were splashing in the river."

He'd seen that, had he?

She tried on a dozen different answers, finally settling on, "He deserved it."

"A lot of boys like Brama deserve a beating, but you can't be the one to give it to them, Çeda. People in Sharakhai have long memories, and sooner or later, the city will end up the master and you the student, and I'll wager you're old enough to know how that lesson is likely to end."

"I thought you'd be grateful. It was *your* package I was protecting."

"First of all, the only time you'll find me grateful is when none of my packages go missing. Second, that was no favor you were doling out back there. Not for me, at least. You were nursing a wound to your precious ego. You fight in the pits, and if I'm being truthful, I've rarely seen someone with the gifts the gods themselves surely bestowed upon you, but don't think that trading blows with dirt dogs helps you at all in the shadows of this streets. You're shrewd enough when you put your mind to it, but you'd better start putting that quality to better use before I find that you've been given back to the desert."

Given back to the desert, a phrase that spoke of bleaching bones, of men and women forgotten and swallowed by the Shangazi's ever-shifting dunes... She was so angry she wasn't sure she wouldn't still give *Brama* back to the desert. "You do this to everyone, then?" Çeda asked as a wagon train rumbled past. "Set them up to see how they dance?"

Osman shrugged, not even looking at her. "I had to know what you'd do if you lost a package."

"And?"

"And what?"

"How did I do?"

"Poorly. It's the *package* I care about, Çeda. Let *me* decide who needs a beating and who doesn't. Understand?"

"Yes," she said, forcing the words through her teeth.

Osman stopped walking. They were on a small lane now, a well-worn one used by laborers to head to and from Sharakhai's sandy northern harbor. Men and women passed them by like the Haddah's waters around a pair of particularly surly stones. "Tell me you understand."

She stared into his eyes, ready to answer with another petulant, barking reply, but she stopped herself. This was no small thing he was asking. Osman might have been a pit fighter once, but he was a shademan now. He'd taken Çeda under his wing, but he would toss her to the dogs if he thought he couldn't trust her.

She'd been foolish with Brama. She saw that now. She needed to watch out for Osman's interests, not her own.

"I understand," she said.

"Good, because there's something a bit more delicate we need to discuss."

"*That* doesn't sound good."

Osman shared a wolfish smile and bowed his head like old Ibrahim the storyteller did before beginning a tale. "How astute of you to notice."

They passed out of an alley and onto the cobblestone quay surrounding the northern harbor. A line of eight sandships were just setting sail, their long runners carrying them swiftly over the amber sand toward the gap between the two tall lighthouses. "Two days ago," Osman continued, leading them over a meandering rank of stones that marked the dry yard around the lighthouse, "a man named Kadir came to me. He works for someone who is… Well, let's just say she's a powerful woman, indeed. Kadir's visit was regarding a package that was delivered to him three weeks ago, a package delivered by you." Osman came to a stop short of the door to the lighthouse. Beside them lay an old mint garden that years ago had been well-tended but had since lain forgotten, so that its contents looked little better than a forgotten pile of brown twine. "He also claimed that the contents had been poisoned."

Suddenly Çeda felt very, very small. She felt under scrutiny, like a dung beetle crawling over open sand. "Poisoned?"

"Poisoned."

"By whom?"

"That's the question, isn't it?"

"Well, it wasn't me! I remember that package. It was delivered as you asked!"

"I know."

"I didn't tamper with it."

"I *know*, or we'd be having a very different conversation."

"Is this why you had Brama steal the purse?"

Osman shrugged while waggling his head. "I would've done it sooner or later in any case." Çeda opened her mouth to deny it again, but Osman held up his hand. "Kadir wishes to speak with you. He believes he knows who sent the poison but would like to find more clues from you if there are any to be found."

Çeda stared deeper into his eyes. "And you told him I would? What if he thinks I *did* poison the contents of that drop? What kind of fool would I be to simply walk into his arms?"

"As I said, he works for a powerful woman. If *she* thought you had done so, she wouldn't have done me the courtesy of having Kadir ask to see you. He and I spoke for a long while. I believe him, Çeda, and you will be under my protection. You'll be safe enough, though I'm sure it won't be a comfortable conversation to have."

"And if I refuse?"

"Then Kadir doesn't get what he wants and life goes on."

"With no repercussions?"

A sad simulacrum of a smile broke over Osman's broad, handsome face. "None for *you*."

"But you would lose her as a client."

Osman shrugged. "In all likelihood, yes."

Çeda took a deep breath. She didn't like this. She didn't like this one bit. She knew her shading with Osman would get her into some trouble sooner or later. She just hadn't expected it would come from Osman himself. Still, she owed him much, and if this Kadir really *did* wish to speak of clues to the one who'd meddled with the package, then it seemed safe enough.

"Very well," she said.

Osman nodded, then put his fingers to his mouth and whistled sharply. From the lighthouse came Tariq, a boy Çeda had grown up with and who had joined the ranks of Osman's shades around the same time she had.

"Bring them," Osman said.

Tariq nodded and ran off down the quay before ducking into an alley. Soon, a rich, covered araba led by two horses was trundling up the quay toward the lighthouse with Tariq hanging off the back. When it had swung around the sandy circle in the yard and pulled to a stop, Tariq dropped and ran back to stand in the lighthouse doorway. Osman swung the araba's door open and Çeda climbed inside.

"Come see me when it's done," Osman said, closing the door and knocking twice upon it. "I'll stay until you return."

As the araba pulled away, Çeda saw someone standing on one of the empty piers in the sandy harbor—again, the Kundhunese boy with the bright blue eyes. He had a scar running near his left eye and down his cheek. Strange she hadn't noticed it before, as it was long and puckered in places. The pier and the boy were both lost from sight as the araba passed a long train of wagons loaded high with cord after cord of bright white wood. When the wagons had passed, the boy had vanished.

———

IN A TASTEFULLY appointed room Çeda sat in a high-backed chair of ornamented silk. The estate to which she'd been brought had surely been built centuries before. She could tell not only from the architecture, but from the paintings on the walls, the vases on their pedestals, the occasional weapon. They were elegant, all, but had clearly been born of another age.

Ashwandi, the beautiful, dark-skinned woman who'd led Çeda here, lingered in the arched doorway, staring at Çeda with a strange mixture of piqued curiosity and contempt. "Kadir will see you soon," she said, and bowed her head. No sooner had she left than a slender man strode in scanning a sheet of vellum. As he swept behind an opulent desk, Çeda stood and bowed her head, for this was surely Kadir. He ignored her, his eyes continuing to scan the tightly scripted words while holding his free hand at attention behind his back, the pose a steward would often take while standing at attention. His brow creased as he finished. Only then did he set the vellum down and regard Çeda with a critical eye. He hid a frown as he looked her up and down. "Osman sent you?"

This was a man who took his position seriously, Çeda could tell, and it made her even more curious to know who his master was. "He did."

"It was you who delivered the package, then?"

"Yes."

"Your name?"

"Çedamihn Ahyanesh'ala."

He nodded as if knowing her full name had incrementally raised her status in his eyes. "Osman was to tell you our purpose here. Did he?"

"To a degree."

A frown appeared on Kadir's refined face. "Tell me what he told you."

"That the package I delivered had been poisoned. That it had been discovered early. That I was not under suspicion."

"The first two I'll grant you. As to the third"—he swept the back of his damask coat as he sat—"let us see what we see."

Çeda bowed her head once more. "Forgive me if I overstep my bounds, *hajib*, but my master informed me that I had come to help you find the one responsible. Was he mistaken?"

Kadir gave her the smallest of smiles, but it seemed genuine. "He said you were direct."

"My mother always told me there's little point in waiting when a hare needs chasing."

"There are times when that's *exactly* what needs to happen, but your mother was wise. So tell me, do you remember much from that day?"

Çeda shrugged noncommittally. "I remember it, but I recall nothing amiss. I came for the box at Osman's estate at nightfall as he'd bid me and, after the moons had set and full night had come, brought it to the drop near Blackfire Gate."

"Did you notice anyone following you?"

"No, or I would have delayed and come the following night."

"Did you notice anything strange in the days before the drop?"

Her mind went immediately to the strange, blue-eyed Kundhuni boy. She remembered where she'd seen him now: at the spice market just before Brama had nicked her purse. She'd seen him again at the river, and then a short while ago at the harbor. How many times had she missed him? Had he been watching her for days? Weeks?

"What is it?" Kadir asked, his dark eyes suddenly sharper.

"It's nothing to do with your package. At least, I don't think it is."

"Just tell me."

"There was a boy. I've seen him several times these past few days."

"He's been following you?"

Çeda shrugged. "I suppose he must be, though I have no idea why. I've never seen him before."

Kadir seemed eminently unfazed by this. "He's a head and a half shorter than I, with closely shorn hair and cinnamon skin and bright blue eyes. And a scar"—he ran his little finger down the left side of his face, neatly bisecting the skin between temple and eye—"just here."

"Yes... But how did you know?"

Kadir pursed his lips, staring down at the desk for a moment, then he took in Çeda anew, his eyes roaming her form, lingering not only on her face, but on her hands as well, which were riddled with small scars from her time in the pits. She balled them into fists and held them by her side, which only seemed to draw *more* notice to her scars. Kadir smiled a patronizing smile. "The boy you saw is from Kundhun, and the poison on the package you delivered was not meant for my mistress, but for Ashwandi, the woman who delivered you to this room."

Ashwandi had been beautiful, but she had also eyed Çeda uncharitably from the moment she'd stepped foot in the estate.

"Why?" Çeda asked.

"My mistress hosts social gatherings, and in these she has had cause to take on protégés. In her wisdom she took on a Kundhuni girl named Kesaea, a princess of the thousand tribes. Years ago Kesaea had come to Sharakhai with her sister, Ashwandi, and here the two of them have remained, vying for my mistress's attentions. When Kesaea left our employ, there was some, shall we say, *acrimony* over the decision."

"She was forced from her lofty position...."

Kadir nodded, granting her the smallest of smiles. "Just so, and as you might have guessed, Ashwandi took her place. You can see how this might cause more than a little bit of strife between siblings, especially one—may my mistress forgive me for saying it—as petulant as Kesaea."

"But to poison her sister?"

Kadir shrugged. "Surely you've heard worse stories in the smoke houses of Sharakhai."

In point of fact, she doubted Kadir would be caught dead in a Sharakhani smoke house. "Yes, but from a princess?"

"Are not those who wield the scepter most likely to strike?"

"I suppose," Çeda said. "What of the boy, though? Why should I still find him following me?"

She left unsaid the fact that the boy had likely been following her for quite some time, a logical conclusion that bothered her greatly, not merely for the fact that she hadn't noticed him before today, but because she hadn't a clue as to the reason behind it. If she was to become the unwitting accomplice to this boy's plans, why follow her at all and give Çeda the chance to become wise to it? And for that matter, how would they even have known that she would be the one to take the shade from Osman that night?

Kadir steepled his fingers. "Now that *does* give me pause. Have you no guesses of your own?"

Çeda shrugged. "None," she said. And then the strangest thing happened. A moth flew into Çeda's field of vision. Where it had come from she had no idea, but it landed on her sleeve and sat there, wings fanning slowly. The top of its wings were the deepest indigo Çeda had ever seen, with a bright orange mark akin to a candle flame.

Çeda was loath to shoo it away, partly from the sheer surprise of it, but more so from the realization that Kadir was staring at it as if it were about to burst into flame and take Çeda with it.

"They're called irindai," Kadir said with an ease that made Çeda's hackles rise. "Some call them cressetwings, and consider what just happened to you a sign of bountiful luck."

"Others call them gallows moths," she replied, "and consider them a sign of imminent death."

"Well," he said, standing and motioning to the way out, "as with so much in the world, surely the truth lies somewhere in between." As Çeda stood, the moth flew away and was lost in the fronds of a potted fern in the corner. "I'll only ask you for one more thing. Keep an eye out for the boy. I would not recommend you approach him—there's no telling how Kesaea might have armed him—but if you discover that he's following you still, return to this estate and inform me."

Çeda might have granted Kadir that if she'd been planning to leave this matter alone, but she refused to allow some Kundhuni child to use her as his plaything. She couldn't tell that to Kadir, though, not leastwise because it might get back to Osman, so she nodded obediently and said, "Very well."

As Kadir joined her at the arched entryway, he held his hands out to her, as if asking her to dance. It was such an odd and unexpected gesture that she complied, lifting her hands for him to take. He did, then considered her with deliberate care. "They say scars have tales to tell, each and every one." He examined not just her hands, but her face, her body, her legs, even her ankles, which somehow made her feel unclothed. "What would yours tell, Çedamihn Ahyanesh'ala?"

"Tales are not told for free in this city, Kadir."

"If it's money you want"—he leaned toward her—"you need but whisper the price."

"The price of their telling is something you cannot afford."

Kadir laughed. "You'd do well not to underestimate the size of my mistress's purse, nor her will to follow a scent once she's gotten wind of it."

"My tales are my own," she said finally.

For a moment, Kadir seemed prepared to press her, but then he raised her hands and bowed his head. "Forgive my boldness. A habit most foul, formed from years of service."

"Think nothing of it," Çeda said, though somehow she doubted he would heed her words. No matter what he said, his eyes were too hungry, too expectant of submission.

Kadir raised his hand high and motioned to Ashwandi, who stood further down the hall. She came and put on a smile, motioning for Çeda to follow her. Her smile vanished, however, when the moth fluttered out from Kadir's office to flitter around the two of them. As they walked toward the entrance to the estate, the moth continued to dog them, and it became clear it was fluttering around Çeda much more than it was Ashwandi, a thing that appeared to please the Kundhunese woman not at all.

———•———

THE CLACK FROM the strike of wooden swords filled the desert air, strangely deadened by the surrounding dunes where Çeda and Djaga, her mentor in the pits, fought. The sun shined off Djaga's dark, sweat-glistened skin. The sand shushed as they glided over it, a strangely calming sound amid the rattle of armor and the thud of their shinai as they engaged then backed away.

Çeda fought with abandon, hoping to impress, pushing herself more than she had in a long while. When Djaga retreated, Çeda closed the gap. When Djaga pressed, Çeda countered as soon as the flurry had ended. When Djaga ran backward, Çeda flew after her. She thought she'd timed her advance perfectly, but just as she was lunging forward, Djaga did too, beating aside her blade and sending a nasty swipe of her shinai over Çeda's thigh.

Çeda, thinking Djaga was going to press her advantage, slid quickly away as the pain blossomed, but instead the tall black woman stopped and stood, chest heaving, her face a sneer of disgust. "You invite me to spar," she said in her thick accent, "and this is what I get? You're not watching *me*."

Çeda opened her mouth to explain, to apologize, but Djaga abruptly turned away and headed for the skiff they'd sailed from Sharakhai's western harbor. Together they stepped over the runners of the sandship to reach the ship's side, at which point Djaga leaned over the gunwales, popped the top of their keg of water, and filled a gourd cup. "You're distracted," Djaga said after downing the cup and running the back of her hand over her mouth. She refilled the cup and held it out to Çeda. "Why?"

There was no sense denying it. She *was* distracted. Çeda took the offered cup and drank down the sun-warmed water.

"Tell me it's a man," Djaga went on, a smile making her full lips go crooked. "Tell me you've decide to take your Emre to bed. He's disappointed you, hasn't he? I knew he would. Haven't I always said it? No man as gorgeous as that knows his the way to the promised land."

Çeda laughed. She shared a home with Emre, and he meant much to her, but not *that*—they'd probably never be *that*—yet it never stopped Djaga from digging her elbow into Çeda's ribs every chance she got.

"Come, come. What's there to think about? He's a pretty boy... You're a pretty girl...."

"Well, if you must know," Çeda said, desperate to move the conversation beyond these particular grounds, "it *is* about a boy."

"A boy..."

"A Kundhunese boy."

"Well, well, well... A *Kundhunese* boy..." Djaga laughed, then bowed and flourished her arms to the desert around them. "Then know this, oh Çeda the White Wolf. The desert is wide enough to hold your secrets. Tell us both your tale if you're bold enough."

Where to begin? In the days that had followed her meeting with Kadir, she would swear by her mother's own blood that she'd seen the blue-eyed boy a half-dozen times, but always from the corner of her eye, and when she looked with a keener gaze, she found someone or some*thing* else entirely—boys or even girls with similarly dark skin, lighter-skinned boys wearing dark clothes, even the simple swaying of shadows beneath the odd acacia tree. Once she'd even spotted him in the ceaseless flow of traffic along the Trough, but when she'd caught up to him and spun him around, it had been a Sharakani boy with closely shorn hair who looked nothing like the bright-eyed Kundhuni. The mother had shoved Çeda away, and Çeda had retreated under the angry glares of those standing nearby, wondering what was happening to her.

She'd spent the next few days wallowing in confusion and fear while a small voice whispered from the corners of her mind—*you're going mad, mad, mad, you're going mad*. A fury born from her own helplessness grew hotter by the day, but what good was fury when there was nothing to direct it against? She needed a change. If the winds were blowing across one's bow, one didn't simply stay the course. One turned and tacked until the safety of port was reached once more.

And who better to help steer this strange ship than Djaga? So much of this tale seemed to be wrapped up in the people of Kundhun, their customs, their norms, and Djaga was Kundhunese. She might see any number of things Çeda was blind to. So she told Djaga her tale. She spoke of the shade, of Osman's confession after, of her visit with Kadir. She spent a long while describing the strange blue-eyed boy with the cinnamon skin, hoping Djaga would somehow know him, but there was no glimmer of recognition in her eyes.

When she was done, she asked Djaga, "Have you heard of her, this princess Kesaea?"

"No," Djaga replied, "but you know what we say in the backlands. If you stand our princesses shoulder to shoulder with our princes, they will drown the land like blades of grass."

It was true. There were as many kings and queens as there were hills in Kundhun, or so it seemed. "It was so strange," Çeda went on. "When I left, a moth followed me."

Djaga smiled her broad smile. "Good luck be upon you."

But Çeda shrugged. "So they say, but it was a gallows moth."

"An irindai? A cressetwing?"

"Yes. Why are you making that face?"

"Who did you say is this Kadir's mistress?"

"I don't know her name."

Djaga's expression pinched from one of confusion to outright worry. "There's a woman who hides in the shadows of the lords of Sharakhai. A drug lord named Rümayesh. Have you heard the name?"

"I've heard it," Çeda lied.

"I can tell you don't know enough, girl. Not nearly enough. Those who enter her house pay fistfuls of rahl to do so—not the silver of the southern quarter, mind you, nor the coppers of the west end, but *gold*. Her clientele is exclusive. The lords and ladies of Goldenhill, those of noble blood, rich merchants and caravan masters that paid their way into Rümayesh's good graces, and in return she feeds them dreams, dreams she summons and all share in. Dreams taken from the souls that Rümayesh herself selects."

"Why did you think of Rümayesh?"

Djaga's face was staring out at the sand, her eyes distant, but now she pulled her gaze away and stared down at Çeda. "Because she uses irindai, Çeda."

Someone, somewhere danced over Çeda's grave. "How can you know?"

"There was one in the pits, the one who taught me, as I teach you. Her name was Meliz, and one day she disappeared. For weeks we searched for her. She was found at the bottom of a dry well two months later, still alive, the crushed body of a cressetwing stuffed inside her mouth. We nursed her back to health, but she was never the same. Her mind was gone. She remembered nothing—not why she'd been taken, nor who had taken her. She couldn't even remember who she was, not much of it, anyway. It had all been taken from her. She did whisper a name, though, over and over."

"Rümayesh."

"Just so. She took her own life two months later"—Djaga drew her thumb across her neck—"a crimson smile, drawn with her favorite sword." She looked Çeda up and down, as if she were in danger even here in the desert. "You say he's left you alone, this Kadir?"

"As near as I can tell."

"Then make no mistake, girl, the gods of the desert have shined upon you!" Djaga took the gourd cup from Çeda and set it onto the keg. In unspoken agreement, they strode away from the skiff and began loosening their limbs. "Watch yourself in the coming days, and when we return to Sharakhai, go to Bakhi's temple. Give him a kind word and show him a bit of silver, or gold if you can manage, lest he take it all back."

Çeda had no intention of doing so—she didn't believe in filling the coffers of the temples any more than she believed in giving the Kings of Sharakhai their due respect—but she nodded just the same.

"Now come!" Djaga brought her blade quickly down across Çeda's defenses, a swing Çeda beat aside easily. "You've a bout in two weeks." She swung again, and again Çeda blocked it, backing up this time.

"People know we spar with one another, girl." A third strike came, a thing Djaga put her entire body into, but Çeda skipped back, avoiding the blow. "I'll not have it said the White Wolf is some poor imitation of the Lion of Kundhun!"

Çeda retreated and bowed, arms and shinai swept back while her eyes were fixed on Djaga. "Very well," she said, and leapt in for more.

———•———

THE DAYS PASSED quickly after that.

Çeda saw the boy again—several times, in fact, and now she was sure it was him. Once, she was sure she'd caught him in the Well, the quarter of the city that held Osman's pits. She chased after him, yelling for him to stop, and when she'd turned the corner, her hand nearly upon him, she found the alley ahead empty. He'd disappeared. At a whistle, she'd looked up and found the boy staring down at her with a wide smile. And then he was off, leaving an awkward knot inside her she couldn't untie, a knot composed of anger and impotence and foolishness.

He must be a warlock, she decided—it ran thick in some areas of Kundhun—and now for some reason he was toying with her. She vowed to find him, but for the life of her she had no idea how she would manage it. Every time she tried to lie in wait, she ended up spending hours with nothing to show for it.

She lost herself in preparations for her upcoming bout instead—running in the mornings, sparring in the afternoons, lifting Djaga's stone weights beneath the pier in the western harbor in the evenings. Osman had told her she'd have no shading work until after her day in the pits, a thing that had bothered her at first, but given that there was nothing she could do about it she threw herself into her training with an abandon she hadn't felt in months.

Djaga noticed, and even allowed a grudging nod once or twice for how focused Çeda's technique had become. "Good, girl. Good," she had said. "Now keep your rage bottled up. Release it in the pits, not before. It's not so hard as you might think."

Çeda thought she understood, but as the day for her bout approached, she found herself becoming more and more nervous. It wasn't because of her opponent—some Mirean swordmaster who'd had some success in Sharakhai's pits before. It was because she couldn't shake the feeling that she was being watched, that something was about to happen.

And it wasn't from the Kundhunese boy this time. She kept seeing men or women watching her. When she looked, however, they seemed to be doing completely innocent things, apparently oblivious to her presence. The experience so unnerved her that, despite her plans in the desert, she took Djaga's advice and went to Bakhi's temple and dropped three golden coins into the alms basket at the foot of Bakhi's altar. She thought to speak with the priestess, but she looked down at Çeda's kneeling form so uncharitably that Çeda just stood and left the temple.

It was all in her mind, she decided. Her mind and her worries were conspiring to play tricks on her. Yet slowly, the strange calmness she'd shown with Djaga began to slip as the day of the bout approached.

"Enough," Djaga said two days before the match. "We've practiced enough. Too much, in fact. There are times when you can overtrain, and I think I've done it with you, girl. Take this time before your match. Stay away from the pits, think of anything but fighting, and you'll return to the pits a new woman."

"And if I don't?"

"Then you'll be no worse off than you are now. You're in your mind too much. Go to your Emre. Fuck him like you should have done long ago. Or take another to your bed. But for the love of the gods, let your sword lay untouched."

Near dusk that evening, as Çeda wended her way through the tents of the bazaars, waving to those who had stuck throughout the dinner hours hoping to catch a final few patrons, she felt someone watching her: a woman who Çeda could tell was thin and lithe, but little more than this, for her head was hidden in a deep cowl, her hands within the long, flowing sleeves. Çeda had no idea who the woman might be, but she wasn't about to lead her toward the home she shared with Emre.

She kept her pace, moving along a narrow street that would head down toward the slums of the Shallows, and when she came to the next corner and turned, she ducked into an elaborate stone archway, the entrance to a boneyard that looked as though it had stood longer than Sharakhai itself.

She glanced over the yard for the telltale glow of wights or wailers—one didn't treat boneyards lightly in the desert—then peered out through the arch from behind a stone pillar marking one of the graves. She saw the form soon enough, a shadow in the deeper darkness. The woman slowed, perhaps realizing she'd lost her quarry. She pulled her cowl off her head and turned this way, then that, then continued down the street.

Çeda hadn't seen her clearly, but she knew it was Ashwandi, the woman who'd led her to speak with Kadir, who'd led her out of the estate when they were done. What by Tulathan's bright eyes would she be doing chasing Çeda through the streets? And why was she doing it so clumsily?

Çeda drew the knife from her belt and followed, padding carefully in time with Ashwandi's footsteps but with broader strides, until she was right behind her. Ashwandi turned, eyes wide as she raised her hands to fend Çeda off, but she was too late. In a blink Çeda had slipped her arm around Ashwandi's neck and pressed the tip of her knife into her back—not enough to draw blood, but certainly enough to make Ashwandi intimately familiar with just how sharp Çeda's blades were kept.

"You might get away with such things east of the Trough," Çeda whispered, "but not here." She pressed the knife deeper, enough to pierce skin, drawing a gasp from Ashwandi. "Here, women like you are as likely to end up on the banks of the Haddah staring sightless into a star-filled sky as they are to make it home again."

"I'm not the one you should be worried about," she rasped.

"No?" Çeda asked, easing her hold on Ashwandi's throat. "Who, then? Your mistress, Rümayesh?"

"I am no *servant* of Rümayesh! I am her love, and she is mine." Her Kundhunese accent was noticeable, but more like a fine bottle of citrus wine than the harsh, home-brewed araq of Djaga's accent.

"She wants me, doesn't she? That's why I'm being followed."

"You begin to understand, yes? But I tell you, you have no idea the sort of trouble you're in."

Çeda shoved Ashwandi away. It was then that Çeda realized that a bandage was wrapped tightly around her left hand. With a pace that spoke of self-consciousness, or even embarrassment, she used her good hand to tug her sleeve back over her bandaged hand, then pulled her cowl back into place. Only when her face was hidden within its depths did she speak once more. "Do you know who Rümayesh is? She has *seen* you, girl. She is *intrigued*... And nothing will draw her attention away now, not until she tires of you."

Çeda felt suddenly exposed and foolish, a fly caught in a very intricate web. "What would she want of *me*?"

"You're a tasty little treat, I'll give you that. She's taken by this girl who shades at night but fights in the pits by light of day." Even in the dying light, Çeda was sure Ashwandi caught her surprised expression. "Yes, she knows of your *other* pursuits with Osman, and now she's taken by the pretty thing that came to her estate, by the White Wolf who sank her fangs into the Malasani brute."

This implied much… That Rümayesh likely knew of Çeda's time with Djaga, her training for her coming bout, her time in the pits, perhaps. Çeda didn't merely feel off-balance; she felt like the world had been tipped upside down, and now the city was crashing down around her. "I came to Kadir to speak of a *package.* That was all."

"You've been set up, girl, as have I."

Çeda closed the distance between them with one long stride. "Make some bloody sense before I rethink how very nice I've been treating you."

"Kadir told you of my sister, Kesaea. For years *she* held the fa-vored position at Rümayesh's side, longer than any other, if the stories I've heard are true. But Rümayesh grew bored of her, as I knew she would, and *I* stepped into her place." Ashwandi shrugged. "Kesaea was angry. With Rümayesh, with me. But after a week of her typical petulance, she returned home to Kundhun, and I hoped that would be the end of it."

"But it wasn't, was it? *She* sent the boy."

"Boys. There are two of them. Twins. And she didn't *send* them. She *summoned* them. Our mother has the blood of witches running through her veins, and Kesaea inherited much of it. Their names are Hidi and Makuo. Hidi is the angry one. He has a scar running down his cheek, a remnant of the one and only time he disobeyed his father, the trickster god, Onondu, our god of vengeance in the savannah lands."

By the desert's endless sand, *twins*… And born of a trickster god. It explained, perhaps, why she'd been unable to do any more than see them from the corner of her eye. They'd been toying with her all along. "But why?" Çeda asked. "What would those boys want with me?"

Ashwandi looked at her as if she were daft. "Don't you see? They were sent by my sister to harm *me*. They've been sent to find a way for me to fall from grace, and in you, they've found it, for if Rümayesh becomes entranced with you…"

"She'll what, forget about you?"

Ashwandi shrugged. "It is her way. There isn't room in her life for more than one obsession."

"You wish to be that? An obsession?"

"You don't know what it's like… It's wondrous when she turns her attention to you, if you don't fight it, that is. To be without it…"

Çeda's head was swimming. "Tell Rümayesh what your sister has done! Surely she'll see that she's being manipulated."

"I have"—Ashwandi turned, as if worried someone was watching— "but it isn't Rümayesh that's being manipulated. It's us. All of us. You, me, Kesaea, even Onondu, which surely pleases her to no end. Don't you see, girl? Rümayesh *enjoys* this, seeing us squabble and fight."

"She acts like a god herself."

Even from within the cowl, Çeda could see Ashwandi's eyes growing intense, and when she spoke once more, her words were very, very soft. "You aren't far from the mark, but there's something you might do."

"Out with it, then."

"The boys, Hidi and Makuo. I know how to bind them."

"And how might you do that?"

The tall Kundhunese woman reached into her robes. "I've already done it." She held out a small fabric pouch for Çeda to take. "Search for them. And when you are near, use this to send them home."

Çeda stared down at the pouch. "What is it?"

Her only response was to take Çeda's hand in hers—the bandaged one—and forcibly press it into her palm.

Staring at the bloody bandages around her left hand, Çeda had a guess as to what was inside. "Why don't *you* do it?"

"Because they're not here for me. They're here for Rümayesh, and now you, and they will avoid me when they can, for the blood of my mother runs through my veins as well." She nodded toward the pouch. "Onondu will listen to this, and so will Hidi and Makuo."

Çeda had heard how cruel the gods of the savannah were. They demanded much for their favors. Blood. Fingers. Limbs. Sometimes the lives of loved ones. How desperate Ashwandi must be to do such a thing just to remain by Rümayesh's side...

No, Çeda realized. This was no fault of Ashwandi, nor even Kesaea, but rather the one they both longed for. How strong the lure of Rümayesh to make them both do this, for surely Kesaea had gone through a similar ritual on her return to Kundhun.

Rümayesh had cast a spell that had utterly bewitched them both, these princesses of Kundhun.

Çeda stuffed the pouch, heavy as a lodestone, into the larger leather bag on her belt. "What do I do?"

"Wear it in their presence. They will listen to you, and they will grant you one favor."

"A *favor*? What am I to do with that? Can I ask them to simply leave?"

"Perhaps, but that would be unwise. They must be turned to Rümayesh now, to make her forget about you. I fear that is the only way for you to survive this."

"And for you to return to her good graces..."

Ashwandi shrugged. "We want what we want, and I've given up much for that to happen." She began stepping away, her eyes still on Çeda. "The twins are drawn to water. You'll find them along the

Haddah, often at dusk or dawn."

And then she turned and was gone, swallowed by the growing darkness over Sharakhai.

———•———

WITH THE EASTERN sky a burnished bronze and the stars still shining in the west, Çeda pulled the black veil across her face and crept along the edge of the Haddah, watching carefully for signs of movement along the riverbank. She had arrived hours ago, hoping to catch the godling twins either in the night or as the sun rose. She still hadn't found them, and soon the city would be waking from its slumber. She didn't wish to be skulking along the river when it did, but the desire to find them was palpable as a canker, and every bit as maddening.

The talk with Ashwandi had so shaken Çeda she hadn't gone home last night, preferring to sleep in a hammock at the rear of Ibrahim the storyteller's tiny mudbrick home. She'd unwrapped the rolled bandage and found Ashwandi's severed finger resting there with a leather cord running through it like some depraved version of thread and needle. She'd held it up to the starry sky, looked at it beneath the light of the moons, Rhia and Tulathan, wondering if she would feel the magic bound to it, or through it that of the twin boys. She'd felt nothing, though, and after a time she'd slipped the cord over her neck and worn the finger like a talisman, which was surely what Ashwandi had meant for her to do.

It rested between her breasts, a thing she was all too conscious of, especially when she walked. It tickled her skin like the unwelcome touch of a man, and she longed to be rid of it, but she couldn't, she knew. Not until this was all over.

She parted the reeds and padded further down the Haddah. She passed beneath a stone bridge, looking carefully along its underside, which the boys might use to hide, but when she found nothing she moved on, heading deeper into the city.

Above her, beyond the banks, a donkey brayed. A woman shouted at it, and the sounds of a millstone came alive, dwindling and then replaced by burble of the river and the rattle of stones as Çeda trekked onward. The sky brightened further. Carts clattered over bridges. Laborers trudged along, lunches bundled in cloth. A boy and a girl, both with wild, kinky hair, headed down to the banks of the Haddah with nets in hand. She even saw one of the rare Qaimiri trading ships rowing toward a pier, her lateen sails up, catching a favorable wind.

But of the twins she saw no sign.

She was just about ready to give up when she saw movement near an old acacia. Half the branches were dead, and the thing looked as though it were about to tip over and fall in the water at any moment. But in the branches still choked with leaves she could see two legs hanging down, swinging back and forth. The skin was the same dark color she remembered, and when she looked harder, she saw movement in the branches above—the second twin, surely, sitting higher than the first.

She took to the damp earth along the edge of the bank to silence her footsteps, then pulled her *kenshar* from its sheath at her belt, whispering a prayer to fickle Bakhi as she did so. Reaching past her mother's silver chain and locket, she slipped Ashwandi's severed finger from around her neck, whipping the leather cord around her hand with one quick snap of her wrist.

She stood twenty paces away now.

As she approached the godling boys, she wondered how vengeful the god Onondu might be. She hoped it wouldn't come to bloodshed, but she'd promised herself that if they wouldn't listen to her commands, she would do whatever she needed to protect herself, even if it meant killing his children. Her identity was her most closely guarded secret, after all—no different than a chest of golden rahl, a chest these boys had tipped over with their mischief, spilling its treasure over the dirt for Rümayesh and Ashwandi and perhaps all of Sharakhai to see.

Ten paces away.

Then five.

The nearest twin faced away from her, looking downriver to the trading ship, which was just mooring, men and women busying themselves about the deck, a few jumping to the pier. She'd grab him first, drag him down and put her knife to his throat, then she'd grip the finger tightly and speak her wish. The moment she took a step forward, though, something snapped beneath her foot.

She glanced down. Gods, a dried branch off the acacia. How could she have missed it?

When she looked up once more, Hidi, the one with the scar, was turned on the branch, looking straight at her with those piercing blue eyes. In a flash he dropped and sprinted up the bank.

Çeda ran after him and was nearly on him, hand outstretched, ready to grab a fistful of his ivory-colored tunic, when something fell on her from behind. She collapsed and rolled instinctively away, coming to a stand with her *kenshar* at the ready, but by the time she did both of the boys were bounding away like a brace of desert hare.

She was up and chasing after them in a flash. "Release me!" she called, gripping Ashwandi's finger tightly. "Do you hear me? I command you to release me!"

But they didn't listen, and soon they were leading a chase into the tight streets of the Knot, a veritable maze of mudbrick that had been built, and then built *upon* so that walkways and homes stretched out and over the street, making Çeda feel all the more watched as men and women and boys stared from the doorways and windows and balconies of their homes.

Çeda sprinted through the streets, wending this way, then that, coming ever closer to reaching the boys. She reached for the nearest of them—her hands even brushed his shoulder—but just then a rangy cat with eyes the very same color of blue as the boys came running out from behind a pile of overturned crates and tripped her. She fell hard onto the dirt as the boys ahead giggled.

She got up again, her shoulders aching in pain, and followed them down the alley they'd sprinted into. When she reached the mouth of the alley, however, she found not a pair of twin boys, but a strikingly beautiful woman wearing a jeweled *abaya* with thread-of-gold embroidery along cuff and collar and hem. She looked every bit as surprised as Çeda—almost as if she too had been following someone through the back-tracked ways of the Knot.

"Could it be?" the woman asked, her voice biting as the desert wind. "The little wren I've been chasing these many weeks?"

Çeda had never seen this woman before—tall, elegant, the air of the aristocracy floating about her like a halo—but her identity could be no clearer than if she'd stated her name from the start.

"I'm no one," she said to Rümayesh.

"Ah, but you are, sweet one." From the billowing sleeve of her right arm a sling dropped into her hand. In a flash she had it spinning over her head, the sound of its blurred passage mingling with Rümayesh's next words. "You certainly are."

Then she released the stone.

Or Çeda *thought* it was a stone.

It flew like a spear for Çeda's chest, and when it struck, a blue powder burst into the cool morning air. She tried not to breathe it, but she'd been startled and took in a lungful of the tainted air. As she spun away its scent and taste invaded her senses—fresh figs mixed with something acrid, like lemons going to rot.

Çeda turned to run, but she'd not gone five strides before the ground tilted up and struck her like a maul. The world swam in her eyes as she managed with great effort to roll over. Blinking to clear her eyes of their sudden tears, she stared up at the blue sky peeking between the shoulders of the encroaching mudbrick homes. In the windows, old women and a smattering of children watched, but when they recognized the woman approaching Çeda, they ducked their heads back inside and shuttered their windows.

Çeda's *kenshar* was gone, fallen in the dusty street two paces away, though it might as well have been two leagues for all her leaden limbs would listen to her. She'd somehow managed to keep Ashwandi's finger, though; its leather cord had surely prevented it from flying away like her knife. Her throat convulsed. Her tongue was numb, but she chanted while gripping the finger as tightly as her rapidly weakening muscles would allow. "Release me, Hidi... Release me, Makuo... release me, Onondu..."

The only answer she received was the vision of the beautiful woman coming to stand over her, staring down with bright eyes and a wicked demon grin.

———•———

ÇEDA WOKE STARING at the ceiling of a dimly lit room.

She was lying on something cold and hard. She tried to sit up, tried to *move* but was unable to. Her legs felt as though the entire world were sitting atop them. Her arms were little better. Even her eyes moved with a strange listlessness, brought on, no doubt, by the powder that had erupted when the sling stone had struck.

The light in the room flickered strangely.

No.

The ceiling itself...

It was covered in some strange cloth, undulating like the fur-covered skin of some curious beast.

No.

Not cloth...

Wings. By the gods who breathe, they were *wings.*

She was lying in a room, and above her, covering the ceiling as far as the lamplight revealed, moths blanketed its surface, their wings folding slowly in and out, flashing their bright cresset flames over and over and over. They did so in concert such that waves appeared to roll across their surface, as if they were not thousands upon thousands of individuals at all, but a collective that together formed some larger, unknowable consciousness. She couldn't take her eyes from them, so hypnotic were they, not even when she heard footsteps approaching, the sound of it strangely deadened.

It was cool here. And humid. She was underground, then, in a cellar, perhaps, or one of the many caverns that could be found beneath the surface of Sharakhai.

The footsteps came nearer. "Do you like them?"

Rümayesh...

Soon the tall woman was standing over Çeda, staring down with an expression not so different from what a caring mother might share with her sick daughter. The urge to reject the very notion that this woman held any similarities whatsoever to Çeda's mother manifested in a lifting of Çeda's arm in an attempt to slap the look away. Her right arm shifted, but no more than this, leaving Çeda to fume as Rümayesh reached down and brushed Çeda's hair from her forehead.

"They're wondrous things," she said, looking up to the ceiling, to the walls around them, every surface awash in a landscape of slowly beating wings. "Do you know what they do?"

Çeda tried to respond, but her mouth and tongue felt thick and rigid, like hardening clay.

Rümayesh went on, apparently unfazed by Çeda's silence. "They are taken by the mouth, eaten, in a manner of speaking, but when one does, she is changed, drawn into the whole of the irindai, drawn into a dream of their, and your, making. Some think they're connected, all of them, anywhere in the world, like threads in a grand weave, though I doubt it goes so far as that. These, though... My lovely brood..." She stopped near the wall and stretched out her forefinger until one of the moths crawled upon it, then walked slowly across the room until she was standing once more at Çeda's side. "*They* are certainly aware of one another, as you will soon see."

"Wuh..." Çeda tried forming words. "Wuh... Wuh..."

Rümayesh stared at the moth as if she hadn't heard Çeda's graceless attempts at speech. "The effects of the powder will wear off in time, certainly soon enough for you to select the irindai you wish to consume"—she flicked her hand and the moth took wing, fluttering in the air for a moment, circling her, then flying back and returning to the very same location it had roosted before crawling onto Rümayesh's outstretched finger—"though if experience has taught me anything, it's the irindai that choose *you*, not the other way around.

"Relax, now. The ritual will start soon. I'd ask that you choose a memory for us to share. My patrons wait years to partake of someone as captivating as you, so choose well. Make the memory dear. I wouldn't want them to leave disappointed." She strode away, heading for the arched entrance to the room. "And I hope you're not thinking of denying me this small request. If you refuse, I'll simply find one on my own, but it's less special for my patrons when I do. The memory is dimmed. More importantly to you, the experience will, I'm afraid, leave your mind ravaged, possibly beyond repair."

When she reached the archway, she stopped and turned until she was staring sidelong at Çeda. "Perhaps the tale of the White Wolf's first fight in the pits. Yes, I think that would please them a great deal. There will be plenty of time for the rest in the coming weeks."

Dear gods, it was true then. It was all true. Rümayesh was going to force her to take one of these moths and relive her past. Like a dream, except her *patrons* would dream them as well. How many? A dozen? Two dozen? They'd witness her trips out to the blooming fields to harvest adichara petals. They'd see how she dried them and used them in service of Osman's shades or her own needs. Either was a high crime in Sharakhai, punishable by death.

But that wasn't the worst part.

She didn't wish to die, but she was horrified by the thought of someone forcibly taking her memories from her. By Tulathan's bright eyes, would she still have them when they were done with her? Or would they rob her memories and leave her some useless husk like Djaga's mentor, Meliz? Would she go to the farther fields not knowing her mother? She couldn't bear it. She'd lost her mother eight years ago, but at least she still had her *memories* of her. At least she'd *know* her when they were reunited in the world beyond.

As a door somewhere boomed shut, she commanded her muscles to move. She felt her legs shift, her arms twitch, but they would do no more than this. She tried over and over and over again, and soon it was bringing on a dull pain that grew with each attempt.

She saw movement to her right and managed to loll her head in that direction. Gods, a *mound* of irindai were rising, pulling away from their brethren. It was vaguely man-shaped, she realized.

Or *boy*-shaped.

As the form came forth, the moths began fluttering away, returning to their previous positions, and a second form began to emerge. Whole flocks of moths peeled away, revealing two boys with dark skin and bright blue eyes, and one of them, Hidi, with his terrible scar running down his cheek.

Hidi glanced to the archway where Rümayesh had recently went. Makuo came straight for Çeda, a gentle smile on his lips. "You are here," he said in a Kundhunese accent so thick Çeda could barely understand him.

"Yuh…" Çeda licked her lips and tried again. "You wuh-wanted me here…"

Hidi came and stood next to Makuo. "Yes, and now you come."

"Buh… But I commanded you. Ashwandi…"

"Yes," said Makuo, "and we are bound. We listened."

"I s-said to release me."

Hidi tilted his head, as if speaking to a child. "And we will obey. We will give you the keys."

"What do you mean?"

"You must release yourself," said Hidi in a sharp tone. "Rümayesh is not so easy to move as that."

"H-how?"

Hidi ignored her, choosing to step around the perimeter of the cellar, while Makuo reached into Çeda's black *thawb* and pulled out her mother's locket.

"Luh-leave that alone!"

"Calm yourself, girl." He pried it open, revealing the two petals Çeda had placed inside. She'd normally have nothing inside, or perhaps one if she was expecting trouble, but she'd started carrying two for the fear that was constantly running through her.

Makuo took them, then whistled two sharp notes. A flurry of cressetwings descended from the ceiling, one of them alighting on

Makuo's outstretched finger, the rest continuing to fly around and above his head. With care, Makuo set the two petals onto the wings of the moth. The petals remained there, as if they'd been a part of the moth from the moment it crawled from its chrysalis. Makuo whistled again, and the moth on his finger flew to join her sistren.

Bit by bit, the swarm retook their positions, but in doing so Çeda completely lost the one with the petals. She searched frantically, but couldn't find it. "Where is it?"

At this they both smiled and spoke in unison, "And what fun would we have by giving you that?" They glanced to the archway, and Hidi began backing away. Moths flew toward him, landing on him, layering his form as if consuming him.

Makuo touched his hand to Çeda's cheek. "Look to the flames," he said while backing away. "Look to the flames and you'll find it." Soon both of them had been consumed by the irindai.

And all was still.

She could hear her own heartbeat, so complete was the silence.

She looked among the irindai, one to the next to the next, trying to find the one to which Makuo had fixed the petals, but it was so bloody dim she couldn't tell if one merely had a bright mark of flame or if it was indeed the one she needed.

While she searched, she worked her muscles—her legs, her arms, her neck, her torso. It was slow in the coming, but she managed to bend her limbs, to regain some sense of normal movement, even if it was slow, even if it felt as though her muscles were made of bright, molten metal.

Just when she was ready to sit up, she heard the door opening, and this time many sets of footsteps approached. Kadir came first, but others followed, men and women dressed in white thawbs or full-length kaftans, and with them came the reek of the sort of tabbaq that would make one high. Some wore *niqabs* or veiled turbans to hide their faces, but most were unadorned, and came holding flutes of golden wine in their hands or stubby glasses filled with araq. Others still held nothing at all, preferring to cross their arms or hold them behind their backs as they stared at the irindai or Rümayesh or Çeda.

In her desperation, Çeda tried to lift herself from the cold slab upon which she lay, but before she could do more than curl her head and shoulders off the slab, Kadir came rushing to her side and pressed her back down. Those gathered watched with jackal eyes, hyena grins, as Kadir leaned in. "Stay where you are until spoken to," he whispered, "and perhaps you'll leave this place whole." Unlike Rümayesh, who was soft velvet, a knife in the dark, Kadir was a cold, bloody hammer, every bit as blunt and every bit as deadly.

She grit her jaw and stared up, not wanting to give Kadir the satisfaction of seeing the fear in her eyes, and that was when she noticed it. Makuo's irindai, slowly fanning its wings almost directly overhead. How could she have missed it earlier? Now that she *had* seen it, though, it was like a bloody great beacon. A fire on the horizon.

With care, praying Kadir wouldn't notice, she averted her gaze and lay still. Kadir did glance up, but then retreated to one corner of the room. From a pedestal he picked up a heavy bronze cymbal and a leather-wrapped rod of the same metal. He ran the rod around the edge of the cymbal, creating a strangely hypnotic sound. The irindai responded immediately, their wings moving at a slower pace in time to the rhythm of the cymbal.

"The festivities are over," Rümayesh said. "I trust you'll enjoy what I've found for you, a rare little bird indeed. A Sharakhani through and through, with mystery upon mystery we can unravel together. Please"—she motioned around her to the walls, to the low ceiling— "choose, and our young maid will follow."

Those gathered began walking about the room, looking up to the ceiling, plucking a single moth from the writhing mass. Çeda tried as well as she could not to stare at the moth with the adichara petals, but she was so worried that someone would take it that she found her eyes flicking there every so often. One of the women noticed. Eyes glazed, she stared up at the ceiling where Çeda's gaze had wandered. Her hand wavered near Çeda's cressetwing, but the gods must have been watching over Çeda, for the woman chose another less than a hand's-breadth away.

One by one, those gathered opened their mouths and placed the moth within, taking great care to prevent harm to the delicate wings. Without exception, their eyes flickered closed as soon as the irindai was taken within them. Their lids opened and closed like the wings of the irindai, then they stood still, watching Çeda or Rümayesh or one another in a half-lidded daze.

Rümayesh strode to Çeda's side.

"Choose," was all she said.

Çeda stared defiantly, as if she were conflicted, as if she might very well do something desperate at any moment. She would take the cressetwing the boys meant for her but, when she did so, she wanted Rümayesh's eyes on *her* and nowhere else. With care, Çeda stood. She felt strangely alone with Rümayesh, even with so many of those gathered staring dazedly at the two of them. With as much speed as she could manage, she grabbed the cressetwing with the petals and stuffed it into her mouth.

She had planned to chew it immediately, to devour it, but the moment the moth's delicate wings touched her tongue, a rush of euphoria welled up from somewhere deep inside. It brought with it a rush of thoughts and memories, all flickering like the surface of a sun-dappled river.

Her mother raising her wooden shinai in the air, waiting for Çeda to do the same.

Running through the dusty streets of Sharakhai with Emre, each with a mound of stolen pistachios cradled in their arms, shells dripping like rain as they sprint along.

Peeking through the parted blankets of a stall in the spice market late at night as Havasham, the handsome son of Athel the carpetmonger, thrusts himself over and over between the legs of Lina, a girl three years Çeda's elder who is not beautiful but has a way of talking with the boys with that sharp tongue of hers that makes them want her.

Çeda felt her consciousness attempt to expand to encompass all of who she was, all she'd experienced. She wondered, even while her mind raged, whether everyone experienced this same thing or if it was to do with the petals she'd also consumed. She could feel it now—the verve the petals granted her, the strength, the awareness.

Through the irindai she could feel others' minds as well: those closest, their eagerness to feel more from Çeda; those beyond, who had done this many times before but hungered for more; and Rümayesh, who was someone different altogether.

Where Rümayesh stood, there were two, not one.

Two minds, sharing the same body. One, a lady of Sharakhai, high-born, a woman who'd lived in her estate in Goldenhill her entire life.

And the other...

A chill rushed down Çeda's frame even as more of the memories jumbled past.

The other was something else. Something Çeda had never seen or experienced before. How could she have? This mind was deep, foreign, and by the gods *old*—not in the way Ibrahim the storyteller was old, nor even in the way the Kings of Sharakhai, who'd seen the passage of centuries four, were old, but in the way the city was old. In the way the desert was old.

This was no human, but some creature of the desert, some vestige of the desert's making, or one of the *ehrekh* that haunted the forgotten corners of the Great Shangazi.

Çeda knew immediately that few others had ever felt this being's presence, for it now awoke in a way it hadn't been moments ago. It grew fearful, if only for the span of a heartbeat, and in the wake of that realization, Rümayesh—or the woman Çeda had *thought* was Rümayesh—strode forward and placed her hand around Çeda's neck, gripping it tightly enough to limit Çeda's breath. She leaned down and stared into Çeda's eyes, imposing her will, sifting through Çeda's memories.

Çeda couldn't allow this.

She couldn't allow Rümayesh to have her way. Çeda would be lost if she did.

This was the gift of the adichara petals that Hidi and Makuo had granted her—the ability to remain above the effects of the irindai, at least to some small degree.

But what to do about Rümayesh?

As more memories were examined, then tossed aside like uncut jewels, Çeda thought desperately for something that might divide these two, something that might give the highborn woman a reason to throw off the chains Rümayesh had placed on her.

She found it moments later. A memory flashed past—of stepping into the blooming fields to cut one of the adichara flowers. It was discarded immediately by Rümayesh, but the woman huddling beneath that greater consciousness, a highborn woman of Sharakhai, flared in anger and indignation. Rümayesh tried to settle on Çeda's first fight in the pits, but Çeda drew her mind back to the twisted trees that grew in a vast ring outside the city's limits. Had Çeda not had the effects of the adichara running through her, she would surely have succumbed to the onslaught Rümayesh was throwing against her defenses, but with the petals she was able to focus on that memory, to share it with all those gathered within the cellar.

She pads along the sand as the twin moons shine brightly above. The adichara's thorned branches sway, limned in moonlight. They click and clack and creak, a symphony of movement in the otherwise still air. Çeda looks among the blooms, which glow softly in the moonlight, a river of stars over an endless sea. She chooses not the widest, nor the brightest, but the bloom that seems to be facing the moons unshrinkingly, then cuts it with a swift stroke of her kenshar, tucking it away in a pouch at her belt.

Çeda had expected anger from the woman Rümayesh controlled. What she hadn't expected was anger from all the others as well. She should have, though. Nearly everyone gathered here would have the blood of Kings running through their veins; they would know every bit as well as Çeda the sort of crime they were witnessing. A woman stealing into the blooming fields to take of the adichara insulted not only the Kings, but all who revered the twisted trees.

They began to mumble and murmur, more and more of their number waking from the dream they shared. At first they stepped forward like boneyard shamblers, but with every moment that passed they seemed to come more alive.

Behind them, the highborn woman Rümayesh controlled railed against her bonds. She was more angry, more aware of herself, than she'd been in years, but she was buoyed by the anger of those around her. Rümayesh's will was still strong, however. She held against the assault, the two of them at a stalemate. Soon, though, the woman's anger would ebb. Soon Rümayesh would regain the control she'd had over this woman for so long.

Çeda had lost track of those around her. She realized with a start that one of the men was holding a *kenshar*. A woman on Çeda's opposite side drew a slim knife of her own. A remnant of Çeda's earlier lethargy still remained, but fear now drove her. She rolled backward, coming to a crouch, waiting for any to approach.

A moment later the man did, the woman right after, but they both gave clumsy swipes of their blades. Çeda leapt over the man, snaking her arm around his neck as she went. She landed and levered him so that he tipped backward, then controlled him, moving him slowly toward the door.

He tried to use his knife to strike at her arm, but she was ready. She released his neck at the last moment and snatched the wrist holding the knife with one hand, closed her other hand around his closed fist, the one wrapped around the weapon. Then she drew his own knife toward his neck. He was so surprised he hardly fought her, and by the time he realized what was happening, it was too late. The knife slipped into his throat like a needle through ripe summer fruit.

For a moment, everyone stared at the blood running hot over Çeda's hands.

They were not only *witnessing* his death; they *felt* it through their shared bond. As his heart slowed and finally stopped, the irindai burst from the walls and from the ceiling. The air became thick with them, fluttering, touching skin, batting eyes, becoming caught in hair.

Çeda's mind burned in the thoughts and the emotions of all those gathered. They were of one mind, now, sharing what they'd known, what they hoped to be, what they feared in the deepest recesses of their minds. It was too much, a flood that consumed them all, one by one.

Çeda screamed, a single note added to the cacophony of screams filling this small space, then fell beneath the weight of their collected dreams.

———•———

ÇEDA OPENED HER eyes, finding a dark-skinned boy with bright blue eyes staring at her.

"The sun shining bright, girl," Makuo said. "Time you return to it, let it see your face before it forget."

"What?" Çeda sat up slowly, her mind still lost in the land of dreams. She remembered who she was now—her name, her purpose here—but it seemed like an age and a day since she'd fallen to the weight of the minds around her.

Across the floor of the cellar, bodies lay everywhere like leaves tossed by the wind. Layer upon layer of dead moths covered their forms. Hidi stood by a sarcophagus, staring into its depths. It was what Çeda had been lying upon, she realized. The lid had been removed and now lay cracked and broken to one side.

Çeda stood and took one step toward the sarcophagus, but Makuo stopped her. "This isn't for you," the boy said.

Within the sarcophagus, she saw the crown of a head, wiry black hair, two twisted horns sweeping back from the forehead.

She thought of pressing Makuo. They'd won, she knew. They'd beaten Rümayesh with her help, and until now they'd considered her their ally, but that could change at any moment.

Steer you well wide of the will of the gods, old Ibrahim had always said after finishing one of his tragic stories. She'd heard dozens of those stories, and none of them ended happily. She'd always thought it a trick of Ibrahim's storytelling, to end them so, but now she wasn't so sure.

"What of Ashwandi?" Çeda asked.

Hidi looked up from whatever it was that had him transfixed, his scar puckering as he bared his teeth. "She free now. Her sister's wish was always for Ashwandi to leave the *ehrekh's* side, to return to the grasslands."

An *ehrekh*, then…

Rümayesh was an *ehrekh*, a twisted yet powerful experiment of the god, Goezhen. Few remained in the desert, but those that did were powerful indeed.

"Is she alive?"

"Oh, yes," the boys said in unison, their eyes full of glee.

"What will you do with her?" Çeda asked, tilting her head toward the sarcophagus.

At this they frowned. Hidi returned his gaze to Rümayesh's sleeping form, while Makuo took her by the shoulders and led her away. "The sun shining bright," he said. "Time you return to it."

Çeda let herself be led from the cellar, but her tread was heavy. Rümayesh may have tricked Çeda, may have wanted to steal her memories, but something didn't feel right about leaving her to these godling boys.

Makuo led her up a set of winding stairs and at last to a metal door. Çeda paused, her hand resting above the handle.

Steer you well wide of the will of the gods.

There was wisdom on those words, she thought as she gripped the door's warm handle. Surely there was wisdom. Then she opened the door and stepped into the sunlight.

THE
LOYAL DAGGER

Zin E. Rocklyn

T HE BOY FOLLOWED directions and found her 'round back of the inn as promised, face hidden by the hood of her cloak as she violently threw up all her guts had to offer. It wasn't much other than mead, by the smell of it. He recoiled from her retching and the overpowering stench of waste, bodily and otherwise. When she appeared to have finished, left gloved hand clasping at the brick wall, breath heaving from her chest, he stepped forward, cautiously avoiding the crawling puddle of bile, and handed over the tea-stained scroll.

"Don't want it," she said, swatting at him.

"I got three pfennigs for this, and I aim to deliver," he spat, chest swollen as he wagged the neatly coiled paper in her direction.

"I'll give you four if you fuck off," she said, voice gruff as she bent up at the waist. "Oh good fuckin' Mary, the world needs to stop spittin' spinnin'."

"Gotta do better than that," the boy pushed. "This comes from on high."

She fell back against the wall, then eased the hood back from her head. The boy gasped and stepped away. She smirked. "Still got a duty to fulfill?"

He blinked at her, jaw loose, then snapped to attention. "Yeah, I do. I got brothers. Don't care if you's a Moor or a fuckin' gyp, I--"

The boy had obviously underestimated his receiver, for within the blink of an eye, she was on him, large hands wrapped tightly around his throat, back pinned to the cold brick. "You wanna see them brothers again, you watch your fuckin' mouth and get from my sight, you hear?"

The boy's neck crunched as he tried to nod against her tightening fingers. She let go, dropping him hard onto the cobblestone, her bile warming him.

"Fuck 'on high.' And fuck you, too." She spat in his direction for good measure, then pulled her hood back up before stumbling out of the alleyway and disappearing into the night.

<hr />

YOU KNOW THAT tingling sensation you get when someone's unclothing you with their eyes? Like a heavy breath laced with fresh cream rolling across the back of an exposed neck. Thick and wrong and hot, cloying, yet it chills you to the quick?

Yeah, that.

That's the sensation that wakes me at an unjustly hour, sand settling in my limbs and mouth. I must've slept wrong; my shoulder is killing me and my bed reeks of mead and this new spirit *gin*. Bless the Dutch, the ruthless fucks. A few of them are donning clogs and stomping their way through the mush of my head when someone clears their throat.

Two things happen then: Charlotte three doors down perfects

the high, final squeal of her performance of the early morn and I sit to attention, arms raised, eyes half-lidded.

"Exit my quarters, interloper," I mumble, then grimace at the smell of my own breath.

"You sent away my messenger. My presence is your punishment," he says.

I smirk, then wipe the gunk from the corners of my lips. "Surprised you'd sully your reputation, arriving here."

"I have the cover of pre-dawn hiding me, and I arrived on foot."

"Brave of you."

"Or foolish. Either way, this message is important."

I sigh, my shoulders falling heavy, and flop back into the down of my comforter and goose-feather stuffed mattress. Only the best for Madame Flora's whores and guests. She and her girls and boys and those in between entertain dignitaries, royalty, diplomats, and high-standing officers of Her Majesty's brigade.

And then there is me, basking in it all and tasked with protecting the bodies of her wards and the reputations of her clientele. A bed with three meals a day and all the tipple a woman like me could manage was nothing less than a match made in Hades.

"Aelian!"

I jolt upward again, mid-snore of a surprise nap, and groan. "What is it you *want*, Jolyon?"

"Your services, Aelian, for the Royal Court," he says, patience thinner than the skin of a piglet.

Finally, I open my eyes. He's sitting in the vermillion wingback chair at the end of my bed, a freshly roaring fire warming his crossed legs, fingers steepled in annoyance. His liquescent blue stare cuts icicles through me, blonde hair neatly tied with a velveteen royal-coloured bow, the blue as pale as his eyes. He is infuriatingly good-looking with a strongly chiseled jaw and plush, almost feminine lips. The sight of him in fine silks embroidered with gold thread heats my blood, and I fling the covers away from me.

He winces at the sight of me naked, and I want to laugh in his face. This is the game we've played for years, especially when my circumstances were much different. Now, he has the freedom to ogle me a bit harder.

I stretch my torso for good measure, my full breasts on display and free from the cloth bindings I stifle them in, then stomp my way to the basin and pitcher full of crisp, clean water. I can feel his gaze still on me, and I know he sees the fullness of my high backside, the corded muscles of my thick thighs and calves, the litany of scars marring my wide shoulders and muscled arms. I am unlike the women he is used to, the fair and willowy. Delicate. I am as black as the night I was born into and just as cold. I confound him and his ilk, the attraction and curiosity driving some to anger and violence.

I'd learned from youth to defend myself, as no one was coming to my rescue. Ever.

"You're telling me nothing, and I remember no messenger."

He clears his throat and I hear him shift against the chair. "That's because you nearly killed the young boy in your drunken rage."

I frown in the silver-backed mirror as I wipe my face. Then it hits me. The gin. "Oh. Right. Well, perhaps you shouldn't send a sectarian little fuck to handle such business. Now what is it?"

He shifts again, this a different kind of discomfort. "I do not know."

I lift an arm to smell the pit and immediately grimace. A full bath is necessary. "Aren't you the most trusted advisor to the Queen?" I say mockingly. Before he can answer, I open the door to my quarters and yell below, "Annabelle, fetch me a bath!"

Annabelle hates Blacks, yet Annabelle has no choice but to serve me, and I revel in her muttering anger while stewing in water drawn by her hands and flavoured with her spit. Makes no matter to me. Her spit cleans my cunt so I'd consider us both quite satisfied.

I slam the door shut and stalk back towards Jolyon, sitting in the matching chair across from him. I spread my legs and dig my elbows in my thighs, my chin resting in the basket of my woven fingers. "I don't like the sound of this, Jolyon."

"Neither do I, but I have no say when it comes to Queen Lady and her desires. Please. Take this from me so I can be on my way. Dawn quickly approaches."

"Fine. Tell me."

Jolyon sits back into the chair, eyes rolling into the back of his skull, mouth hanging open, as I stand and reach for the golden urn sitting on the mantle. I peel back the top carefully, wetting the tip of my pinkie with moist lips, then dipping it into the ashes. I quickly replace the lid and carry the ashes to Jolyon's awaiting tongue. I smear the contents, then shut his jaw, waiting the precious moments for it to hit his blood stream.

It takes quickly, and Jolyon begins to speak, yet the voice is not his. It is higher with a lilting accent of the North, like silks through mud.

"Drizana. Before week's end. Poison. Peaceful."

And his head flops forward, the tip of his ponytail dangling in his face. He will need to rest, but he cannot do it here. More than likely, someone has followed him, awaiting the moment he expels the message in order to kill him. A message such as this would stay between three people: the solicitor, the assassin tasked, and the poor soul dispatched from our living plane. I have severed plenty a messenger, blood-print or no. The risk for gossip is too high, as memories before and after the edict are intact.

"Jolyon!" I say, slapping his pale cheek ruddy. "Jolyon, you must wake!" He groans at me, head lolling. "You must leave here!" I pop his cheek again, but it's hopeless. A moment later, there is a knock at my door. I hurry to it, opening it a crack to see not Annabelle, but Catherine with my bath water behind her. Catherine is a pleasant surprise, but a complication nonetheless. Her peaches-and-cream complexion roseys once she sees the condition I'm in as I widen the door.

"Good-lookin' lad there," she says, tiptoeing over. She gasps slightly, dark brown eyes widening. "You do 'im in?"

"No, Catherine, he's resting," I say, hauling the water in myself and shutting the door behind me. "His life is in danger and I need you to keep a watchful eye on him. And by eye, I mean the pair in your head not either of those lips, you hear me?"

Catherine snorts a laugh, then nods. "I hear ye, but look at 'im, will ye? How can a girl like me resist?"

I grimace. "Easy. Now help me drag him to Patty-Anne's room, then fetch my clean clothing. I may be gone for a few days, yet."

Catherine stops, fists deep in her sides. "I get anything out of this?"

"I come back alive, you do. I don't, you get my bed. On my honour."

Catherine rolls her eyes and blows a stray red hair from her face. "Full of shite, you are."

I wink at her, then set about to saving Jolyon's pale ass once again.

———————

THERE'S AN ACHE blooming from the right side of my skull by the time I set out that evening. One of the other girls has fed and cleaned Augustus, and while I'm grateful, the massive raven is still cross with me.

"Come now, Gus-Gus," I coo, stroking her opalescent plumage. She cocks an amber eye at me, squawking shortly, then snorting in my face. I swipe the muck from my forehead and flick it away. "You done?" I swear she laughs, the trill in her throat mocking me. "Whatever." Still, she does not allow me to climb her, her wing pushing me back each time I attempt. "Oh, for bleedin' Mary's sake, fine!"

Pleased with herself, Augustus tucks in, lowering her head so I can push back the few feathers covering her ear. Softly, I sing to her, the ache of a time lost settling deep in my breast, yet I ignore it to comfort my companion.

> *my body was your egg*
> *and your cries broke the sky*
> *at your birth*
> *my hatchling, see your first feathers*
> *wait for me before you fly*

She coos back at me, nuzzling her head against my side. I nuzzle back briefly, getting a strong whiff of the vomit still deep within her plumage. No wonder she's irritated with me. To make up for it, I scratch just above her throat, then smooth my palm against her beak, both top and bottom. She eases even further, forgiving me just a little bit more for sullying her rather impressive coat. I smile as she opens her wing. I find the tiny step implanted in her side and swing the other leg over. I do not fully straddle her by any means; I had her bridle removed ages ago, allowing her to grow bigger and healthier than most of her engineered kind. Still, she manages to blend in with most others, never quite giving me away until it is too late for most.

I lay against her back, the warmth of her body, the steadiness of her breathing grounding me, and for a moment, the nerves that had erupted within me after hearing Jolyon's message calm, and I'm able to focus, able to envision my destination. I stroke the two hidden short feathers at the top of Augustus's head and whisper, "Let's go home."

She bristles, then takes off into the night air.

———

I SIT ON the lip of the lead-paned window, my dagger poised in my grip, tip carving out the gunk beneath my nails. I steal a glance at my target through the distorted glass and feel an inordinate amount of emotion writhing within me.

Drizana.

Or rather, Princess Drizaniella of the Third House Torner.

My sister. Half-sister, to be precise.

To say we dislike one another is to be coy. There are no proper words within the confines of language to describe what we feel toward one another. At the thought of her, I find my fists impenetrable, the skin of my face taut with the heat of fury.

I cannot speak for her, as I am not as well-versed in forked tongue, but I'm certain she feels something like the same for me.

Bored, I ease the lock with the same dagger, the gunk silencing the shriek of ore against rust. Three crane women cluck at her, one fastening fresh water pearls against Drizana's pale neck with her bright orange beak, the other fluttering her pale feathers fingers along Drizana's severe cheeks, rouging the sickly white with expensive tinted powders. Yet another crane woman watches it all, her curved neck nearly straight as her beady eyes scrutinize every move.

I shudder at a memory.

My father's creations and acts of heresy, these crane women, my Augustus, and many others. Until the kingdom found use for them, at least. Of course, this was after he'd been imprisoned and executed for his crimes against the nation, leaving the crown to my stepmother, Lady Mayne. I cannot say times before then were pleasant either. They hadn't been since the death of my mother, seemingly ages ago. Yet, I can see her face as clear as the day dawns, her night black skin, her even blacker eyes. And the gentleness of her smile. My father took to reminding me I looked like her every night he tucked me in after

THE LOYAL DAGGER + 57

she died, even in whisper once her name was banned from Kingdom Torner by Lady Mayne. Things only worsened with the hex of my sister's birth. She took on my father's ears and plump lips, while the rest of her is all her mother. All grace and ice and as white as the sun.

Suddenly, Drizana's cold eyes flick up in the mirror, meeting my heated gaze. She counts a moment, then gasps rather dramatically, the tips of her fingers brushing the plane of her adorned breastplate.

My mother's sapphires.

Hex and doom, this creature astounds me with her audacity.

The crane women flutter at Drizana's alarm, wings flapping uselessly and shedding white feathers everywhere in the massive room.

"Oh, calm it, Jacqueline!" I groan, dropping from the window sill. The crane women back away, crowding around Drizana as she pretends to weep, ready to sacrifice themselves in honour of the kingdom that enslaves them. I stop advancing, truly sickened by the sight of them and their so-called honour. "I have no business with you women, only my sister."

Jacqueline, the head mistress, rears up, plumage raising high from her narrow head. Her neck curls. "You have no sister here, Aelian," she says, the voice of a brief point in my childhood nearly bringing me to tears. My bladder wishes to void itself as my back and arms remember the peckings. So much torn flesh, too many nights fighting fevers of infection from that disgusting bill.

"Fuck off, Jacqueline, and let me have my say. Then you'll never have to see me again," I say, gripping the handle of my dagger even tighter, my arm curled behind my back.

She huffs, flutters, but makes no move to leave. The other women stay as well, though I can feel their nerves from across the room.

"Leave us, Jacqueline." Drizana. She's over her vapours. Amazing turnover. I'm rather impressed.

Jacqueline lends me her left eye as she gathers Drizana under a wing. "Are you sure?"

"I am," Drizana says staunchly. The women separate to reveal my sister's glare. Those hazel eyes refuse to blink, even after the doors to her chambers close with a thud. "What in the seven hells brings you here?"

I smirk. Such unbecoming language from a lady-in-training. "Your death, dearest sister."

Still she stares, unmoved. "You speak in riddles, and I have no time. Prince Christopher awaits my company." She turns on her ottoman and resumes her primping. She's quite adept at it alone. The thought of the crane women angers me even more.

"Someone wants you dead, Drizzy."

She stops mid-tuck of a wavy curl, her fine fingers twitching just slightly. She hates the nickname almost as much as she hates me.

"Then you've clearly failed your mission, stealing my attention like this," she resumes, voice even haughtier than before. I want to stick her neck, cut out the muscle to her condescending lilt. Feed it to Augustus.

"Because I am not entirely stupid, you see," I say, taking a slow step towards her. She glances at me quickly.

"The drink hasn't rotted your brain quite yet? Pity."

I'm on her before she can stick the pearl comb into the tufts of her perfectly coifed hair, my gloved fingers deep within the bouffant, curling and tugging to expose her long neck. She gags on air, eyes widened in shock as I slowly drag the dagger's flat edge against the delicate flesh.

"Trust, I have no qualms in killing you, dear sister, but first, I must clear this slate. I want your death clean and the blood strictly on my hands as I dance in it. Do you hear me?"

She has no choice; my breath is hot against her cheek, my lips brushing against the shell of her ear. I want to bite it, tear it off with my teeth, chew on its flesh. But I let her go instead, flinging her head forward.

"Pray I do not solve this soon. For your sake and your mother's." I turn, tempering the temptation to take my mother's necklace, and walk back from whence I came, jumping out of the window with one leap. I duck back in. "And don't you *dare* call the guards on me. There are others looking for you. I merely have a head start," I lie. I want to strike the fear of several Hades within her. By the look on her face, I am successful. "Enjoy your courtship, Drizzy."

And I slam the window closed before falling below to Augustus's awaiting back to fly back into the night.

———

I RETURN TO my quarters to find Jolyon sitting on the edge of my dressed bed, stripped of his fine silks and garbed in a night gown. It's freezing in the room, yet he doesn't seem affected by it. I pause at the threshold until better sense hits me, and I shut the door.

"Do not blame the girl. I asked to be in here," he says as I cross the room to strip myself of my weapons.

"Why?" I start a fire and rub my gloved hands against the burgeoning flames.

"I feel… safer," he says. He sounds as if he's in a trance. As if he's been traumatized and cannot face reality without shattering.

"What is it, Jolyon?" I ask, sitting in a wingback. I ease my boots from my feet, rub the arches, then stick them close to the fire.

He doesn't move for a bit, and I don't make him, exhaustion eating my bones. "I remembered something."

I look at him, yet he is still unfocused. This isn't good. The carrier of a blood-print is to never remember the words spoken. Aside from sensitive information that puts their lives in certain danger—and in Jolyon's case, it is already too late—the act itself is harsh and unforgiving in memory. It can drive a person mad, those chemicals floating about, the flashes of the ritual performance tearing at their sanity.

A single tear drops from his unblinking eyes, and I rush towards him, the tug of affection beating my pride into submission. I cup his cheek, turning his face just so until he has no choice but to look at me.

"What is it, Jolyon?" I ask again. "What do you remember?"

He watches me, eyes tracing mine, then my lips until he captures them in between his. The kiss is sloppy, shy, like the first one from ages ago. He settles in quickly, remembering our unofficial lessons behind the rose garden, and I kiss him back until we're both breathless.

The son of a gravedigger and a nursemaid. The broken, orphaned princess violating her exile.

How tragic of us.

He holds my face between large, calloused hands, his eyes swimming as he watches me.

"You will not survive this, in body or in mind or in both, I fear," he whispers. I frown, and he presses his lips to mine one more time. "Woodrow. The name I recall is Woodrow."

For a moment, I cannot breathe. My throat becomes impossibly dry, and the bed disappears from beneath me.

The name I recall is Woodrow.

My father.

He is alive. After all these years. After his *execution*.

My father is alive.

And he wants my half-sister, his own daughter, dead.

"Sweet bleedin' Mary," I say just before sliding to the floor.

———•———

MY FATHER WAS a broken man long before his marriage to Lady Mayne.

The advisors of our old House, turned common servants, entrusted to me the idea that my mother's death had done him in. His heart was never to repair itself, no matter the circumstances. No merger of kingdoms, no mad creations, not even the birth of his precious porcelain daughter. He carried on mumbling to himself, hobbling from one end of the Torner castle to the other until nightfall, when he'd poke and prod and scheme until the morning light. He ignored his frosty wife, scowled at his newborn daughter, balked at servants decades in his care.

He never cooled to me, though, still calling me his little birdie and teaching me to fly on back of Augustus and others like her, others less fortunate in their fate.

He whispered lovely stories of my mother, of us all together in a kingdom of ebony skin and lush oases in a landscape of unforgiving sands. He told me of riches of the earth, a hot sun, and cleansing rains. I longed to be in these places, especially during the weeks upon weeks of heavy, silver clouds in this God-forsaken country.

He'd sing me to sleep with the same refrain every night:

> *my body was your egg*
> *and your cries broke the sky*
> *at your birth*
> *my hatchling, see your first feathers*
> *wait for me before you fly*

But eventually his madness caught up with our stolen moments of affection.

The night before he was arrested in the name of Torner, my father sat the foot of the bed, not looking at me, seemingly mesmerized by the roaring fire.

"I have failed you, my sweet Aelian," he'd said.

"Papa?" His voice scared me. I didn't like the way it sounded, as if he were crying.

"They killed your mother, little birdie, and I tried so hard... so *hard* to bring her back, to avenge her—"

He broke down then, his broad shoulders shaking with his sobs.

I held the comforter to my mouth, shivering with the ferocity of a fever until he left an hour later.

It would be the last time I saw my father alive.

———•———

I AWAKEN WITH the smell of the devil in my nose.

"Bleedin' Mary, that shit stinks!" I scream, flailing my arms for fresh air. Too many bodies crowd me, and I push out again.

"That's the whole bloody point, Aelian," a gruff voice snaps back.

I hiss as my head explodes red with pain. "How lovely of you to grace me with your presence, Madame Flora."

"Shut it, Aelian, and eat some food. You refused the plates from your drink night and you're not dying on my property." The large, red-headed woman in an impeccable jade-green dress moves with familiarity around the room that has been mine for ten years, setting a small table near the fire with four dishes (three meat, one vegetable), a decanter of red wine, and a ripe, beautiful orange.

"Where in Hades did you find that?"

"'Twas a gift. Don't ask too many questions. I've girls knockin' on scurvy's door," she says in one breath. "Your guest saw his way out after tendin' to you. Left you this." She waves an envelope just out of my reach. "You'll get it once you eat. Both his and my orders."

I snort, pushing against the warmth filling my chest. "Fine."

She leaves the room and my stomach betrays me, growling loudly at the scent of succulent braised lamb, stewed oxtails, and roasted chicken. I devour all three, pick at the vegetables, and polish the decanter, a slight buzz enlivening me.

I knock on the door twice, and Madame Flora waddles back in. She inspects the plates, sniffs at the fire, and then, once satisfied, hands over the envelope.

"Gussy's resting, so you'll not bother her tonight, yeah?"

I nod, though I'm hardly paying her any mind. I turn the envelope over twice before breaking the plain black seal. My breath is stolen at the sight of my father's script. I quickly read the contents, then throw the sheet of paper and the envelope into the fire.

"I will need Fauna," I say without looking at her. I am mesmerized by how quickly the words are devoured by heat and flame. "And I will need my dagger."

Madame Flora nods, then hurries away.

I, in turn, prepare to see my father, the man who I thought had been executed thirteen years ago.

———•———

THE CLOISTERS WAS a place of mystery and thrills for me, before it became synonymous with my mother's tomb. She'd been found hanging in the open center, a threadbare noose swaying from the extended arm of my father's statue. It was poetic in a sense. My mother had always hated this country, had wished to return to our true home, a home I barely knew myself.

This is where I find my father. In the open. Sitting below where my mother's feet had been.

He's paler than I remember, most likely from hiding, the olive of his tanned and scarred skin turned sickly green. His curly mop is now long and scraggly, his green eyes rheumy and unfocused.

He looks like death. And I want nothing more than to hold him.

But as I approach, an all-encompassing fury takes hold and before I know it, I strike him across the cheek, twisting his head hard to the left, blood spurting from his nose. The wine runs hot in my veins, but I stop myself from striking him again.

"I deserve that," he whispers. Whether it's lack of use or fear that tightens his throat, I'm not sure, but I hate the sound of the scratchy baritone that used to sing me to sleep. "And more." He chortles. I want to hit him again. I slide to cobblestone with him instead.

"They don't deserve this land," he says after three crows land near our feet. He is barefoot, three of his toes missing. I want to weep. "They don't deserve you."

It is my turn to chortle. "They've exiled me. I spit in their faces and stay, murdering their constituents for a few pfennigs."

"More than a few, from what I've heard, and more than mere peasants," he says with a smile.

The pride in his voice almost makes me smile back, but I staunch it. "Where have you been?"

"There's no time to explain that. I've already spent too much time in the open." He turns to me, but I stare straight ahead, afraid to look into the eyes I inherited. "You did not do as I asked."

"No."

"Smart girl."

I shrug one shoulder. "Always have been."

"Then why are you here?"

I turn to him then and my heart stutters, my vision clouding. "You *left me*," I say. "You left me to those... *things*, to her heartlessness, to the very dungeon they cast you in before your—"

I stop, realizing I have no idea how he's here. How did he escape those flames? How did he break free of the chains that bound him to the stake he screamed against? I can feel the heat, feel the iced fingertips of Lady Mayne holding my head in place so I was forced to watch. When I closed my eyes, Jacqueline was ordered to peck until I opened them.

"My death, little birdie," he says with a sad smile, a glimmer of maddening light sparking in his eyes. It's the look I remember during his mumblings. "They must pay." He cups my cheek, wipes my tears. "Kill her. Kill Drizana in the name of the Brenton Empire and we can dance in the ashes. This place can be ours once more."

Yet this place was never ours to begin with. It was a promise of power, a promise that was a lie, a lie that brought us here and left us a dangling footnote in their history. My father knew this, having felt the repercussions of their betrayals, yet as I stare into the eyes like mine, I see he still he hungers for a power that would never be his. A power that cost our standing, our lives, *his* sanity.

All for nothing. All for him to hide in the shadows of this city for thirteen years, hide in the place we both died a little.

I have stayed loyal to the memory of a man living and breathing the same wretched air as me, who chose to rob me of what little warmth I might have had left within me for the sake of his selfish intentions.

Who would have one daughter kill his other to complete that task. My heart aches as I turn into his palm, kiss it with a tear and say, "I cannot, Father."

THE AIR STILLS between us, his eyes watering, thick eyebrows twitching as he studies my face. His rough hand slips from my cheek, bits of blistered flesh scraping my sensitive skin.

"Wh-*why*?" His voice is wounded, and I feel the weight of it in my chest.

"Where have you been?" I ask again. He frowns, then opens his mouth, anger contorting his face, and I stop him with another slap. Its impact is minimal, considering the odd positions we sit in, but it does what I need. "We have time for this. *Make* time for this or, so help me Hades, I will turn you in myself."

"Your own *father*?" he has the fucking nerve to gasp.

I grit my jaw. "My father died at the stake thirteen years to the day the eve before this. Do not *tell* me of my father."

He smirks, the expression nearly violent. I now know where I get it from. "Correction, my little birdie. Your father died long before."

"Answer my question," I push, my jaw tight.

"He died when his love's belly was robbed of his son—"

My jaw hangs loose, eyes filling with moisture. "Wh-what?"

"—when they stitched her up, yet let her bleed in their marital bed—"

"I-I don't understand! I had a brother?"

"—when they took his son and flung him into the depths of the waters surrounding the Castle of Torner—"

"Stop it!" I slam my hands against my ears, and instantly I smell burning flesh, *his* flesh. A memory, yet effective. My shoulders sting.

"—when they took his love's body from that funeral bed, dragged it through the streets, and strung it from the statue made in his own image, the statue they commemorated him with for his *con-tributions to the **crown**,*" he sneers. "The same contributions they executed him for."

And it is then I stop whimpering, my anger renewed.

"How old was I?"

He eases back, swallows soundly. "What?"

"How old was I when Mum—" I choke on the word, the taste of it like dust. "—when she died?"

"Aelian—"

But I can't stop, not now. "How long were you married to Lady Mayne? How did you make love to her make that... *thing* that is my sister? How many times before she fell pregnant with *her*? How long did you watch me suffer? How many times did you watch me being beaten and pecked at? How long did you wait before seeing me take a john for a loaf of bread? How long have you watched me suffer? HOW LONG HAVE YOU BEEN ALIVE, FATHER?"

He shifts next to me, but I am fogged by tears, my eyes on Fauna. The Friesian's ebony coat and knee-long mane shine in the pre-dawn light, further distorting my vision.

"I-I did not... *see* you, per se, I just—"

"Learned of me from afar? Kept distant tethers through—" My eyes widen as it clicks. I turn to him. "Your birds."

He grins, then stills, remembering himself. "Yes."

"Augustus?"

"She only did what she was made to do," he says, eyes dropping from mine. "Do not be cross with her."

"You still haven't answered me. Where have you been, Father? How are you alive?"

That mad gleam goes off again and he giggles. "I perfected it!"

I shake my head. "Perfected *what*?"

He clicks his tongue, a gesture of impatience I recognize from his lessons. "The formula to *raise the dead*."

I gawp at him, lost for words.

"Yes, my little birdie! The formula I'd so frantically tried for your mother—but she was much too gone for it to work. One must ingest the potion *before* the time of death. When I knew I had no chance of surviving, I drank it. It wouldn't hurt either way, yeah? They doused the fire once my screams stopped, believing me vanquished, which I was but... it hardly matters, does it?"

I glare at him. "To my scars? No."

He deflates, his head falling back against base of the statue.

"Have you tried this... *formula* with any other living beings?"

"Not since my own resurrection, but with your help—"

"I will do no such thing."

"What?"

"You are not *God*, Father," I growl. "You are no Fate to any *living being*. How *dare* you?!"

He opens his mouth, but I hold up a finger, giving one short shake of my head. "No more, Father. No. More."

I stand.

"You *let* her die." He twitches, affronted. I hiss back, annoyed. "You needed a specimen. With all your knowledge of the body, you could have helped her. You've made *birdwomen*, for fuck's sake! Long before the Kingdom turned on you! On *us*!" My chest is heaving from lost breath, from the pent-up anger of abandonment, from abuses unspeakable, even to myself, even in the dark. Most of all, I weep. I weep for the family I lost and for the family who left me to the cold, bitter winds of a country not mine. Never mine.

My father chuckles from behind me and I turn to see him on his side, knees tucked under his chin. "Smart girl."

I shrug. "I had the best teacher."

He shifts, eyes pleading. "Me?"

"Myself," I spit.

———•———

I GAVE HIM a choice before walking away and mounting Fauna to ride back to my home, the brothel.

In seventeen hours, he is to show at my doorstep with his decision.

It is then I will either save my father by exiling him to the pillaged lands my mother had longed for or kill him where he stands.

Sleep doesn't find me as I await the early evening hour.

At hour fifteen, there is a knock at my door.

TROLL TROUBLE

Richard Lee Byers

THE FOREST OF Thorns is well named. Briars scratched and snagged me with every step, or at least it seemed that way. Meanwhile, the soft ground mired my boots, and cold rainwater dripped on me from the weave of branches overhead.

In other words, this little excursion into the wild was unpleasant enough to remind me of one reason why I'd abandoned the life of a mercenary—marching in the snow and heat, eating half-spoiled rations or none at all, and sleeping rough—to set up shop as a fencing master in Balathex, City of Fountains. I strove to stay alert lest discomfort distract me.

Yet despite my caution, when I first glimpsed the troll peeking out at me, he was only a few strides away. It seemed unfair that a creature so large could nonetheless hide so successfully, even behind the broad, mossy trunk of an ancient oak.

Truly, though, there was no reason why he shouldn't, because he wasn't as tall as a tree. Such towering specimens may have existed long

ago. They may still, in far corners of the world. But in all my wandering, I've never seen one.

No, his long arms knotted with muscle, hide mottled brown and gray, red eyes shining under a ridged brow and fanged mouth smirking and slavering at the prospect of cruel sport and fresh meat, this fellow merely loomed half again as tall as I was. That was still big enough to make a sensible man turn tail.

I didn't, though. Nor did I reach for my broadsword in its scabbard, though my fingers itched for the hilt. Instead, as the creature shambled into the open, I gave him a nod and said, "Hello. My name is Selden. I come as an envoy of the August Assembly of Balathex."

Then I studied his brutish face in an effort to determine whether he believed the lie, and if so, whether it mattered.

———

MY ERRAND BEGAN three nights earlier, in the shop I'd rented and through hard and fumbling work—I'm no carpenter—transformed into a space suitable for teaching swordplay and associated arts. Effort wasted, it seemed, for no students had presented themselves to study there.

The problem was that I was a stranger. No one in Balathex knew me as a successful duelist or an instructor capable of raising others to proficiency. The obvious remedy was to pick a few quarrels, but I was reluctant to go down that path.

I'd grown tired of killing for no better reason than to put silver in my purse, and besides, I was loath to start my new life by instigating feuds. I didn't need vengeful brothers, sons, and friends of the deceased leaping out at me for years thereafter.

Unfortunately, that unsatisfactory scheme was the only plan I'd been able to devise. Thus, on the night in question, I sat alone drinking cheap Ghentoy red laced with raw spirit, and never mind that I'd squandered coin originally intended for next week's rent to purchase the jugs. Morose as I was, I had more immediate needs.

Someone rapped on the door.

My first half-tipsy thought was that I'd lost track of the date, and the landlord had come for his due, but a moment's reflection assured me that couldn't be so. Perhaps here was my first pupil, then, unlikely as that seemed at this late hour.

I straightened my jerkin, smoothed down my hair, and hurried to answer the knock. When I did, a stooped old woman squinted at me from the other side of the threshold.

She wore charms, talismans made of bone and feathers and other items hidden in little cloth bags, dangling around her wrinkled neck. But had you seen her, you wouldn't have thought *sorceress*. You would have thought *witch*.

For there was nothing about her to suggest the sort of citified mage who pores over grimoires, compounds elixirs from rare ingredients, and commands devils via complex ritual and force of will. Rather, she was manifestly a village wise woman who knew only the patchy lore her mother passed down to her, brewed dubious remedies from whatever happened to grow nearby, and dickered with goblins in a manner little different than she'd haggle with a neighbor.

Surprised, I said, "Mother Elkinda."

She sniffed twice. "You stink of drink."

"Whereas you stink of the usual." It was true. There are rustic folk who give the lie to the insult *dirty peasant*, but she wasn't one of them. "And I suppose that, as we both smell already, a hug won't make it any worse."

We put that to the test, and afterward, I ushered her inside.

"How did you know I was in the city?" I asked.

"The wind whispered it to me, and then I dowsed my way to your door." She hefted a gnarled walking stick.

"Well, it's good you came when you did," I said. "In a week or two, I'll likely be gone." Soldiering again, if I could find a captain to take me on this late in the season.

I don't think she even registered the glumness in my tone. "I need your help," she said. "I...may have done a bad thing."

Concern nudged aside my self-pity. I waved her on toward the rickety table.

She stumbled before she got there. It was a long hike from her little forest village to the city, and she'd exhausted herself making it. I caught her, got her into a chair, poured her a cup of wine, and sat back down across from her. "Tell me," I said.

She took a long drink first. When she set the goblet down, she said, "There are trolls in the wood."

More concerned now, I nodded. "I know."

"Well, what you may not know is that sometimes they need blessings and medicine just like people do. Then they come to me."

I frowned. "That's like trafficking with outlaws, only worse. People would hang you if they found out."

She glowered. "I give the trolls things they need, and in return, they leave the village alone. We couldn't live where we do, otherwise."

"I can believe it," I said. "And I wasn't condemning you, just worried for your sake. Please, go on."

"Well...two of the trolls who came to me were Skav Hearteater, their chieftain, and Ojojum, his mate. Their problem was, she couldn't conceive."

"And that upset them?"

"Yes. In some ways, trolls and people are alike. Through my craft, I discovered the fault lay with Skav, but when I tried to quicken his seed with the usual remedies, nothing happened."

"So you tried something unusual?"

"Once I was fool enough to tell the trolls the notion that had come to me, they insisted. Had I refused, how do you think it would have ended?"

"With your flesh in their bellies," I said. "So what did you do?"

"I called a spirit of lust and fertility and put it inside the Hearteater. My thought was that he would share the imp's vigor the next time he and Ojojum coupled." She smiled. "And I was right. She's with child."

"Then what's the problem?"

The smile disappeared. "Skav changed. He'd always doted on Ojojum. But afterward, he started beating her until, fearful she'd lose the baby, she ran away."

"Ran away and came to you. Because she suspected your magic was to blame? More to the point, do *you* think it's to blame?"

Elkinda sighed. "Perhaps. When the spirit came, I sensed it was something crueler and less biddable than I meant to catch. Something from the netherworld and not just out of Nature."

"You should have tossed it back and tried again."

"That's easy to say now, but I'd had trouble summoning anything. I didn't know if I'd be lucky a second time, and with the trolls watching and waiting…"

"I understand," I said. "Well, partly. Do you believe the spirit's touch poisoned Skav's mind?"

"Worse. I fear it didn't leave his body when it was supposed to. I need you to find out if it's still inside."

"What, now?"

"I can fix it so you're able to see the incubus once you're close enough. I need to know for a fact that it's there and how it looks before I can set about casting it out."

"Then go peer at Skav yourself. You're the one who's friendly with him."

She shook her head. "The spirit would be suspicious of me."

"Whereas the trolls will eat me simply because they're hungry."

She grimaced. "I know what I'm asking. But dangerous as trolls are, the ones hereabout mostly leave people alone. They won't do that much longer if a demon has possessed their chief. They'll start hunting humans every chance they get, and you're the only one I can ask to help me keep it from happening."

She didn't add that I owed her my life. Apparently she trusted me to remember that for myself.

I came down with the plague called the Bloody Noose when my mercenary company was chasing bandits on the fringe of the Forest of Thorns. For fear of contagion, my comrades abandoned me. Mother Elkinda found me a day later.

She always claimed the foul potions and gruels she gave me cured me of my affliction. I had my doubts. But I didn't doubt that after the delirium passed and I was breathing normally again, my lingering weakness would still have killed me had she not nursed me through the two long months of my recovery.

Now the debt had come due. I poured us each another drink and said, "Tell me how I'll be able to spot the imp."

NOW YOU KNOW how I came to find myself deep in the woods facing a troll. But you may still wonder why I approached the creatures openly when I might have spied on them instead.

This was my thinking. Mother Elkinda knew the trolls; she watched the trails in the heart of the wood, but not where they laired. I could have crept around for days before I found the place, and even when I had, I might not recognize Skav. I'd never seen him before, and to human eyes, one naked beast-man tends to looks like another. And once I did identify him, I'd still need to come close to discern the incubus inside, close enough to make concealment problematic.

Thus, passing myself off as an emissary seemed a better option. Or at least it did until the troll roared and rushed me with ham-sized, jagged-clawed hands outstretched.

I jumped aside, and he lunged past me. As he lurched back around, I snatched my sword out. He hesitated, but not, I judged, because the blade frightened him. He was simply considering how to contend with it.

At least that gave me another chance to talk. "I know where Ojo-jum is," I told him. "I think the Hearteater will want to hear, don't you?"

"Yes," he growled, then instantly swatted at the sword in an attempt to knock it aside.

I twitched the blade above the arc of the blow and sliced him across the knuckles. He snatched his hand back, and in that instant, I lunged closer and set sharp steel against his dangling, warty genitals. He froze.

"Give me your word," I said, "that you'll take me to Skav without any more nonsense. Or I swear I'll geld you."

"I'll take you," he said. His voice still sounded like growls and coughs. It reminded me of the lions I'd seen in the grasslands of Lazvalla.

I shifted my sword away from his maleness and returned it to its scabbard. I didn't like doing it, but it seemed unwieldy to approach Skav as an envoy and a hostage taker, too.

To my relief, the creature before me didn't try another attack. Instead, he led me on down the path. Evidently the feel of a blade against his tender parts had made a lasting impression.

His cooperation notwithstanding, I never dropped my guard. But eventually I relaxed somewhat, and then I asked, "What sort of mood is the Hearteater in today?"

My guide gave me a glower. "Angry. Hungry." Then he stepped into a spot where the tangle of branches overhead was thin and winced at the wan light leaking down from the sky.

That's how trolls are. It's a myth that sunlight turns them to stone, but they're sensitive to it. Had my companion not been charged with keeping watch on the trail, he might well have opted to sleep by day and roam around at night.

Certainly, that was the case with the majority of his fellows. They lay snoring in heaps of leaves and pine needles in a particularly shady portion of the forest floor.

Despite the crudity of the sleeping arrangements, the place had the air of a home and not just a camp where nomads had stopped for a day. The trolls had taken the trouble to wedge racks of antlers and skulls, some of them human, in the crotches of trees and to scratch crude drawings on the trunks.

That was all I had time to take in before one of the wakeful trolls noticed me. He roared a warning, whereupon his fellows roused and, glaring and slavering, came shambling to surround me.

I didn't realize when one reached to grab me from behind. Fortunately, my guide noticed. He snarled, slashed with his claws, and sent my would-be assailant reeling backward with a gashed face.

It was more assistance than I had any right to expect. But I'd entered the trolls' home at the side of my reluctant escort, and maybe that meant an attempt to harm me implied disrespect for him.

The balked troll swiped at his flowing blood and gathered himself to lunge. Fearing that a general brawl was imminent, I shouted, "I speak for the lords of Balathex, and I can tell you what's become of Ojojum!"

Some part of that was surprising or intriguing enough to make the creatures around me falter. Then another troll, one who hadn't rushed to encircle me with the others, prowled out of the gloom.

Upon observing him, I decided I'd been wrong about one thing. I would have recognized Skav Hearteater on sight. He was even bigger than the others and had dried blood and yellow earth streaked on his face and chest.

I couldn't tell if he also had an incubus riding him. I hoped Elkinda's witchcraft would answer that question in due course.

"What do you know about my mate?" Skav demanded.

"One thing at a time," I said. "Do you understand that I speak for Balathex?"

He flicked his hand in an impatient gesture I chose to interpret as *yes*.

"So do you promise to receive me hospitably and allow me to depart in peace," I persisted, "as the rulers of men deal with one another's envoys?"

"Tell me where Ojojum is!" he bellowed, "or my people will tear you to bits!" The trolls surrounding me poised their hands to rip and snatch.

"Kill me," I said, "and you won't find out about your mate. More, if I don't come home in one piece, Balathex will avenge the affront to its sovereignty by sending an army to scour the forest clean of trolls, as many of my folk believe we should have long ago."

Skav glared at me. I stared back while trying to look like a dauntless idiot who'd enjoy nothing more than dying hideously for the sake of the Whispering City.

Finally the Hearteater said, "I promise not to hurt you. Why not? What does a little turd like you matter either way?"

"Thank you for your courtesy," I replied. "May I approach?"

"Come," he said, and, looking disgruntled that I might not be supper after all, the other trolls opened the way for me. I walked forward until I was near enough to converse comfortably, which in this circumstance wasn't comfortable at all.

Without taking my eyes off Skav, I bowed. "My lord—"

"Ojojum!" he snapped. "Where?"

"Balathex," I replied.

"You captured her." His clawed fingers flexed, and growls and muttering sounded from the trolls behind me.

"No," I said. "She came to the city of her own free will seeking sanctuary, and the August Assembly gave it to her."

He hesitated. Then: "You're lying!"

I certainly was. Had his mate presented herself at a city gate, the guard would have attacked her on sight. But I hoped ignorance of human society would prevent Skav from realizing how preposterous my claims actually were.

"Admittedly," I said, "it's a novel situation. But your mate's petition came to the attention of the Hand Maids of Rendeth. The welfare of mothers and children is their particular concern, and they pleaded on Ojojum's behalf."

"For a troll! And the leaders heeded them?"

"Yes. They respect the temples, and honestly, I think the very strangeness of it all intrigued them." Trying to look casual about it, I drew a handkerchief from my sleeve, ostensibly to wipe sweat from my face. In reality, Mother Elkinda had soaked the cloth in something she'd brewed in an iron pot, and I needed to get the fumes into my eyes.

When I did, my eyes burned, and tears dissolved the world into blur. I daresay blindness is never desirable, but I can attest that unexpectedly losing your sight in the midst of a mob of man-eating brutes is particularly disconcerting.

Fortunately, none of the trolls availed itself of the opportunity to attack me before the stinging faded and I blinked and wiped the tears away. Instead, Skav asked me, "What ails you?"

"Pardon me," I said. Meanwhile, inside my head, I was cursing Elkinda for not warning me. "Apparently something's blooming hereabouts…"

Suddenly, midway through my excuse, Skav's face changed. A second set of features shined through it like firelight glowing through a paper lantern, and remarkably, the one underneath was even more disturbing. With his crooked fangs and piggy crimson eyes, the troll chieftain was ugly and intimidating but not unnatural. In contrast, the long, narrow visage of the incubus twitched, oozed, and flickered from moment to moment in a way that was both wrong in some fundamental manner and sickening to behold.

But I couldn't let the demon know I beheld it. I held myself steady and finished my thought: "…that disagrees with me."

"I'll disagree with you," said Skav, jumping back to the actual point of the conversation, "unless you prove you're telling the truth."

"Just think about it," I replied. "If Ojojum didn't come to Balathex, how do I even know her name, let alone that she's gone missing?"

Apparently he couldn't think of an alternative explanation. For after another pause, he snarled, "Send her back! Or I'll kill every human in the forest!"

Now that I had the information I'd come for, I would have liked nothing better than to assure him Balathex would bow to his wishes and make a speedy departure. But alas, the emissary I was pretending to be wouldn't behave that way.

"We've been over this," I said. "If you trolls make pests of yourselves, the August Assembly will do whatever is required to exterminate you. But it needn't come to that. Ojojum wants to return home."

Skav grunted. "What's stopping her, then?"

"You are. She says you've been beating her for no reason, and she's afraid she'll miscarry."

He hesitated. Then: "There are reasons. But maybe I've been too strict. I don't want to hurt the child." Behind its mask of flesh, the incubus grinned.

"Good," I said. "But it won't be quite that easy. When Ojojum returns, six Hand Maids will accompany her. They'll ask you to swear on a lock of Rendeth's hair that the abuse will stop."

The incubus's leer stretched until it split his seething face in two. "If that's what it takes."

After negotiating the details of the fictitious rendezvous, I took my leave and, once I was a little way down the trail, quickened my pace. Shortly after that, I had to stop and puke. The devil's face had been that upsetting.

———

WHEN I TOLD Mother Elkinda about the palaver, she said, "You didn't tell me you were going to talk to them. It's a wonder you're still alive."

I shrugged. "I made Skav believe he had to let me go to seize a bigger prize, namely, Ojojum at his mercy once more, six nuns to eat, and a sacred relic to defile. What I don't understand is why he and the tribe aren't rampaging through the woods killing people already."

The witch shifted on the only chair in her hut. "Maybe the incubus wants to get used to being Skav first," she said. "Or spend more time enjoying it. The spirit may believe that once the slaughter starts, an army truly will come running to wipe out the trolls, its host included."

"Too bad that isn't so."

When the residents of Balathex thought about the forest dwellers at all, it was as poachers, runaway indentured servants, and mad hermits whose welfare was of trifling importance. In time, I supposed, the August Assembly might send sufficient troops to put an end to the trolls, but by then, whole settlements would lie dead.

"No use crying about it." Throwing her head back, Elkinda emptied her jack of the bitter beer they brewed there in her village, then used her walking stick to heave herself to her feet. "I'll just have to clean up my own mess." She started hobbling around gathering the ingredients for a spell, a clump of moss from this shelf, a piece of stag horn carved with a rune from the table in the corner.

I stood up from the earthen floor so I could stay out of her way. My head jostled a dried lizard hanging beneath the thatched roof.

When Elkinda had collected everything she needed, she carried it outside to the crackling yellow fire she'd built, and I followed. She gazed up at the moon and stars, or what we could see of them through crisscrossing branches and wisps of cloud, then motioned for me to stand in a particular spot.

I couldn't tell what made that bit of ground special. She hadn't scratched a circle of protection in the dirt or anything like that. But I obeyed without asking the reason why. Once mages set to work, it's dangerous to distract them.

With me positioned to her satisfaction, the wise woman started chanting words in a language I didn't recognize. Periodically, she tossed one of the items she'd collected into the flames until they were all gone. Afterward, the incantation droned on.

Then, in an instant, the fire turned from gold to scarlet and shot up high over Elkinda's head. At the top, the pillar of flame spread into a fan shape in a way that reminded me of a hand poised to swat a fly.

Elkinda gasped and jerked backward. She recognized the threat as quickly as I did, but that didn't mean she was spry enough to avoid it.

I lunged, threw my arms around her, and drove onward until balance deserted me and we fell. Behind us, fire hurtled earthward with a hiss like a cataract. A wave of heat washed over me.

But when I checked, neither Elkinda nor I were burning, nor had the plunging blaze left a sheet of flame licking at our feet. Some tufts of grass were charring and smoking, but mostly, the fire was gone. In the pit where the witch had lit it with a word of command, only coals remained.

I stood up, offered my hand, and hauled her to her feet. "Are you all right?" I asked.

"No," she said.

"Did I hurt you? I didn't want to knock you down—"

"I'm fine!" she spat. "But don't you understand what just happened? I can't cast out the incubus! It's protected. Too much darkness stuck to it when I pulled it up from the places underneath."

"Maybe if you try again?"

"I will. I owe everyone that, no matter what the danger. But it won't work."

"Then don't be foolish. Think of a different tactic."

She shook her head. "There's only one. I'd need to attack the incubus close up, with Skav in front of my eyes. That might tip the balance in my favor. But how could I do it without the trolls spotting me?"

How indeed?

Curse it, it wasn't fair. I'd called on the trolls once and lived to tell about it. That should have been sufficient.

But there isn't much in life that counts for less than *fair* and *should*. I took a breath and said, "Well, plainly, you can't creep up on them, not tottering along with a cane. We'll need to hide you where the creatures will come to you. And then I'll need to distract them."

———•———

MY SECOND MEETING with the trolls was set for dusk. Plainly, that was stupid. Even if a man survived the parley itself, he'd start the night in the deep forest for the man-eaters to stalk as the temptation seized them. But when Skav and I negotiated the details of the rendezvous, I hadn't imagined I'd actually be keeping it.

As Ojojum and I advanced up the trail, I resisted the urge to look for other trolls. It didn't matter if they were already shadowing us. The important question was, had the creatures stumbled across Mother Elkinda in the thicket where I'd hidden her that morning?

Unfortunately, there was no way of knowing, and perhaps Ojojum realized as much, for she, with her tangled steel-gray tresses and unborn child swelling her belly, looked as nervous as I felt. After a while, I noticed she was shivering.

It sounds asinine to say I felt sympathy for a troll, but perhaps it was because we were comrades in a dangerous venture. I touched her on the forearm, above the spot where some animal's teeth or horns had scarred her, and said, "It's going to be all right."

She shook her head. "I didn't tell Mother Elkinda everything Skav did to me. Beatings weren't the worst of it."

"It wasn't truly him," I said. "That's why we're here, to bring the real Skav back."

"I know." She spat in the dirt as a soldier will try to spit away fear. I shifted my hold on the chest tucked under my arm, and we headed onward.

I'd carried the box around through years of campaigning, and though I'd done my best to clean it up, it still looked like the scratched, utilitarian article it was. But I hoped that to troll eyes, it would pass for a reliquary.

After another bend, the trail widened out to make a clearing. Concealed by brush, a stream gurgled nearby.

Skav was waiting with much of his tribe but not, I was relieved to see, with a killed or captured Elkinda. Upon sighting Ojojum and me, he asked, "Where are the Hand Maids of Rendeth?"

"I apologize," I said. "When the time to set forth arrived, it turned out that even holy sisters are susceptible to human frailty. By which I mean, they were afraid to meet trolls. But surely that doesn't matter. You see Ojojum is with me. I also brought the relic." I held out the chest.

Meanwhile, I prayed my nattering had fixed everyone's attention on me. That Elkinda had lit her fire—she'd said she could manage with a small one, but the exorcism required at least a bit of flame—and started whispering her incantation without anyone noticing.

Skav glowered as though pondering whether there might be some way of forcing me to produce the absent nuns. Finally his red eyes shifted to Ojojum. "Have you truly come back to me?" he asked.

She hesitated, and the thought came to me that our deception was about to fail because she was too afraid to lie convincingly. But then she said, "You hurt me and shamed me, but a child needs a father. I'll come back if you take the oath."

"Good." The Hearteater looked back to me. "Open the box."

"As you wish." I set the chest on the ground slowly, feigning reverence. Then I slipped the iron key into the lock and tried to twist it.

It wouldn't turn. Since I'd previously broken the lock with the point of a dagger, that didn't surprise me.

But I did my best to feign surprise. As I jiggled and shifted the key, I said, "I'm sorry. I didn't try this before I left the temple. The Hand Maids didn't warn me the lock sticks."

Skav endured my clicking the key back and forth for a bit longer. Then a clawed hand gripped my shoulder and flung me backward. The troll chieftain dropped to one knee beside the chest and started trying to turn the key himself.

Why, you may wonder, did he bother? He surely intended to end this farce by giving Ojojum the most vicious thrashing yet and telling his fellow trolls to tear me apart. Why not get on with it, then?

I can only speculate, but maybe the incubus simply wasn't very clever. With the right bit of mummery, you could fix its attention on something insignificant.

Or maybe it enjoyed toying with its victims and so didn't care to reveal its true intentions just yet. It wanted Ojojum and me to enjoy false hope a while longer.

While Skav fiddled with the key, I silently implored Elkinda to hurry and fought the urge to glance in her direction. I wanted to know if there were at least wisps of smoke rising from the thicket, but I couldn't risk some troll looking where I was and spotting them, too.

Skav eventually snarled, sprang to his feet, and grabbed the chest. His claws digging into the wood, making it snap and groan, he swung it over his head.

"Please, don't!" I cried. "The chest is sacred in its own right!"

Ignoring me, he dashed the box to the ground. It smashed apart to reveal the emptiness inside.

The Hearteater rounded on me. "What does this mean?" he growled.

It meant I needed to improvise a new stalling tactic.

"It's a miracle," I said. "Rendeth whisked the lock of hair out of the chest and back to the temple."

Ridiculous as that assertion sounded, it gave Skav pause. His true plans for the relic had surely been impious to say the least, and perhaps in his mind, that bad intent lent my claim a trace of plausibility.

As before, his hesitation didn't last long. Then he said, "The hair was never in there."

"It was," I insisted. "I saw it myself before the Hand Maids closed the chest. And I know what this means." I turned to Ojojum. "You said you had to return to Skav for the baby's sake and so we could never be together. But the Bright Angel has given us a sign that our love is meant to be."

The trolls gaped at me. The notion of romance between one of their kind and a human was as bizarre to them as it is to you and me.

But grotesquerie was helpful. Anything to keep Skav off balance.

Ojojum was as surprised as everyone else and needed a moment to reply. When she did, though, she followed my lead: "Yes. You're kind, and Skav's cruel. You're clever, and he's stupid. You'll make a better mate and a better father."

Seemingly furious and dumbfounded in equal measure, Skav looked like he was struggling to work out a suitable response. Eventually he opted for the obvious.

"Enough of this!" he roared to his followers. "Come eat." He sneered at Ojojum. "You're going to eat his face, eyes, and pizzle, and afterward, I'll fix it so you never run off again."

Some of the trolls, the hungrier or less befuddled ones, started toward me. I drew my broadsword. The blade glowed white in the gathering gloom.

"Another miracle!" I cried. "Rendeth charged the sword with holy power."

I wished. The humbler truth was that Elkinda, loath to send me back among the trolls without some semblance of a magical defense, had muttered over the weapon and then set it outside for the better part of a day, during which time it had soaked up sunlight like a sponge holds water.

The trolls balked. The radiance stung and dazzled them, and maybe they feared the Bright Angel truly was watching over me.

But then Skav decided she wasn't. Or else the infernal spirit inhabiting him was game to try its luck against an agent of the divine.

The troll chieftain advanced on me. I came on guard, my sword held high to shine as much light in his eyes as possible.

This was pretty much the situation all my trickery and lies were supposed to avert. The sole difference between it and my grimmest imaginings was that I was only fighting Skav. For the moment, his followers were holding back, but it was far from certain that would change the outcome in my favor, especially when I couldn't even try for the kill. I still hoped that, given enough time, Elkinda would cast the demon out.

Squinting against the glow, Skav came closer still, then, with a quicker, lunging step, snatched for the broadsword. Though I didn't want to kill him, I was willing to wound him if that would slow him down, and I spun the blade to avoid the grab and slice his hand as I'd previously cut the watcher on the trail.

Skav spun his hand, too, and swept the sword out of line. He sprang and raked at my chest with his claws. The other trolls roared in anticipation of the killing stroke.

I leaped backward, and the attack fell short by a finger-length. He kept charging and slashing, and I continued my scrambling retreat. I tried to open up the distance so I could interpose my blade between us again, but he was pressing too hard.

Then I attempted a shift to the side that would cause him to blunder past me. He compensated.

In desperation, I suddenly reversed direction, advancing instead of retreating. That spoiled his aim, and his talons slashed harmlessly behind me. I bashed the broadsword's pommel into his jaw. If the impact stunned him, it would win me the instant I needed to separate myself from him and come back on guard. If not, I'd positioned myself perfectly for him to gather me into a flensing, bone-breaking bear hug.

The attack did stun him. Even so, simply by stumbling on forward, he nearly knocked me to the ground. But I wrenched myself out of the way and even managed to cut the back of his thigh as I did.

Unfortunately, though, when Skav shook off the daze produced by the clout on the jaw and whirled in my direction, he moved as fast as before. The leg wound didn't hinder him.

The thing that was hampering him was the sunlight stored in the sword. That became apparent when it dimmed and disappeared.

The trolls bellowed and howled to see the enchantment exhaust its power, and Skav came at me even harder. He could now see me better.

Whereas I was seeing him worse. With the glow in the blade extinguished, I discovered that if the sun hadn't quite set yet, it might as well have with the trees obscuring it.

Curse you, Elkinda, I thought, and curse my stupidity, too. Why had I staked my life on a second exorcism succeeding when the first one had been an abject failure?

I belatedly decided I should try to kill the Hearteater. If I succeeded, the trolls wouldn't have a demon for a leader anymore and presumably wouldn't go on a rampage. That would be victory of a sort even if I doubted the creatures would let me survive to celebrate it.

Since I'd been fighting defensively, when I came on the attack, it surprised Skav. A stop cut met a clawing hand and left the little finger dangling. He hesitated. I stepped in, feinted high, then low, then spun my blade high again to deliver the true attack at the juncture of his neck and shoulder. The cut landed where I'd aimed it.

But Skav drove at me once more. Leathery hide and dense muscle had kept the sword stroke from shearing deep enough to kill.

I jumped back. His claws still grazed my chest, though, and that was enough to dump me on the ground.

Skav threw himself on top of me. The hand I'd maimed retained sufficient strength to pin my sword arm, and the Hearteater raised his other hand to rip me to pieces.

Then Ojojum rushed in behind him, grabbed his wrist, and strained to keep him from clawing me. Her intervention roused the rest of the trolls from their passivity, and they charged forward, too. I had no doubt it was to pull her off Skav and enable him to get on with butchering me.

But that was when the incubus finally came swirling up out of the troll chieftain's head like steam from a kettle.

The spirit's long, rippling face seemed even ghastlier than before, because now it was full of rage and the rage was directed at me. Its cloudy arms stretching, it reached down and plunged its fingers into my head.

Its touch felt like what it was, filth slithering into me, but there was even more to the unpleasantness than that. Every nasty thing in my mind—emotions it had shamed me to feel, perverse impulses I didn't even realize I had—welled up to join with the intruder.

Given time, that dual onslaught would surely have crushed my will. But when Elkinda dragged the spirit out of him, Skav had gone limp. His grip on my sword arm had relaxed, and I was able to jerk it free.

I thrust the blade through the demon's torso and felt nothing. It was like stabbing fog.

Still, perhaps because Elkinda's magic rendered it susceptible, the incubus screeched, a shriek heard not with the ears but with the mind, and disappeared. To my relief, the vile sensations in my head vanished along with it.

Afterward, the trolls stood flummoxed by astonishment and, conceivably, even horror, for it seemed to me that the incubus's appearance had appalled them, as well.

In that moment of quiet, Elkinda emerged from her thicket.

"There," she declared, "all better."

Still heedless of his various wounds, Skav got up off me and embraced Ojojum. "I couldn't help it," he growled. "The spirit had me in its grip."

"I know." She ran her talons through his greasy black hair, dislodging a nit or two. "I know."

Skav rounded on Elkinda. "I should have said," he growled, "the spirit had me in its grip thanks to *you*."

I clambered to my feet. "You're right," I panted. "The wise woman's magic didn't work precisely as intended. But she and I risked our lives to save you, and at the end of it all, you and Ojojum have the child you wanted. That being so, I ask you to let us go in peace."

Scowling, the troll mulled it over. Then he asked, "All the things you said before. About being an envoy, the relic, and loving Ojojum. Was any of it true?"

"Not a bit," I said.

He laughed a grating laugh. "The demon believed, but I didn't. All right. Go."

I took a long breath and strode toward Elkinda.

Then Skav said, "Wait."

Heart thumping, I turned.

"We have gold," said the troll. "Some our fathers took fighting your fathers. Some, we took from city fools who hunt too deep inside the forest. Do you want some?"

I did. I knew just what to do with it.

With gold, I could rent a more fashionable space for my school, buy elegant clothes, and cut a stylish figure to attract the notice of Balathex's gentry. I could stage fencing exhibitions and demonstrate my skills. Gold was a second chance to achieve the life I wanted.

I smiled at Skav. "Well, if you're offering," I said.

HIS
KIKUTA HANDS

Lian Hearn

I N THE EAST they call him The Dog," the older brother said.
"He lived with the Kikuta family in Matsue for months and was
trained by Akio. The Kikuta master requested it. Apparently he
is his nephew and has all the Kikuta skills and more."

The Kuroda boy, who was a great scoffer, scoffed now. "You all go
on about his talents but I don't believe he has any. Why would he leave
the Tribe if he had? My guess is he wasn't good enough, he couldn't
take Akio's training and he ran away."

The man they were discussing was the new lord of Maruyama, by
name Otori Takeo, though to them he would always be known as The
Dog. Maruyama was the only great domain in all the Eight Islands to
be inherited by the female line, an anomaly which infuriated many in
the warrior class. When the last lady, Naomi, died in Inuyama, several
of the clan's elders wanted to change the system quietly and install
as lord someone from the Iida family, whose wife had a slight connection with Maruyama through marriage but not by blood, thereby

Illustration by ORION ZANGARA ▸

saving themselves the trouble of finding the next female heir, for Lady Maruyama's daughter had drowned with her.

Now Otori Takeo had turned up in the city with a Shirakawa wife, Kaede, claiming she was the heir to the domain, in which he was supported by the Sugita family, senior retainers to the Maruyama.

"I told you to kill the Sugita boy," the older brother said.

"His father and the other guard took us longer than we expected," the Kuroda boy replied. "When we'd finished with them the son had vanished. We could hear Otori's horses; we had to get out of there."

There had subsequently been a huge and bloody battle in which most of the warrior class had been killed, including the Iida pretender, resulting in the Tribe not receiving payment for dispatching the two guards, an omission which annoyed Jiro's father immensely. Soon it would be the least of his worries.

The young men were chatting before training. If people thought about the Tribe at all, for very few even knew they existed, they probably imagined their skills came to them magically at birth. It was true that talents were innate but they were nothing without training. Hours were spent every day in gruelling routines to build up muscles needed for leaping, bare hand fighting, and garrotting; even the less common talents like invisibility and the *second self*, though they seemed effortless when they first appeared, usually just before puberty, withered away without constant practice.

Jiro's elder brother usually led the sessions. There were not many pupils – Jiro himself, three Muto boys, and two Kuroda: the scoffing boy and a girl who someone thought might have some talent, though so far there had not been much evidence of it. Mostly she was used to run errands and make tea. Jiro was interested in her as she was the same age as him, and he'd heard whispers in the kitchen where the women gossiped that she would be married either to one of the Muto boys or to himself. His older brother was already married to the only Muto girl in their generation.

They did not use names much, just the common ones: Taro, Jiro, Saburo. When they became elders they would be given names that meant something to the Tribe. Jiro hoped he might be called Shintaro after the famous assassin who had died in the failed assassination that had brought The Dog to the attention of the Tribe. He was thinking about this as he began to limber up. It was already very hot. The training room had a wooden floor but the walls were plastered and painted white — if you could maintain invisibility against a stark white background, you could do it anywhere.

It had been believed that it was impossible for Shintaro to fail. He had murdered hundreds flawlessly throughout the Three Countries, yet The Dog had heard him and he had been apprehended. He had immediately bitten into the poison capsule, aconite encased in wax, which they all kept at the back of the jaw where the molar tooth had been extracted to make space for it. His death had sent shock waves through the Tribe, even as far away as Maruyama.

There were few families in the West. Their father feared they were dying out and wondered if they should not move east to Inuyama, but the years went past and he never made that decision. In Maruyama at least he was the sole ruler of his empire, even if it was a meager one. There was not a lot of work: the Seishuu clans of the West were an easy-going lot who settled their differences with marriage alliances, ceremonies, hunts, and feasts. The attack on the guards had been an exciting event — it was too bad they weren't going to get paid for it.

His brother cuffed him round the head, hard enough to make his eyes sting.

"Concentrate! Get to work! You're always dreaming about something or other. One day you'll wake up with a knife in your throat."

He faced up to his older brother, the Kuroda girl to hers. By the end of the session they both had bruised knuckles and ringing ears. He had been knocked down three times, the girl twice. He was seething inwardly.

The older brother said, "Hate me as much as you like. Hate your opponent, have no pity, and no hesitation." Then he went to the targets and loosed a few shafts. He was far and away the best marksman among them and loved his wisteria-bound bow and his eagle-fletched arrows.

Jiro spent a lot of time hating him but at the same time would die to save his life — in the Tribe that went without question. No one liked or had much affection for anyone else, but their loyalty was complete.

The girl gave him a quick glance. He thought he saw contempt in it, though maybe it was pity, which was no better. Her brother's back was tattooed in the Kuroda fashion. He wondered if hers was too. The thought obsessed him and he began to daydream about slipping the jacket from her shoulders and exploring the inked skin. He was at that age.

Maybe since she was the same age her glance showed interest.

Their skins were slick with sweat in the heat. The cicadas from the grove around the shrine were deafening. The thick woods cast dense shade on the rear of the house. It was on the edge of the city and, from the front, seemed a typical merchant's store where rice was fermented into wine, stored in casks and sold. The Tribe had the monopoly on its production in Maruyama, just as they had for the soybean paste that flavored everything they ate. Both had lately become more profitable than their other traditional trades of spying and assassination.

Behind the storefront were the living quarters, including several secret rooms and closets, and at the back were the indoor and outdoor training areas and the well.

Jiro lowered the bucket into the well, drew it up, and poured cold water over his head. He did the same for the Kuroda boy, admiring how the wet tattoos gleamed. Then he turned to the girl.

"Take off your jacket. I'll cool your skin."

She ignored him.

Inside the house the midday meal was waiting, trays and bowls set around the room. Their father was already taking up the wooden eating sticks. The men sat down. The girl went to the kitchen to eat with the other women. One of them said something to her that made her laugh.

Their father selected a morsel of grilled eel and ate deliberately and slowly, then he said quietly, "I've received a message from the Dog, and so have my colleagues in the Muto family, summoning us to consult with him tomorrow. I am a little surprised he knows about us and where to find us."

"What is there to consult about?" the Kuroda boy said cheekily. "Does he want us to tell him how we plan to kill him?"

"Will you go, Father?" Jiro asked.

Before he could answer the girl came from the kitchen and said, "Master, someone is here to speak with you. He says it is urgent."

Their father laid down the eating sticks and made a beckoning gesture. The man entered and fell to his knees. Jiro knew him by sight. He was of solid build with a plump face that looked dull apart from his glinting, deep-set eyes. He was from the Imai family and worked at Maruyama castle as a groom.

"What do you have to tell me that can't wait till I've finished eating?" the Master said.

Imai whispered, "There is a box containing records, made over the years by Otori Shigeru."

"Everyone knows Shigeru made records of everything, all his farming experiments and his crop yields." The Master drank his soup.

"And all his failures. That would make a long list."

"These are different. They are of the Five Families, of the Tribe."

"It is not possible," the Master said. "Nothing has ever been written down. The structure of the Tribe means no one knows more than they need to, at any time, not even myself and the other Kikuta masters."

"Yet the records exist. They are in the current Otori lord's possession. His wife carries them hidden among her clothes, and she has begun making copies."

Jiro sensed his father's unease. The Tribe's power depended on secrecy, on the ability to strike without warning and disappear without trace. As he said, no one, even within the Tribe, knew everything. How could an outsider?

The Kuroda boy said, "It would not be difficult to steal the records or get rid of The Dog or, better still, both. Shigeru was a failure: this Otori is a weakling, we know that much."

Jiro's father smiled. Maybe he was a little uneasy but he was not yet truly concerned.

"May I?" said the Kuroda boy.

The Master nodded. "It will have to be tonight."

The girl spoke from the doorway. "He will hear you, as he heard Shintaro."

"He will not hear me or see me," boasted her brother.

No one slept that night at they awaited his return. At dawn there was a clattering in the street outside, men pounding on the gate. The two brothers and the girl fled over the roofs on the father's orders while he took refuge in one of the secret rooms. They went to a Muto house nearby. The girl and Jiro were quickly hidden away in a cavity in the wall while the elder brother donned merchant's clothes and went out into the town to gather news.

The girl said nothing but he could smell her fear and her grief, not for herself but for her brother who they both knew must be dead.

The house smelled of fermenting bean paste. Normally it would have made him feel hungry but now it nauseated him.

"Killed by the guards outside the wall," the older brother said when he returned. "Better than being captured." He had changed from his town clothes into a dull-colored jacket and leggings like that of a farmer, but he carried his bow and a quiver of arrows. "I am going into the country for a while."

"Is Father safe?"

"He was discovered and arrested."

The two Muto men looked at each other in disbelief.

"How...?" said one.

"It is not possible," murmured the other, his voice petulant. Jiro could see how slow and inflexible they had become. They thought they were invulnerable; they thought they could outwit everyone, but now Otori had appeared like a fox in a flock of ducks, and soon they would all be headless.

"You are not safe here," the older Muto master said. "It seems he has been informed about every house and its secrets."

"Someone has betrayed us," said the girl. "Someone from the Tribe." Her face was contorted with fury. "Wasn't he close to your family, the Muto, in the Middle Country?"

"Save the accusations for later," the older brother said. "I will deal with Otori." He embraced Jiro, an action so unusual Jiro feared it meant they would never meet again.

"He has offered to spare anyone under the age of sixteen," the younger Muto master said, his eyes on his own son.

"I would sooner kill them myself." The older brother spoke as if he were already the head of the Kikuta family, but he would die three days later and the following day his father would be hanged.

The older Muto master took poison, the younger fled with his son to the east.

"Your brother took a shot at him but Otori heard the bowstring," the girl said to Jiro. "His horse, who is as cunning as he is, heard it too. I could have told your brother that. Not that he would have listened to a girl. Now he's dead — he took poison."

Better than being captured.

"I suppose that means you are the last of your family," she said. "I wonder if I am the last of mine."

I am the Kikuta Master, he thought. It brought him not the slightest shred of consolation.

They had moved from house to house, from wells to lofts, escaping the slaughter that took place in their wake. Even their ruthless upbringing could not inure them to the shock of witnessing the extermination of their kin. He saw in her his own blank eyes, dulled wits, and numbed limbs. On their last night she crawled into his arms. At dawn he traced the Kuroda tattoos of the five poisonous creatures that covered her back; snake, scorpion, centipede, lizard, toad. She took her hands in his and pressed her lips to the line across his palms that marked him as Kikuta.

"We'll be married," he said dreamily. "We'll start again, a new family of our own, maybe in one of the other islands, free of the Tribe."

"No one is ever free of the Tribe," she replied.

Even as she spoke they heard Otori's guards breaking down the doors.

That was the moment when they should have bitten into the poison capsules, but neither of them did. Jiro waited to see if the girl would, and then he would follow, but she didn't. Perhaps she was waiting to see if he would. Then it was too late. Their bodies wanted to live and be joined again. Desire betrayed them into hope.

So they were brought into Otori's presence alive and forced to their knees, their mouths held open with sticks and cords. He, The Dog, extracted the poison with gentle, Kikuta marked hands.

He had never been inside the castle before. There were fleeting glimpses of luxury in the cypress wood floors, the woven wall hangings, a smell of sandalwood, but the room they were taken into was unadorned, white walled, like a training hall. He knew instinctively that was what it was, and that Lord Otori, his Kikuta relative, trained here. And that The Dog could take on invisibility and not be perceived by any of them. And that he heard now the same soundscape that Jiro did, the tread of guards on the walls, street cries from the town, horses neighing in the water meadows, the surge of the tide against the rocks in the bay, just as he had heard the chock of the bowstring drawn by Jiro's older brother.

Jiro had expected him to be older, more brutal, more like a demon; this man was not much older than his brother, and there was a resemblance. You could see he was from the same family, perhaps a distant cousin. But he had an unexpected lightness to him, a dazzling, multi-faceted quality, very different from the dour single-mindedness that was demanded of the Tribe.

There were two other men, the senior retainer Sugita Haruki whom he knew by sight, and another man who looked like a monk, though he was dressed like a warrior. But it was Otori himself who loosened the cords that bound their wrists. He studied them both, saying nothing.

"So you are the last two," he said finally, with no air of pleasure or triumph, but something more akin to sorrow. "I will give you the choice I gave your relatives. You will renounce the Tribe and serve me, or you can die by poison or the sword."

He gestured towards a small table where the wax tablets had been placed in a celadon bowl. Next to the bowl lay a short sword with an unadorned handle and a blade so sharp it was almost transparent.

When neither of them replied he went on. "You are both young. You will find working for me has many benefits and rewards. Your talents, which I know are considerable, will be respected and put to use."

"Against the Tribe?" the girl said, her voice tiny and defiant.

"If I am to rule the Three Countries, and I intend to, I have to break the Tribe." He said it calmly, without vindictiveness, and smiled at them.

How did we misjudge him so? Jiro thought. *Why did we take him for a weakling?* The gentle demeanor, he saw, masked a complete ruthlessness. This would be a man worth serving. It would not be a betrayal: he was, after all, Kikuta. *If he commands me, I must obey.*

He felt desire to live flood through him. Never had the flow of his breath, the surge of his blood, seemed so precious. He looked up and into Otori's eyes, holding his gaze for a moment, before wrenching his own away, fearing the sleep the Kikuta could deliver. Certainly The Dog would possess that skill as he possessed all the others.

"They call you Jiro, don't they?" The Dog leaned towards him.

"Lord Otori," Sugita said in warning, taking a step forward.

The Dog gestured him to stay back.

"I already have a young man called Jiro in my service," he said. "He is about the same age as you, but of course not with the same talents. I need young people like you. Swear allegiance to me. I will give you your own name." His voice was compelling and calm.

Jiro felt a weight lift from his shoulders as he drew breath to speak. His new life stretched before him. But with a movement of incredible swiftness, taking even Otori by surprise, the girl grasped the knife and stabbed herself in the throat. The blood, shockingly bright, vermilion, sprayed across his face and threw a splashed pattern against the white wall.

Jiro looked again at The Dog, saw the regret and pity in his eyes and felt tears spring into his own for everything that might have been. The girl reached towards him even as her eyes glazed. The sword fell from her hands into his.

"I'm sorry," he said, and used the blade before regret could un-man him.

"Believe me, so am I," said The Dog, the last words Jiro heard before his sharp hearing finally failed, and his spirit fled after hers into the realm of the dead.

TAKE YOU HOME

David Dalglish

J ULIANNE SAT WITH hands folded across her lap, just as her mother had instructed, as their carriage rolled through the streets of Veldaren. The stone road was uneven and crowded, their driver lucky to keep them at a consistent pace for more than a second or two. The curtains were drawn, preventing her from seeing out, which left Julianne incredibly bored.

"Will we be there soon?" she asked.

"Your asking won't bring us there any sooner," her father said, head leaning against the side, cradling by his large hand.

"It won't be long," her mother said, casting an annoyed look to her father. She looked tired, dark circles underneath her blue eyes, her long brown hair lacking any luster as it fell past her neck. Julianne sensed the tension, and she prayed it wasn't her fault. Her parents had bickered about this trip to Veldaren for weeks, with neither seeming like they wanted to go. *Veldaren is dangerous,* her father had said over and over again. But her mother always countered with language of

tradition, trade, contracts, things far beyond nine-year-old Julianne's understanding. All of it must have meant something, though, for her father had relented, and together they'd traveled south from Felwood to the city of Veldaren.

Not alone, of course. They'd had their house guards, plus some servants, most of whom followed in the carriage behind them. The only strange addition was the man who sat beside Julianne to her right. He was a quiet man, having entered their carriage just before they drove through the gates of the city. She'd flushed upon first seeing him, for he was very handsome, his blonde hair cut to the neck, his blue eyes sparkling whenever he smiled, which was never enough for Julianne's taste. Whenever she could she peered at him, and she swore he was always watching from the corner of his eyes. Sometimes he ignored her. Sometimes he'd wink at her and smile.

The man was so charming it made it easy to ignore the long blades belted to his waist, to forget that she didn't know his name. Whatever the reason he'd joined them, Julianne had a feeling those swords were involved.

"*Get out of the way!*" she heard the driver shout, and the carriage lurched to a stop for the thousandth time that day.

Her father sat up, pulling back on the curtain so he could look out.

"Gods damn it," he muttered.

"Want me to take a look?" asked the blond stranger.

"It's probably for the best," her father answered.

The stranger pushed open the door and stepped out. The sounds of the city rushed in, louder than ever. She heard shouting, arguing, an intermixed bustle of motion and footsteps. The daylight was almost blinding, and she squinted and turned away. Wishing she could go with him, Julianne thumped her head against her door and lifted the curtain slightly. She was so short, she could only see the upper portions of the square wooden homes built on either side of the road.

Her mouth opened to ask again how long until arriving at their temporary home in the city when a shadow covered the door. She spotted a hooded man wearing a green cloak for the briefest of moments before the door ripped open. Instinctively, Julianne let out a cry and tried to scoot back, but hands were on her, a bag pulled over head. Her parents screamed, and she joined them as rough hands pulled her out of the carriage. Throat burning, she fought as coarse strings at the bottom of the bag tightened, choking out her cry. She gasped for air as her feet bumped along the stone, her tiny body easily carried. As the world turned brown, and then black, she heard the distant sound of swords clashing, coupled with the screams of men dying, dying just as she was now.

———•———

WHEN JULIANNE CAME to, the bag was no longer over her head. Her eyes slowly opened and she fought waves of nausea in an attempt to gain her bearings. She was in an empty building, dark, dusty, and with a tall ceiling. Her last few moments of consciousness flickered through her, reawakening her fear. Letting out a gasp, she pushed her eyes fully open to take in her surroundings. Her gasp made hardly a sound, for a gag was tightly wound about her head and shoved into her mouth. She sat in a chair, hands tied behind her with a large piece of rope. All around her were men with dark clothes and long green cloaks. At their waists, tucked into belts and loose hanging sheaths, were daggers and swords.

"The girl's awake," said one of the four men, glancing over. He had a hood pulled over his head, much like the others. His face was badly scarred, and when he smiled at her, it was the ugliest thing she'd ever seen. Immediately she tried to stand and flee, without thought or reason. The binds held her down, and all she accomplished was rocking her chair from side to side.

Casually, as if it were nothing at all, that same man walked over and backhanded her across the face. Tears ran down as she cried into the gag, and she felt her right cheek starting to swell.

"No need to rough her up, Jack," said another of the men.

"Nothing says I can't, either," Jack shot back, and he winked at Julianne. "The rules of the job say she has to be alive when he gets here. I don't remember hearing she had to be dolled up and pretty, though...."

The way he was looking at her, smiling, filled Julianne's stomach with bile. As Jack took another step toward her the door to the warehouse burst open, and a fifth cloaked man rushed inside. His hood was down, his short red hair wet with sweat. He looked young to Julianne, easily younger than all the others.

"What the fuck, Lee?" asked the oldest of the five, a man with wrinkled skin and gray hair who leaned against the wall beside the door.

"The Watcher!" Lee shouted, turning about and kicking the door shut. "The Watcher's on our tail."

Jack took a step back, a hand dropping down to the sword at his side.

"How do you know?" he asked. "He drop in all nicely to tell you?"

"Fuck you," Lee said, wiping a hand across his forehead. "I found Kirby's body three streets over, and the Watcher's Eye was carved into his stomach."

"That doesn't mean anything," said the older man. "The Watcher's killed plenty of Serpents in his day. What makes you think he's looking for us?"

"If you'd let me finish I'd tell you," Lee said. "There was a message written with Kirby's blood in the dirt beside him. '*Where's the girl?*' it said. We're fucked, all of us, we're gods-damn *fucked!*"

Julianne's eyes were wide as they bounced from one man to the other, trying to make sense of the situation. Who was the Watcher? And why would these five be so scared of him?

"Let me get this straight," the older man said, as he drew his sword and stepped closer to Lee. "You found Kirby killed by the Watcher, recently killed I might add, and then you ran straight here?"

Lee's face, already pale to begin with, paled even more.

"Not...straight here," he said. "I ducked through a few alleys first. I'm not stupid, Stan."

The others drew their own weapons, and there was no hiding the frustration on the older man's face.

"Ducked a few alleys?" he asked. "You wet-nosed moron. Did you hang out a sign at the door asking the Watcher to come in for a mug of ale, too? Shit. We're leaving, now."

Jack gestured toward the door.

"What about our payment?" he asked. "If we're not here when—"

"We'll set up another meeting," Stan said. "Something we can't do if we're fucking dead. Have I made myself clear?"

"Perfectly clear," said a voice belonging to none of them. The men in the green cloaks froze, and in that sudden calm the intruder descended from the rafters. He was a swirling chaos of gray cloak and boots and flashing swords. He landed in their center, and though she never saw the hit, Jack fell backward, clutching at his neck as it gushed blood.

Then Julianne knew. The way the others hesitated to act. The way Lee let out a horrified scream as a large urine stain darkened his trousers. The way the intruder smiled beneath his dark hood, as if merely amused by the weapons they raised against him.

This had to be the Watcher.

Stan had the courage to lead the attack, and all but Lee joined in. The Watcher spun in place, cloaks whipping about the air. Julianne could not follow his movements, and it seemed neither could her kidnappers. The men were beaten back, one losing his hand, another screaming as a wound on his chest seemed to open on its own. Stan continued on, stubbornly refusing to be overwhelmed by the display, and then suddenly the Watcher lunged into him. Their bodies crashed together, rolling. When they came to a stop, it was the Watcher who stood, shoulders hunched, cloaks falling forward to hide his body.

His smile was gone.

"Get back here," he said, his voice a whisper that somehow Julianne heard with ease. She wondered a moment who he spoke to, then saw Lee flinging the door open to the warehouse. A slender dagger flew end over end through the air, stopping in Lee's neck. The young man let out a cry, then dropped to his stomach.

With that, it seemed the fight was over. The Watcher walked from body to body, checking for signs of life. Only Jack made noise, weeping as he clutched his bleeding neck. He lay not far from Julianne's bound feet, and the sounds he made, the way his whole body seemed to shiver, filled her with an overwhelming desire to vomit. Only the gag kept her from doing so.

Without saying a word, the Watcher leaned over Jack, curled a blade around his throat, and then cut. Jack's convulsions grew, but only for a moment. Then his eyes rolled back and he lay still, leaving Julianne's stifled weeping as the only sound in the warehouse. The Watcher sheathed his blades then turned to her, and she let out a muffled cry. His face...it was covered in shadow but for his mouth and lower jaw. The grim smile there, so cold, so determined, convinced her this man was not her salvation, but merely another kidnapper. Eyes widening, she kicked and struggled, desperate to free herself from the bonds as the man stepped toward her.

To her surprise, her display halted his approach.

"Calm yourself, Julianne," he whispered. "I'm here to free you."

That whisper...why whisper, when everyone was dead? She stopped struggling, though, for there was no use. Sniffling, she stared at the Watcher, wishing the gag was gone so she could plead with him. The man knelt down so that he was at her height, and then he touched his hood with his hand. It never moved, but somehow the shadows receded, revealing a handsome face, square jaw, blond hair, and pretty blue eyes. Julianne felt hope kindle for the first time in her breast. The man...the man from the carriage?

"Your father sent me," he said, as if he could read her mind. "Now sit still while I untie you."

He walked around her chair, pulling her gag free as he did. She spat several times, wishing she could get rid of the sweaty taste. Behind her, the binds on her feet and hands loosened, and with a soft cry she lurched from the chair and spun about. The Watcher stood there, eyes on her, ropes in hand.

"Take me to my father," she said.

"I will," the Watcher said, the shadows returning to his face. "But I still don't know who hired the Serpent Guild to kidnap you. If I take you to safety, the man or woman responsible may arrive while I'm gone. That means whoever wished you captured could do so again, and next time I may not be fast enough to save you. Do you understand?"

"I think," she said, though she didn't really. "What do you want from me?"

He gestured to the chair.

"If you're brave enough, I can put you back in this chair, and we can wait. When the other party comes, I'll put an end to it, permanently. I need you to trust me, Julianne. I'll understand if you want to leave..."

She thought of going through it all over again, of trying to sleep at night knowing whoever wished her kidnapped or dead still lurked in the shadows outside the window to her keep. Though it made her hands shake, she nodded.

"I'll do whatever it takes to keep me safe," she said. "Just tell me what to do."

He smiled at her.

"A brave girl," he said. "Your parents should be proud. Sit down in the chair and wait."

She did, crossing her arms to fend off the cold she felt despite the warmth of the warehouse. The Watcher removed his large, strange-looking cloak, setting it on top of a crate in the corner. After that he removed Stan's green cloak, checked it for blood, and put it around his neck. Once done, he dragged the bodies one by one to the same far corner where the shadows were at their deepest. Julianne watched with grim fascination. When he was done, the Watcher returned to her chair and stepped around back.

"Put your hands behind you," he said.

She did as she was told, and then she felt the ropes slide once more around her wrists.

"The knots won't be real," he whispered into her ear. "The moment you pull against them they'll come apart, so don't panic or do anything rash. I need you to trust me, you understand?"

She nodded, praying that she did.

The Watcher circled her, examining his handiwork. Apparently satisfied, he picked up the gag and moved to put it her mouth. Julianne turned her head to the side, and as much as she didn't want to, she felt fresh tears roll down her cheeks.

"Please," she said.

The Watcher paused, then tied the gag loosely around her neck instead, letting it hang down as if she'd forced it free.

"Remember," he said. "Stay calm, and no matter what happens, keep your faith in me. You won't die this day, I promise."

And with that they waited, the Watcher hovering over her as he stared at the warehouse's lone door. Julianne didn't know how long they waited, only knew it felt like forever. Her rear hurt from the hard wood, her back ached from staying still so long, but she knew she had to be patient. She was the heir to her family's numerous plantations, and as her mother often told her, suffering through difficulties was part of the life they must live. At last the door creaked open, and she straightened.

Armed soldiers entered, one after the other, until there were six in the warehouse. Her protector watched them with arms crossed over his chest, as if without a care in the world. Last came a man in a finely fitted vest, black pants, and dark hair pulled into a ponytail. A smile was on his face, a face so familiar Julianne could not contain herself.

"Uncle?" she gasped.

The Watcher glanced at her, mouth turned to a frown, and she shrank in her chair. Meanwhile, Uncle Ross chuckled.

"I must admit," he said. "Of all the family reunions we've had in the past ten years, this is my favorite."

The soldiers fanned out, two remaining before Ross to protect him, the other four surrounding Julianne and the Watcher from all sides. Julianne's panic grew, and she struggled to remain seated. The Watcher had just taken on five at once, but that was with surprise against men without armor. Now there were six, and these soldiers carried long blades and wore chainmail beneath their tunics. What hope could he possibly have?

"Good of you to join us," the Watcher said with that strange whisper of his. "Now hand over the rest of the payment."

Ross reached into a pocket, withdrawing a small bag of coins tied shut with a string. He tossed it underhanded, the bag landing near Julianne's feet with a loud, metallic rattle.

"It's all there," he said. "Now do the deed, or get out of the way."

The Watcher's hands drifted to the handles of his swords.

"Consider it done," he said. "You can go."

Ross shook his head.

"Not good enough, rogue. I want my brother's lands, and I want them without any fear of complications. Julianne dies, and before my own eyes. I'm not risking you squirreling her away to ransom back to my brother after I'm gone."

Julianne's eyes widened. Her father's lands? But what did that have to do with her? How did her dying help her uncle? The Watcher seemed to understand, though, and he slowly shook his head.

"Murdering your niece for a chance at an inheritance? You'd fit in well with the people of Veldaren, foreigner."

Ross shrugged.

"I'll consider that flattery. Now if you wish to keep breathing, this is your last chance. Kill the little bitch, or get out of my sight."

The Watcher drew his swords, and he placed one against the skin of Julianne's neck. She tensed, body shivering, teeth chattering. Trust him, he'd said, and she tried to do just that. Looking up, peering into the shadow that was his face, she saw him nod ever so slightly.

"Kill the bitch?" he asked. "If you insist."

The sword vanished from her throat as the Watcher spun into motion. Like a savage beast he flung himself into the soldier at her left, but unlike a beast he made no roar, no sound at all, just the chilling silence and ethereal movements as his body leapt through the air, swords like extended claws. That silence broke the moment he made contact, blood splashing, soldier howling in pain, Julianne screaming at the sudden ferocity as the other guards came rushing toward her with drawn steel. Not him, but *her*.

Julianne leapt from the chair, and true to his word, the Watcher's knots slipped open with ease.

"Watcher!" she screamed, running toward him. The man spun, green cloak twirling, and when he saw her he ripped it from his shoulders and flung it over her head.

"Drop!" he screamed, and she instantly obeyed. As the cloak hit the men behind her she fell to her knees, curled into a ball, and put her hands atop her head. Nothing but a blur, the Watcher sailed over her, twirling midair, and then she heard steel clashing against steel, shockingly close. Teeth clenched, she curled tighter, listening to the battle, listening to the pained screams of another soldier. Something hit her back, and she flung forward, rolling to spin around. It was the Watcher who had kicked her, pushing her away as one of the soldier's swords struck the ground where she'd been. Frozen with fear, she watched as her protector battled two-on-one, swords bouncing back and forth between his foes, and though he was outnumbered, it was clear the Watcher was the one on the offensive. The soldiers looked so sluggish in comparison, so slow and weak and baffled.

The first dropped, blood gushing from his neck. Another took his place, only to quickly find a sword through his eye. Uncle Ross swore, and it seemed he finally realized there would be no victory for him that day. The final soldier leapt back, trying to guard the path to the door as her uncle fled. He shouldn't have bothered. The Watcher slid about him like water around a stone, smooth and quick, and then the sabers slashed out Ross's ankles before he could finish opening the door. As her uncle screamed, the Watcher spun around, anticipating the final guard's rushing attack. Both blades curled around his chainmail, piercing through his armpits and deep into his body. The man froze for a moment, blood gargling from his mouth, and then he dropped.

Yanking his weapons free, the Watcher stood among the bodies, shoulders rising and falling as he breathed in deep. Drops fell from his blood-soaked sabers, and not a hint of his face was visible through the darkness of his hood. Even knowing his reason for being there, even knowing she was safe, Julianne found herself more frightened of him than ever before. He'd killed eleven men, and not a scratch was on him. The only sound now was that of Uncle Ross groaning in pain as he crawled to the door.

The Watcher knelt over him, and without ceremony or hesitation, he plunged one of his swords deep into Ross's back.

"Bitch killed, as requested," he whispered into her dying uncle's ear as he twisted the blade. "Consider yourself lucky to receive such a quick death. You deserve far worse."

The Watcher stood, cleaned his weapons on her uncle's shirt, and then retrieved his original mismatched gray cloak. Sweeping it over his shoulders and clasping it tight, he turned toward her. The shadow around his face receded, and she saw his blue eyes, and in them was a strange sort of sympathy.

"Come, Julianne," he said, hand outstretched. "You're safe now."

It seemed a strange thought, but though his cloak, his shirt, and his arms were all stained, there was no blood on his hands. Rising, she accepted it, and the Watcher smiled.

"Let's take you home."

COMEUPPANCE

Linda Robertson

BRON'S SWEATY PALMS itched. His thighs flexed and his knees tingled, wanting to move. But he dare not. All his suffering, all his rage, every moment of his long, long wait faded away.

The gold was approaching.

His body demanded he charge ahead and be close to the treasure. But that was not the plan. He needed to remain hidden. He needed to watch and count. So, he studied the riding party while holding fast to the tree trunk—lest his desire conquer his mind and he find himself wandering into the enemy's path, drunk from the proximity of the valuable ore.

Accompanying the wagon were six sentinels on horseback, three in front, three behind. Another perched beside the driver, and two more dozed within the carriage. They all looked to be healthy and hearty men.

Ten in all. Ten!

He'd have to get past more men than he'd expected to even breathe on the well-guarded hope. His preparations were already in place.

They would have to do.

⟶·⟵

TIMOR SHIFTED IN his seat, beginning to understand why the other sentinels had quarreled about who rode horses and who sat the wagon. After a morning rolling along this rough terrain, the wheels made every bump an assault. He'd be sitting here the rest of the day, and all of tomorrow as well.

A saddle and an easy-gaited steed had to better than this wooden seat beside Old Hemly. He and the other riders had drawn twigs to determine who would sit up front. Having recently signed on as a sentinel, he was gullible enough to think he'd notched a little victory when he won.

But he hadn't met Old Hemly.

The man reeked of pickled beans.

The rising heat worsened the stench.

By midday, Timor was certain of two things: one, he'd never eat pickled beans again. And two, being *on* a horse was definitely better than being *behind* a gassy one. Let alone six gassy ones. He used to regard horses as majestic animals, but that view was dissipating much faster than the pong of their farts.

What other beliefs will I lose to this drudgery?

His father had died of a sudden illness, and now he and his mother had to repay his debt to the monarchy. King Callos said he would consider the amount repaid when they had both served him for five years—now four years, eleven months and fifteen days.

Timor hadn't wanted to be a sentinel. He hadn't even wanted to be a tailor as his father had been. He'd wanted to be a baker, but most bakers would find him too old to take on as an apprentice when his obligation to the crown ended. This misfortune would ruin his whole life.

He stared into his hands, at the callouses and blisters two weeks of sword-handling had given him. These hands were meant for kneading dough, not bleeding men.

Thinking of his sweet mother toiling in the fields, his eyes threatened to water. Feeling certain that, should this group be confronted, he would be the first to die didn't allay those tears. Worse, his death would do more than grieve his mother. It would extend her servitude.

He understood his father's joy in sewing. Taking flat cloth and creating a garment was like magic. Combining ingredients to make breads and cakes seemed a similar kind of alchemy. As a sentinel, though, he created nothing. He was simply a warm body standing in opposition to anyone who might seek to rob King Callos.

But no one had stopped the king from filching clothes from his father's shop.

Oh, His Highness had asked for the garments and attended fittings, but he claimed that since he had not actually "commissioned" them, he did not have to pay for them. No one forced the king to pay for what he called a "tribute." Apparently tributes neither offset taxes nor garnered royal pardoning where debts were concerned.

And now he sat guarding the gold of a man who wouldn't pay his father.

Just a few shavings of this would have kept his mother from toiling. A few more shavings and he'd have been a baker's apprentice. Instead, at thirteen, he was forced from his home, his dog, and his tutoring, to wear a uniform and carry a sword.

What do I know of weapons? Of stopping experienced thieves? Nothing.

The two weeks of training he and the dozen others new to the service had been given was comprised of how to draw, hold, and sheathe a sword, and a few drills such as stabbing into peasant clothes stuffed with hay.

The captain had said Timor's half-heartedness earned him a place in the kitchen peeling potatoes. His heart soared…until the captain added that the kitchen was already full of boys suffering from the affliction of aimlessness. He assigned Timor a position 'beyond his earning,' and advised him to be grateful for the opportunity to bring himself 'up to the loftiness of the assignment of a red uniform.'

Timor was convinced the captain's speech was as much a ruse as the twig-picking for seats had been.

The only good thing Timor recognized in his new situation was the fact that he would earn the same wage every day whether he sat on a wagon, rode a horse, or stood at attention outside the door of a vault.

Four years. Eleven months. Fifteen days.

He scanned around and sighed as if his spirit could escape on the air.

Old Hemly leaned closer and whispered, "You scared, boy?"

"Of what?"

"This path."

"Why would a bumpy path scare me?"

"*Hmpf.* Do you know why it's bumpy?"

He scanned the path between the horses, expecting to see ruts. Instead he saw an endless series of patches where the soil had been turned. Each dug-up spot was soft and the wheels dipped in, then heaved up onto harder ground.

"It's bumpy because when they felled the trees to get through they barely paused to chop the roots out, let alone waste time trying to level it."

"Why not?"

"Has no one told you of the beast of Brock Forest?"

Timor shook his head. He'd heard old men spin yarns before.

"No one mentioned the carnage the beast wrought on the men making this path wide enough for a wagon carrying the king's gold?"

Timor frowned. "No."

"Bodies ripped and burned and partially devoured. Each new party of axe men found the remains of the last and sent one man back with the news as the others began work. They started at the onset of summer. We're the first wagon through. Took them all those weeks to make way for a wagon and cost the lives of over sixty men. Near the end, any axe men left refused the King's call and he put axes into the hands of sentinels like you."

"Why bother with a new road? The King's Road is smooth."

"Ah yes. It runs through six towns where we might find food and lodging, and that sounds smart, but it takes eight days to travel from the mine fort to the King's castle. In that eight day trip, there are six towns where folks may decide to rob the wagon, and one night on the open road where brigands could lie in wait. A road *through* Brock Forest, on the other hand, means the trip would take merely two days. Only one night of risk. And in a forest known to be inhabited by a cruel beast, even the bravest thieves count the risk as too high." He fixed Timor with a squinty-eyed look.

"I'm too old to be scared by stories." Even so, he checked the position of the sun. There was plenty of light left in the day.

Old Hemly snorted. "I'm not trying to scare you, lad, I'm trying to warn you. Ask the others when we make camp. Ask that man at the lead, the one named Derk. He's the King's favorite nephew, don't you know. A learned man with integrity and character. You have to believe what *he* says."

"I'll ask." Timor wanted to resituate in his seat, but he wasn't going to give a hint that the smelly man's tale might have gotten to him.

"I bet you haven't been told about the curse of the mine, either, have you?"

"No."

"They say the gold from the King's new mine—the gold in the chests within this very wagon—is cursed and that all who come in contact with it will bear the curse."

"What curse? Boils? Hair loss? That all your livestock will fall ill?"

Looking from the corner of his eye, Old Hemly asked, "Are you so brave, lad, are you so powerful that you can mock a curse?"

"If it's so scary, why are *you* driving a wagon in a forest filled with monsters? Why would you risk bearing the curse?"

"A dozen drivers refused this assignment, preferring to be sent to the dungeon for a fortnight. Then they asked me. I said I'd do it…for triple the usual pay. And pay they did." Reaching within his shirt, Old Hemly produced what looked like a poultice. "It may stink, but this amulet ensures no beast will bother me and no curse can touch me." He tucked it away. "Sometimes knowledge is more dangerous than a weapon."

When they made camp as the sun was setting, Timor was sent to gather firewood. He was sure that, while gone, Old Hemly would tell the others the yarn and instruct them in what to do and say to work Timor into a real fright.

He was determined that they would not succeed. He wouldn't let them have such cruel fun. He wouldn't let them create something to ridicule him about for the next four years, eleven months and fifteen days.

Absorbed in such thoughts, he never saw the thin string along the leafy forest floor, but he felt it as his boot triggered the mechanism of the trap.

———•———

SUMMER WAS BEGINNING to wane but the heat remained close,

held in by the dense foliage. Even after years above ground, exiled by his peers, Bron had not developed an appreciation for all the green, let alone the heat. He would never feel safe in the expanse of a forest with the bright open sky above. Every day he longed to be within the walls of a cool, dark cave.

However, living on the edge of the world of men, he had learned much about them.

When they began felling trees, he knew there had to be a significant purpose—and it was not difficult to connect the gold in his cave as the one thing in the area worth the effort of creating a wagon path. He knew the time to act was coming. Using what he knew of men, he adjusted a certain area to appeal as a campsite.

And then he waited.

But waiting was a wretched thing when one's hands were idle and one's mind had nothing to do but wander around the angry landscape of his own head.

He cursed the magician responsible for releasing the enchantment that sealed the mine. He cursed the judges who'd sent him word that, "Due to new information that caused them to reverse their former decision about exiling him," they had opened his mine and it was waiting for his habitation. Because of the time required to travel back to this area, he was not able to secure the mine against human eyes. Filthy men had discovered his birthright and begun plundering it. They had even gone so far as to expand the walls of their nearby fort to encompass the mine's entrance.

Reclaiming the ore already stripped from his mine was the first priority. Removing the men from it was second. Only then would his grief be ended and his fury laid to rest.

Having trailed the wagon the whole way, he kept up on foot because their horses plodded along, slowed by the wagon's weight and the inconsistent ground. In the afternoon, their progress was halted as they had to deal with a tree that had…somehow…fallen to block their way.

They used the wagon team to haul the trunk to the side while the others, suspicious and swords at the ready, remained wary of some enemy about to attack. But no attack came.

The purpose of halting them was to allow Bron time to travel out and around and get ahead of them. It worked perfectly.

As the sun began to set, he was in place when they selected his prepared site for camp. He couldn't have planned it better if he'd been the one in their party deciding who to send out for firewood—they sent the young one. Soon, his cries brought the men of the camp to their feet. Swords drawn, the sentinels raced into the woodland. All but one of them.

Only the old driver remained behind.

Bron's cheeks rounded.

———————

THE NET THAT had captured Timor was still swinging when the sentinels arrived—and halted several paces away. "What are you waiting for? Help me!"

"Spread out," Derk ordered. "Follow the rope and cut him down."

Timor had already visually traced the rope holding him aloft through the thick branches. "It's that one there!" They were working their way to it when a strange sound—like thunder but too high pitched—echoed from the distance.

"What was that?" Derk asked.

"The beast of Brock Forest," one man whispered.

Timor realized they couldn't have made this trap as part of a ruse to heckle him, they'd all arrived at the campsite at same time. His stomach flopped. Old Hemly's story had to be true. "Hurry up!"

Remaining cautious, the sentinels finally arrived at the tree with the rope, but they couldn't reach the lofty binding. Two men dropped down on their hands and knees to allow Derk to stand on their backs and be tall enough that his sword tip could—barely—reach. He sawed at the rope, the distance and angle making it difficult for him to put much pressure behind it.

That sound came again, closer, more screech and less echo.

"Hurry, please, please!"

When Derk had severed more than half of the fibers that made up the rope, they started snapping on their own from the weight and pull of their burden.

Timor fell. His head bounced on the ground. He laid still, dizzy, stunned and hurting everywhere, hoping the sensation would pass.

The strange call came again so loud it resonated along his skin like beats of a drum. Something rustled the trees uppermost limbs. Branches snapped and fell all around them. The men's shouts mixed into the noise. Timor saw boots race past. He kicked at the net, but his senses seemed all backwards and movements seemed delayed. His vision was stuck sideways. He meant to kick the net off but his true motion must have been more like digging his heels in the dirt. The net wasn't going anywhere.

There was shouting, roaring, screeching, screaming.

Please just stop hurting. Get up. Crawl away. You have to crawl away from here. This is bad. Your mother needs you, so you can't just lay here and let this beast rip and burn and devour you.

Then a large shadow darkened the already fading light of the world around him. He feared losing consciousness…then a green-skinned talon with blood drenched claws touched the earth just inches from his nose…and he prayed for oblivion to take him away.

———

BRON APPROACHED FROM the rear, moving in spurts that took him from bush to bush. The nearby screeches had the horses rightly nervous. They shifted about and nickered as they strained their tethers, nicely covering the noise of Bron's movements. The old man had taken refuge under the wagon, but otherwise seemed relatively calm.

One more bush and he would be close enough to make his attack. Ignoring the persistent itching in his palm, he drew his dagger and firmed his grip. He scanned the distance to the next bush and while waiting for the next screech watched the old man.

He couldn't help grinning. Everything was going according to plan.

The roar echoed like thunder. He shot toward the last bush.

But there was one thing Bron had failed to anticipate. He should have recognized earlier that his own reaction to the gold was going to be a problem.

Now, in spite of the thickness of the wood encasing not only the wagon but each of the chests, that precious metal within, that ore that was the very lifeblood of his heritage, was aware of his nearness and aware of its virtually unguarded state, and it called to him…singing an inescapable siren song of doom.

———•——

THE SENTINELS WERE all dead. Timor, still bound in the net dared not move, yet he could not stop trembling.

The dragon growled as it drew near him. He shut his eyes.

Oh, mother.

He felt the talon touch his head, slide across his face, and down to the soft part of his belly.

Death be quick. Don't let it hurt.

The tension in the beast's talon vibrated and the claws pressed and curled…around the net. With a jerk, the creature flung him from the confines. He rolled across the ground, stopping only because of a stout tree trunk that felt like a kick in the gut.

He meant to be motionless, hoping the dragon would think him dead and leave him alone, but his forehead was bleeding and running into his eye. He couldn't help wiping it away. He opened his eyes to a large, snarling reptilian face just inches from his own. It snorted a breath.

Timor squeezed his eyes shut again.

Heartbeats passed. He heard a shifting of leaves.

Daring to look again, he saw the dragon pushing a sword toward him. Put it inches from his hand. Slowly, he sat up, putting his back to the tree trunk.

Take the sword. Die like a sentinel.

His fingers twitched. The strange, catlike eyes before him narrowed. In a swift move he covered his face and cried, "I'm not a sentinel!"

The toothy snout lurched forward to touch the backs of his shaking hands. With a voice like crackling flames, the beast asked, "Then what are you?"

"A boy," he mumbled pitifully. "Just a boy who wants to be a baker. My father died and now I have to work for the king...the same king who stole from my father."

———•———

REKSIAN SNATCHED THE boy and leapt, propelling them through the treetops and into the air. Wings spreading she soared only a short distance before plummeting down and landing beside the wagon.

Horses panicked and reared. A few snapped their tethers and bolted. Some could not. This did not surprise the young dragon.

What did, however, was seeing her friend Bron on his back struggling to hold off the arms of an old man whose gnarled grip held Bron's own dagger.

She dropped the boy to the side and dived forward, jaws open to take the old man's arms off—but she stopped.

A stench that filled her gaping maw which was so repugnant it made her shiver and recoil. Her jaws snapped open and shut, open and shut, but the foul odor plagued her tongue and would not wane.

She had startled the old man, but as she retreated, he returned to his purpose and set about bringing the dagger down on Bron.

Growling, angered by this reaction, and desperate to save the dwarf, she tried again, and again putrid repugnance filled her mouth. This second dose seeped into her skin, flowed up her nostrils, and into her head. She backed up. She stumbled. She dug her claws into the ground, struggling against the sensation that she was clinging to the face of a cliff, about to fall to her demise.

Not far away, the boy wrestled to his feet and staggered toward Bron and the old man. She whimpered and lamented.

The runt of her family and overpowered by her clutchmates, she was regularly denied a share of the meat her mother brought to the cave nest. Though gold was more sustaining, it was unavailable, and they made due on meat…but there was not enough for them all. Poor Reksian had crawled under a crevice to die the morning when King Callos's sentinels came into the cave and killed her mother and her clutchmates.

In the depth of her grief, she was aware that if not for her weakness, she would have died with them. Only she remained. She could lay there, hidden, and die. Or she could accept an unpleasant option and act.

She crawled from what should have been her grave and ate dragon meat. And she vowed to avenge them.

Bron was the one way she had found that she could achieve that goal. In his gold-rich cave, she would grow large enough and strong enough to destroy a kingdom. Dwarven enchantments kept men—as well as dragons—from finding their caves, but in need of help, he'd agreed to house her in his cave and let her feed on a portion of the ore in exchange for her aid and protection.

It was a partnership she'd expected to be rife with success.

The failure at hand, however, hurt every bit as much as watching her family being slain.

"C'MON AND DIE, you filthy, ragged little dwarf!"

Bleeding and aching all over, Timor managed to lift his head and look at Old Hemly.

"Just you and that coward are left…then the gold's all for me!"

The dwarf snarled in response. "That's *my* gold! Stolen from *my* mine!"

Timor struggled onto his feet. He stumbled from tree to tree, feeling dizzy and drained, but he knew the beast of Brock Forest was kept at bay by the power of the amulet the old man wore. Somewhere in the back of his mind, he was aware that the stinking trinket would protect him as well.

But the dragon hadn't harmed him though it could have. Even in the fog of his mind he felt certain that, had he lifted that sword, it would have torn him apart like the other sentinels.

"Help me, lad," Old Hemly rasped.

He thinks I didn't hear him. "Help you? How?" Timor asked.

"Just get something and bash him in the head. I'll do the rest."

Timor turned around, looking for a rock or a log. The dragon remained several paces away, whimpering. He spied no rock. No log. His gaze shifted to his empty hands. He couldn't overpower anyone. *These hands weren't meant for bleeding men.*

"Hurry boy!"

Stepping around the pair, Timor summoned all the strength he had left. He snatched the amulet with a jerk so hard it choked Old Hemly for a second before it broke. Then he ran.

———

BRON'S ARMS QUAKED from the prolonged strain and weight of the old driver. Each tremor shook the hope from his heart.

Then the young human drew near.

Never would he have wagered that the lad would betray the driver. Now he had only to hold the old man off until Reksian recovered and rescued him.

It didn't take long, after the boy reached a certain distance.

One moment he fended off his enemy, and the next there was nothing but forest sky above him.

His arms continued shaking and, slowly, he lowered them, grateful that his last thought would not be a complaint about an old human's stink.

My gold!

He clambered up from the ground and scurried to the wagon. Defying the complaints his body made, he climbed the spokes of the wheel, hauled himself onto the driver's footrest, then crawled onto the wagon top. Flipping over the side, he crashed through the window and landed atop a wide wooden chest. The air was knocked from his lungs, but he couldn't have been more joyous. The gold pulsed rhythmically beneath him and for the first time in many years, he felt a sense of home.

He lay there laughing with what breath he could muster.

Until a human face peered in the other window.

———

REKSIAN SAW BRON thrust a large piece of glass at the boy, and saw the boy withdraw so fast he tripped over his own feet. Sprawled on the ground, exposed and vulnerable he labored to stand, but he'd nothing left. His shoulders tensed in anticipation of the strike.

"Bron, no!" She leapt and landed with wings spread protectively over the boy.

"Out of the way, dragon!"

"I won't let you kill him!"

"What do you care? He's a sentinel!"

"He didn't draw his sword on me. He could have."

"So he's a coward."

"He's not a coward. And he's not a sentinel, either. He's just a boy."

"A big boy." Bron crossed his arms, still holding the glass. "One who knows too much."

"Like you, he's only here now because he lost his father."

Bron spat on the ground, paced away then back. "Dragons aren't supposed to be sentimental."

"Sentimentality has nothing to do with it. He has as much reason to hate the king as you do. Better to let a human like that live. Don't you think?"

Squinting, Bron said, "You know him well for having just met him."

Reksian told him what Timor had said, and the circumstances that brought it on. "Now, you will give him a brick of the gold and one of those horses and let him go."

"Why should I reward the cowardice of a human child?"

"You're rewarding a boy who will remember that a dwarf and a dragon saved him. He'll take that knowledge with him. And," Reksian stepped away so as not to be protecting the boy anymore. "He will deliver a message to the king for you."

He rolled onto his stomach and looked up at her.

Swearing, Bron threw down the glass and clamored back into the wagon. "This is coming out of your share," he grumbled as he returned and handed a gold brick to the boy whose eyes widened in disbelief.

"Tell the king that by the time he gets this message, every man in the fort will be dead. Tell him to forget it exists, because *any* man who enters will forfeit his life."

———◆———

TIMOR BURIED THE gold under a thorn tree twenty paces off the road and twenty paces within the border of the forest. He broke a low branch to mark it.

Satisfied that his treasure was well hidden, he rode to royal fortress.

When he stepped before his sovereign, King Callos looked him over, assessed the dirty and torn state of his clothes and sneered. "I am told you have a message for me, page?"

Page. I'm so filthy he cannot see the red of my sentinel's coat beneath the grime. His chin lowered. "I am Sentinel Timor Bolden, son of your tailor, Farric Bolden, and servant in debt to you for another four years, eleven months, and fourteen days."

Surprise showed only in the marginal lift of his brows. "And what news have you brought, my filthy sentinel?"

The courtiers laughed.

Timor lifted his chin.

He noted the fabric of the sovereign's clothes was one he had seen before in his father's shop, his father's handiwork right before him. The king looked regal, the colors and fit afforded him every detail the appearance of someone just and wise should convey to those who looked upon him. But Timor recognized those threads gave dignity to the man who'd taken advantage of his father. A customer who had not paid and could have. A foe who had made hostages of he and his mother with a few mere words.

Timor's head lowered again, fighting tears even as his hands curled into fists.

"Speak boy. If you can." More laughter.

"I was assigned to the wagon from the mine fort, Your Grace."

The laughter stopped. Silence fell in the hall.

"What happened, boy?"

I may not have the skill to fight with a sword, I may not have the fortitude to charge against a foe, but I can wield words as well as my king.

And my knowledge is more dangerous than a weapon.

Timor firmed his voice and faced the king. "Old Hemly's gone mad. Killed everyone except Derk and me. He said that he'd poisoned the well at the mine fort and everyone there would be dead before he could get back there—but that was where he was going. Gave me a horse and told me ride here and deliver the message. He said if you want your nephew back, you have to come there yourself and negotiate. Said he'd kill Derk if he saw any face other than yours come through that gate."

The king narrowed his eyes at Timor while he considered the words. "Very well. You may go. Leave my hall and clean yourself next time prior to coming before your king."

Timor nodded, casting his gaze to the flagstones in an effort to hide his lie.

"General!" the king called out.

"Yes, Your Grace?" The armored general clattered forward.

"Ready my horse."

"Yes, Your Grace. Ready the king's horse!"

Timor turned and strode from the king's hall as a pair of soldiers hurried past him toward the royal stables. He suppressed a smile, thinking of a dwarf's gold, of his mother finally free from her life-long burdens, and of a worthless king's comeuppance in the belly of a dragon bereaved.

SCREAM

Anton Strout

S O..." THE WOMAN said, drawing the word out with the long, slow hiss of a snake, her eyes dancing with mischievous curiosity. "What *is* your secret, Mister Canderous?"

The crowd of tourists and hipsters seated around us in Katz's chattered away like a gaggle of geese as they stuffed their faces with copious amounts of New York's finest deli fare. I, on the other hand, remained silent as I flecked crumbs of rye off my Ramones 'Gabba-Gabba-Hey!' t-shirt, much to the redhead's annoyance.

I wasn't in the habit of ignoring questions, especially when they came from someone as attractive as the woman who had introduced herself as Mina Saria as she slid in the seat across from me not five minutes ago. Then again, I usually didn't have gorgeous women tracking me down through some of my art dealing fences, either.

Her hawk-like eyes peered out from under bangs of dark red that was a color found more in a bottle than in anything in nature. When I didn't answer her, she sat back in her chair and folded her arms across her chest.

Illustration by OKSANA DMITRIENKO ▸

"What makes *you* so special then?" she asked, changing her tack slightly.

"It's all in the hands, Miss Saria," I said, sliding off my thin black leather gloves and laying them on the smooth surface of the table.

"You've earned quite the reputation out there among the forgers and the fakers," she said.

"Have I?" I asked as nonchalant as I could, trying to mask the swell of newfound pride that rose up in me.

Mina gave me a single nod and a smile. "Yes. It appears they don't like how easily you see through their frauds."

"Sucks to be them," I said, flexing my fingers.

"Most people say you have to have a good eye to do what you do," she said. "Spotting forgeries."

"Well, there are *some* fakes you can tell right away by sight," I said, going for the bowl of pickles a waiter had set down before us, biting into its briny goodness. "For me? It's all about how it *feels*."

The fact that a bit of psychometric tinkering factored into it was not something my potential employer needed to know, but I couldn't help but feel that swell of pride again. This time I gave into it. And why shouldn't I? I had turned a near crippling preternatural power I could barely control into something that was proving quite lucrative among the arts and antique stores up and down Broadway. Not to mention classing up the walls of my newly acquired SoHo loft. Now my growing reputation had put this gorgeous redhead at the table with me, and that was far from something that normally happened in my day to day.

The woman's face was full of skepticism, but I said nothing and continued eating.

"Can you prove how talented you are?" she asked. I raised an eyebrow and she leaned forward. "I like to see things for myself. After all, my team and I want the best at our disposal. Please don't take offense, Mister Canderous."

"None taken," I said with a dismissive wave. "And please, call me Simon. As far as proof…"

The moment I had hoped for, which was why I had picked so notable a meeting spot as Katz's Deli. I gestured to the sign overhead. A red arrow pointed down at where we sat.

Where Harry Met Sally… Hope you have what she had! Enjoy!

Mina looked back down at me, so far unimpressed. "So?"

"We'll see about that," I said and laid my hands back down on the table.

It had taken what little control I had over my power to keep it in check when I had taken my gloves off, but now I gave into it and let the electric connection lash out as it always did, wild and barely containable.

Some objects in this world barely held a psychometric charge, but the fame of this film location saturated the entire deli, allowing me to focus all that raw power down and better direct my vision. My mind's eye filled with a thousand images in an instant. Every person who had ever touched this supposed famous table over the years flickered through my thoughts, and I fought to push through them, sorting as I went.

Like my own personal DVD player, I rewound through the images trying my best not to be pulled in any specific direction. When I caught the bright lights and camera equipment of the film shoot, I focused in until the familiar movie scene was upon me, seeing it from an entirely different perspective than I was used to from watching the film.

I had forgotten how 'Eighties' the Eighties truly looked, but the clothes of the extras were a perfect reminder. It was odd to see a young Rob Reiner directing an equally young Meg Ryan and Billy Crystal in the now famous scene, but one thing was immediately clear. The table I was reading was *not* the one actually being used in the filming. It instead sat about fifteen feet away in use by one of the film's grips to raise and focus a lighting unit on the actual film scene itself.

I had everything I needed and with a force of effort I pushed myself out of my mind's eyes. The strength of the vision held me transfixed in it longer that I would have liked, but with one final struggle I tore free from the historic moment. Gasping, I opened my eyes wide to find Mina Saria staring expectantly at me.

"Are you all right?" she asked. "You looked like you were stroking out."

I wasn't sure how long I had been in the vision, but by the way I was shaking and my head swam, it had been a bit too long. I grabbed my corned beef sandwich and began scarfing it down.

"Blood sugar dropping," I said between bites.

"Hypoglycemia?"

"Something like that," I said and fell back to eating, allowing me to dodge discussing it further, which was fine by me. Why my blood sugar plummeted while using my power was as much a mystery to me as it would be to her. It wasn't like I could just take the issue to my doctor to ask about.

When I was done eating, I licked the last few drops of mustard from my fingers.

"You want to tell me what that was all about?" she asked.

"Let's say this table was up for auction," I said, slapping my hands down on it. "As a piece of Hollywood history. First thing I'd tell you is that this table *wasn't* used in the film."

Mina looked up at the sign overhead and pointed to it. "It wasn't?"

I shook my head. "It wasn't even in the shot," I said.

"Bullshit," she said, and waved a waiter over.

A heavy set man in his late forties lumbered up to our table. His ring of what remained of his black hair was wild and curly, his eyes kind. He smiled at Mina.

"Yes?" he said, the hint of something European in his voice.

"This *is* the table from the movie, right?"

The man hesitated, then pointed to the sign overhead as Mina had, saying nothing.

"Be honest now," I added.

His gaze shifted back and forth between the two of us, then he cautiously looked around the room before leaning in to us, whispering.

"Yes and no," he said with some reluctance.

Mina looked annoyed. "Meaning…?"

"This is the *spot* where they filmed the scene, yes," he said, "but actually the owner took the original table off the floor long ago. It's in his home or the Smithsonian, I believe. Anything else?"

Mina shook her head and the man told us to enjoy our nosh and walked off to clear a table.

When I turned back to her, she appeared suitably impressed, and I tried to contain my smug smile.

"Well?" I asked.

The redhead looked me over. "All that from just the feel of the table, huh?"

"Like I said, it's all in the hands."

Mina leaned forward and held her hand out to me. "Then I do believe we have a deal, Mister Canderous."

"Hold on now," I said, moving my bare hands away from her by leaning back in my chair. "I didn't say I was ready to seal the deal."

"Oh?" she said, dropping her hand to her side.

"You haven't told me what you expect from me," I said.

"Just some light thievery and breaking and entering."

"I don't know what your contact told you about me," I said, pushing my chair back, "but I'm in the business of identifying fakes and forgeries, maybe perhaps keeping the occasional rare find for myself. Why would I steal for anyone's benefit other than my own?"

"Because it pays remarkably well...?"

I stood. "I'm not sure there's a price you can name. Sorry."

"Please, sit," she pleaded. "I work for the Metropolitan Museum of Art."

"Tsk tsk, Miss Saria," I said. "You want me to help you steal from your own job? What must your bosses think? I don't think any price you name is going to talk me into even going near the Met, sorry."

The first rule of Psychometry Club was 'no museums'. With my power and limited control of it, a location so full of history would drain me and leave me a flopping fish on the floor before I could barely make it past the main lobby.

"Thanks, but no thanks."

I turned away from our table and started toward the turnstile exit at the front corner of the restaurant.

"You misunderstand," she called out. "You wouldn't be stealing. Think of this more of a recovery."

I stopped and turned back to her. I leaned over the table, lowering my voice. "If this were legitimate, lady, you wouldn't be trying to hire *me*."

She paused as she collected her thoughts before once more speaking. "This is a delicate situation," she said. "You've indeed heard of *The Scream*, yes?"

Intrigue got the better part of me at the mere mention of the macabre piece of art and I slid back into the seat across from her. "Sure," I said. "Who hasn't? *Der Schrei der Natur.* The Scream of Nature. Gaunt fellow, pulling a *Home Alone* face slap on a long, haunting road. There are four versions by Edvard Munch."

One of Mina's eyebrows raised, disappearing behind her long, red bangs. "Impressive," she said.

I shrugged. "It's a sort of Holy Grail in art thieving circles. They've all gone missing at some point. Always recovered, I might add."

She laughed, but quickly regained her composure. "There are art thieving circles?"

"Not really," I said. "They're all too paranoid, but you get the idea."

She nodded. "One of them is currently on loan from the National Gallery of Oslo to the Metropolitan Museum of Art," she said, then her face fell. "Or was."

"*Was?*"

"You misunderstood me before, Mister Canderous," she said. "I don't want to hire you to steal it. It's *already* been stolen. We need your help retrieving it."

I sat back in my chair as I took her request in, surprised at the nature of it. "From who?" I asked. "From where?"

"As you said, it is highly sought after by the wrong crowd," she said. "Forgeries of it abound. We have some leads, but we need help if we're going to conduct our investigation in an expedient and covert manner. Time—forgive the cliché—is of the essence."

I shrugged. "So send the cops out, round all of them up."

Mina paused before proceeding, and when she spoke, I could see in her eyes the care with which she chose her words. "My higher-ups would appreciate some… subtlety in the handling of this," she said. "If we can recover the painting before it needs to be returned to Oslo, we can avoid a tangle with the Norwegians."

"There's something I never thought I would hear," I said with a chuckle, but Mina didn't laugh, her face remaining stern. "Sorry."

"An international incident would reflect poorly on our institution and the city of New York, Mister Canderous," she said. "Years of diplomacy would be undone." She leaned in and finally let a smile cross her lips. "And be honest…wouldn't you like a chance at getting your hands on *The Scream,* even if it's only for a few moments? How many men can say that? Not to mention the service you would be doing your city…"

She had a point… more than she truly knew. Under the security of a museum's watch, *The Scream* was untouchable. But if I could find it with 'the someone' who had already saved me the trouble of getting it out of there, I just might be able to pull off this dream heist for myself. I'd check out whatever forgeries Mina had in mind, and if I came across the real one, I'd misdirect her until I could secure it for myself.

Mina studied my face, and when she saw me smile, she extended her hand once more.

"My services don't come cheap," I reminded her. "To validate the right painting, especially one as famous as this…"

"Price is no concern," she said, smiling.

I slid my gloves on and took her hand in mine, the sensation of my power dulled to the point where I was back in control of it now. I shook her hand with a wide and wicked grin. "Getting paid to steal *The Scream,*" I said. "Who said crime doesn't pay?"

———

THE MOVIES ALWAYS made breaking and entering look oh so easy and yet it was anything but. Especially with three people watching. Luckily, they were also covering me while I knelt on the steps of a townhouse working the tumblers on its main entrance.

"Can you hurry it up?" Mina asked, her voice hushed under the rustling of wind through the leaves of the tree-lined Upper East Side cross street. "I would think after the first dozen places, you'd have mastered picking locks by now, Mister Canderous."

"Can the three of you kindly fuck off?" I asked, but kept my concentration on my tension control driving the pins under the shear line within the lock.

"Ooh, feisty," she purred, which seemed appropriate given the tight leather cat suit she had managed to squeeze herself into for our evening of burglaries. "I'm sure that mouth will do you well in prison."

"I can feel the three of you watching and it's not helping," I said, not bothering to look back at them. "It's like being pee shy."

"All right, let's all turn away," the one called Kreuger said. His voice sounded as heavy and thick as the man himself. I could picture him behind me, hulking and no doubt buttoning and unbuttoning his black leather coat as he had done a thousand times tonight so far, a habit that I found both annoying and distracting—even when I couldn't see him doing it.

I didn't appreciate Mina bringing along goons for this, but at least they knew how to keep watch so it was one less thing to worry about so I could get my job done.

"Hope you're faster with the interior alarm on this one," the other goon said. Meyers, I thought his name was, although he had spent most of the night watching me in silence.

"Much faster," I replied as the outer door finally clicked open with one last push against the tumblers in the lock. "In. Now!"

The long slow countdown of the alarm system arming beeped away. I ran in before the others could even move and slapped my hand down over the keypad. My psychometric connection snapped to, and my mind's eyes traced the history of the keypad's recent use.

A pale man with dark hair worked the numbers, but at a speed that seemed more than human. I rewound the instance over and over in my head until I could slow it enough to see the number he was keying in.

1337.

I pulled myself out of the vision, only a little shaky from the psychometric reading. Over the increasing tones of the beeping, I keyed the number in, silencing it. My hand shook from my power depletion and Mina held up several rolls of Life Savers.

"Here you go," she said. "I have a diabetic friend who swears by them."

I took a few and crunched them down, surprised at how quickly I felt better. By then she and her cronies were already moving through the dark interior of the townhouse. The main floor looked posh yet normal enough, but once upstairs the building had more of a museum vibe, the walls thick with art and the floor dotted with display cases filled with a variety of antique looking pieces.

"Who *is* this guy?" I asked. I slid my gloves back on, not wanting to trigger off anything in the townhouse by mistake.

"Just another eccentric collector," Mina said, stepping carefully through the room.

On the far wall of the main upstairs room hung *The Scream*, prominently displayed at the focal point as it had been at four of the previous places we had visited tonight. The four of us crossed to it, mindful of disturbing anything as we went.

Not every replica had looked all that genuine, but upon a cursory examination this one held up under my initial scrutiny.

Krueger and Myers kept back, but Mina settled in at my side, examining the painting herself.

"Well?" she asked, her eyes dancing with an anticipatory hope. "What can you tell me about this one?"

"We'll see." The painting itself had its own keypad alarm next to it. I pulled my gloves off, grabbed its code psychometrically to disarm the alarm. I reached for the painting, but before my fingers touched the edge of it, my power crackled to life like tiny jolts of lightning.

The visions associated with the other paintings tonight had varied. One had been reproduced in a loft in Chelsea while two others had been crafted in what looked to be a forgery operation downtown in the Bowery. Another had even been done by a museum staffer who had simply wanted to try his hand at duplicating the piece.

None, however, had screamed with the raw historical power of this one. Its journey to our country form Oslo flashed backwards through my mind's eye, but just seeing it back at the National Gallery wasn't enough for me, I realized. Experiencing this history didn't have to stop there… after all, how often was I going to get the chance to see the actual artistry and creation of a painting like this in action?

I pressed my power further, pushing back through the painting's history until its very creation. The tall, thin man I suddenly found myself as in the vision looked much like the gaunt figure in the painting, only with dark hair combed to one side and a thick mustache. *Edvard Munch himself.* He worked on the painting that would become *The Scream* where it stood alongside several others in a Berlin studio, and I marveled at the artistry unfolding from his—no, *my*—hand as the piece worked its way from swirls of colors to the end result of the painting. My cheeks hurt from the smile that had crept across my own face back in the real world. I had witnessed something no other human ever had—save Munch himself—and the sensation was truly overwhelming which, I realized, did *not* work to my advantage right now. I needed to pull myself out of the vision if I was going to trick Mina into thinking this was just another imitation. Once convinced, I could come back for it later, but first I had to return to reality.

Pulling my mind's eye out of the vision was harder than I imagined and took all my will, the effort driving a spike into the center of my brain to the point that when the connection broke, I stumbled back from the painting, shaking and on the verge of falling over.

Mina grabbed my shoulders to steady me, but I slumped to the floor anyway. I fished for the Life Savers in my pocket with still-shaking hands.

"What the hell was that?" she asked. "You look like you're going to pass out!" She turned from me back to the painting. "That's the real deal, isn't it?"

"That painting…" I managed to mumble through a mouthful of candy as I shoveled it in. Shaken as I was in my current state, I could barely speak let alone muster the guile to try to pull the wool over her eyes. I shut my mouth, and gave a simple nod.

"Are you sure?" she asked, glancing back and forth between me and the painting.

The sensation of being Munch was still coursing through me as I pulled myself up off the floor. "Pretty damn sure."

Like a tree on Christmas Eve, Mina's eyes practically sparkled. "Finally!" she shouted with a squeal, wrapping her arms around me. Her body shook with glee, and in a rush of adrenaline she pulled away, grabbed my face and kissed me hard.

If I wasn't already busy recovering from my psychometric hit, I might have been able to stop my connection from snapping to. Instead my mind flooded with unbidden images of Mina's private life. Images of all her previous art recoveries flickered through my mind, but as they flashed by one thing became abundantly clear.

I pushed myself away from her body, my lips pulling away from hers.

Her face was awash in confusion, no doubt having sensed the psychometric connection.

"You don't actually recover art for the museum," I said through labored breath. "You find it, sell it, or keep it for *yourself.*"

She backed away, her face changing from elation to something wicked—wicked, but confused. "How... how could you possibly know that?" she asked, rubbing her temple. "What did you do to me?"

"You hired me because I was good at finding fakes," I said. "What did you expect? I found the fake. It's you. Let's make something clear... I'm *not* going to help you steal this, Mina."

I reached for the alarm panel next to the painting and just managed to rearm it as a meaty hand closed on my wrist and pulled me away from it. *Myers.*

"And you wondered why I needed the muscle," she said. "Too bad. This could have become terribly lucrative for you, Mister Canderous... now it's just going to be terrible."

I stepped back from her. "I'm not getting paid, am I?"

"Paid in pain maybe—"

I turned to run, hoping to twist out of Myers grip, but he was stronger and quicker, twisting my arm behind me while Kreuger pulled back one of his fists and pistoned it into my stomach. The air went out of me, and all I could do was take it as Kreuger gut punched me over and over.

One thing became immediately clear: I needed to come up with something before they beat me into unconsciousness. There was no way I could take them both on. My only advantage here was my power, which frankly didn't seem cut out to be remarkably helpful in this particular situation.

Unless...

I needed to find an advantage somehow, but for that I realized I would need skin-to-skin contact to activate my psychometry.

Kreuger's next blow to my stomach had me barely able to breathe, but I managed to look up into his eyes and forced myself to speak.

"That ...all you got?"

I kept my head up, daring him to strike me in the face, and he couldn't resist the target. The bone of his knuckles slammed into that of my jaw, the sensation jarring, but it gave me what I needed. A flash of Kreuger's life filled my mind's eye, lingering for a second then disappearing. I needed more.

"You're going to have to rough me up pretty bad with those meat hooks if you want me to be even half as ugly as you, Kreuger."

Another blow, another flash.

"I'd say you hit like a grandmother only that would be an insult to old people."

The blows rained down harder and harder, each one triggering my power. My mind's eye fought to make sense of the flashes, and like going through a kid's flip book, the images began to fit together into a cohesive flow as I sorted back through the thug's day. He might be busy beating me with his fists now, but hopefully Kreuger had not started his day leaving home empty-handed.

I kept searching his memories until at last an image of him strapping a thick, metallic cylinder to his belt hit me. It came to me in the vision just before I watched him leave his dingy Inwood apartment, concealing the tube with his heavy leather coat.

I pulled out of the vision and back to the present. Although I couldn't see the object on him now, it was the only hope I had.

As his next blow came towards me, I let my entire body go slack, my arms slipping out of Myer's hold as my full weight dropped to the floor. My knees screamed with pain as they took the impact, but I was already rolling myself forward, reaching into Kreuger's coat. Thankfully the cool metal of the cylinder was under there in its special holster, secured by an elaborate safety tie, but thanks to my vision I knew exactly how to undo it. I pulled the object free, rolled onto my back and pushed myself across the floor as I examined it.

A safety mechanism sat housed over the single button on the object. I flicked the cover of it off and pressed down. The thick cylinder telescoped out with a metallic *shkkt*, becoming a regulation sized steel baseball bat.

Myers stopped mid-lunge. Kreuger, however, looked more than pissed that I had taken his little toy and came on at a full on charge. I swung, catching him in the midsection with a meaty thud that doubled him over as I wound back and hit him again and again. After my third or fourth strike, Myers finally lunged into action to help, but I twirled the bat in his direction and poked him in the chest with the end of it, driving him back.

"Enough!" Mina called out.

Her voice held enough authority to make me pause and glance at her, while Myers helped Krueger stand. The men's eyes burned through me.

Their boss stepped forward. "Put down the weapon, Simon," she said, her voice calm but commanding.

I shook my head and raised the bat. "So you and your goons can kick my ass some more? No thanks."

From some hidden fold on her cat suit, Mina slid free a long, thin blade. "Suit yourself," she said. "One of us is leaving here with the painting, and here's a hint: it's not going to be you."

Thievery was the furthest thing from my mind. Survival was more my concern, and with three to one odds *and* a knife in the mix now, my chances were looking slimmer and slimmer.

"Fine," I said, backing myself further across the room from the painting towards the second floor windows. If only I had rolled myself across the floor toward the stairs. Stupid 20/20 hindsight. "I don't care if that painting leaves with me, but I'm damned sure you're not taking it either."

Mina sighed. "Your funeral," she said. She flipped the knife around in her hand like a seasoned street fighter until she held it in an aggressive stance with the blade protruding underhand.

Mina and her two thugs started across the room, closing with me and approaching from three different directions using caution.

"I don't think so," I said.

Mina laughed. "No?" she asked. "And why not?"

I pointed to the painting. "I rearmed the alarm system, Mina," I said. "Now you might not be familiar with the finer points of them, but I am." She didn't need to know much of what I had gleaned about this set up had come from being psychometrically in the mind of the townhouse's owner. "In a sweet pad like this, you think the guy who lives here is going to skimp? No, he's going to go top of the line. You try to take that painting… you'll trip the alarm, the front door deadbolts, the windows shutter with steel plating. That sort of thing."

"So?" Kreuger asked with a growl. "We'll still beat you to death before anyone can get in here."

Despite the menace in his face I had to laugh. "I'm not planning on sticking around, guys," I said, raising the bat high. "Sorry to disappoint."

The three of them paused as I swung into motion, but they needn't have worried. None of them were my intended target. With my windup, I turned to the window and swung with all I had.

Glass exploded and fell to the street below as I worked the bat around the window frame, knocking away what I could of its jagged remains. I spun around to find my assailants closing with me again.

Mina raised an eyebrow. "You can't be serious."

I pulled another roll of Life Savers out of my pocket. Taking careful aim, I threw it across the room, toward *The Scream*. It wasn't a heavy enough object to do any damage to the painting itself, but it was enough to trigger its alarm. There was no siren or bells or whistles, but the slamming locks on the downstairs door and windows were enough to tell me it had gone off.

"You won't survive the fall," Mina said, a nervous desperation in her voice.

"I'd rather take my chances out there than in here with you lot," I said, and without waiting jumped into the open air just as the steel window shutters started sliding into place. I was in freefall.

I loved the townhouses of Manhattan, and this street lined with them shared a common trait I had noticed earlier—almost all townhouse streets were lined with trees. I had simply taken in their quiet rustling in the wind as a thing of beauty earlier, but now they were proving my salvation.

Not that the drop was an easy one. My body sailed from the window out over the sidewalk and into the trees next to the street. Branches and leaves poked at my face and eyes as I descended head first. I fell blind as my body exploded with pain, branches breaking some of my fall while others battered and bruised me the entire way down. The final freefall to the sidewalk left me stunned and aching, but I appeared unbroken, alive, and most importantly, not trapped inside with Mina and her thugs.

Already the sound of sirens echoed in the distance, getting me back on my feet faster than anything. I picked up the retractable steel bat from where it had fallen out of my hands.

Tonight had proved a bust, but at least I wasn't going to be busted. Plus I had this nifty new weapon, which I collapsed to its original size and slid inside my jacket before taking my first shaky steps.

"And this is why we only steal for ourselves, idiot," I muttered as I hobbled off.

By the time the rolling reds and blues turned onto the street, I was already rounding the corner onto Fifth Avenue. Shaken, I wondered if perhaps this was a wake-up call, a near miss that the universe had sent down upon me in the hopes I'd shape the hell up. At the very least it was clearly telling me I wasn't built for the life of a career criminal, which I guess I already knew. After all, I didn't look good in stripes or an orange jumpsuit, not to mention that my dating life would probably only get worse if I went to prison over something like this. The idea crept into my head that maybe this power could somehow be turned to something more constructive, to DOING GOOD…not that I had a clue as to the 'how' of all that.

Still, this was *The Scream* we were talking about, *the* Holy Grail of art thievery. Perhaps it wasn't the best painting to go cold turkey on, despite the close call tonight.

Never return to the scene of a crime, the old criminal axiom said, but it was hard to let go of such an opportunity, even after a failed first attempt…

My brain couldn't help but already start planning my return trip to the townhouse. How could I not? Most people would worry about dealing with the changes to a security system or new countermeasures being installed, but when you had psychometry on your side, all those changes are instantly knowable and literally at my fingertips.

Only next time there would be no bullshit stories, no false pretenses, and no partners in crime to get in my way. It wouldn't be about someone else or even the money a painting like that could earn me. In this case, the only way crime *would* pay was because something as special as *The Scream* didn't deserve to be bought or sold. No, it deserved to be appreciated, and as the sole person alive to have just experienced the painting's creation—save Edvard Munch himself, that is—I planned to appreciate the hell out of it on the space right above the mantle in my apartment.

Let the Norwegians be as pissed as they like. They had, after all, lost four versions of *The Scream* over the years. What was one more?

MAINON

Jean Rabe

T HE ROASTED PIKE with green sorrel *verjuice* was amazing; Mainon held a piece on her tongue and relished the flavor. The scents from the other dishes arrayed on the table—artistically prepared marine and freshwater fish—competed for her attention. It had been quite some time since she'd dined in so lavish a place.

The chairs were thickly padded and covered with expensive red brocade, the floor was gleaming marble, and the table made of a polished wood so dark it looked like a patch of a starless night sky come to ground. Soft music drifted from behind a silk curtain, a reed instrument and a harp, and a third instrument she couldn't identify. Everything seemed carefully designed to delight all the senses.

She thought to compliment her host, but remained silent, not wanting him to know she was pleased and impressed. If she'd been in her home city she would have made arrangements to talk to the chef and urge him to share a recipe or two, for the pike in particular. But she was a full day's ride from home, visiting the port city of Nyrill.

So she simply continued to savor the meal, take in the surroundings, and scrutinize her host.

Ilarion was a noble of the merchant house of D'multek, a handsome man with oiled, dark hair, even olive skin, and wide, dark eyes that caught her stare and held it. Despite his voluminous robe, she could tell he had a muscular build. She'd researched him, a man born to wealth who in his relatively short life had managed to considerably increase his family's holdings. Even his upcoming wedding would further expand his business and influence. He had chosen a bride from the nearby country of Crullfeld, from a family nearly equal to his own in riches. Mainon learned of the bride, too—Erleene Hawe—who, at twenty-two, was a dozen years younger than Ilarion. She was said to be the oldest daughter of a cloth merchant. Erleene was not present at this feast.

Mainon was far from her own beautiful self this day. Her long black hair was coiled around her head in a tight braid and tinted by a simple magical glamor that rendered it a flat earthen brown. The same spell made her brilliant green eyes a dull gray and gave her a scar that ran from the base of her right ear down her neck. She wore ash-colored silk robes with a faint green trim, making her appear almost drab.

"I nearly did not come to this meeting, Ilarion," Mainon said. She took a sip from a crystal goblet filled with a pale gold wine. The wine was a little too dry; the only spot of imperfection in the elaborate meal. "I prefer to meet clients on my own terms and in places of my choosing. It is rare I make an exception. And I did not appreciate dealing with messengers upon messengers to set this up." She took another sip and found it a little better. Perhaps it was an acquired taste.

Ilarion quietly regarded her before speaking, creases forming in his brow as if he measured what to say. "There was no choice regarding the situation, the messengers upon messengers, milady."

His voice was rich and deep and Mainon wondered if he sang.

"Given my position in this city, this meeting had to be on my terms, and with my requirements." He leaned forward, elbows resting on either side of his plate. "But obviously my messengers intrigued you just enough. You are here, after all."

Mainon allowed herself a slight smile. "I am here until I finish this meal. Speak quickly."

Before he could continue, the waiter brought dessert, and Mainon did not hesitate to sample it. A mashed pear tart, baked in butter, rose water, and sugar, it was dusted with cinnamon and ginger and served in a small pie shell.

Ilarion watched the server depart. "I've a need to hire you, milady."

"And the target?"

"I have a seer in my employ who I consult on various matters. Three days past he relayed to me a vision most disturbing. He warned me that an assassin has been hired to kill me before my wedding to Erleene. She is not at this dinner because I do not want her to know about the assassin. I wish no worries on my new bride." His once musical voice was strained now. "The seer believes someone does not want our houses joined and my power expanded. Thus I had my messengers find you, she who is said to be the best assassin in this part of the world. I want you to kill the one who has been hired to kill me. Kill the killer, so to speak." He leaned back in his chair and waited for Mainon's response. "You haven't much time. The wedding ceremony is in two days. Please, milady, help me."

She glanced at the men around the table and stationed in corners; considerable security for Ilarion. It would be difficult for an assassin to get past them. With a silent spell, she discerned the noble wore magical baubles to further protect him, as did some of his guards. She wondered why such a man with so many layers of insulation would fear that an assassin could succeed.

Could she succeed?

"I have no faith in seers, Ilarion. Oracular magic is unreliable, and most who claim to command it are fakirs. Prophecies speak only to possibilities. The future is not guaranteed."

Could she succeed in assassinating Ilarion?

Perhaps, she decided, that would be the way to approach it. How would she go about killing Ilarion? That might lead her to the one sent to kill him.

"Nonetheless, Ilarion, consider me hired."

———————

NYRILL'S POOREST LIVED near the docks. Mainon saw that the colors were dreary, the air filled with the scent of fish and filth, and many of the people looked beaten down by their own misfortune. Some had no homes and wore and carried all their possessions; it was the same in her home city, they were just spread out in various districts there, not concentrated in one place.

Farther from the sea, the view improved and the air smelled cleaner. As the land rose, so did the level of society. Like cream, the wealthy floated to the top.

Ilarion's manse was perched high atop the bluffs that overlooked Nyrill. The richest of the city's residents built their homes on the bluffs; the higher their elevation, the more wealth they commanded. Only a few mansions were farther up than Ilarion's.

A veritable palace, she considered his manor house, for it was that lavishly decorated. She spotted crystal and gold in every room, expensive incense burning, and not the smallest speck of dust anywhere. She shook off the unaccustomed envy of his great wealth; she'd been in several such dwellings before, though admittedly none were quite this opulent.

Mainon decided to make a much more thorough inspection of the manse and grounds when she finished meeting Ilarion's staff. She was introduced to advisors and guards, accountants, librarians, poets, artists, musicians ... so many people she could recall only a few names and conjure up flashing images of faces.

Xeno Icculus, however, she had no trouble committing to memory.

The seer politely bowed and extended his hand. "I told Ilarion to hire the very best assassin his coin could buy." Xeno's voice was commanding, but raspy, and that coupled with a yellow tinge to his thin fingers and the corners of his lips showed that he indulged in smoking water pipes. "My incantations revealed that to be you."

"Then reveal something of yourself to me," Mainon returned almost too quickly. "It would only be fair."

The pair sat in a room filled with gilded harps and other musical instruments that appeared to be more for show than intended for use. The walls were painted a dark burgundy, matching the rugs on the floor, but enough light spilled in through the window to reveal the faint lines on the seer's patrician face.

His brown hair and beard were cut short, a little gray showing throughout, but mostly at his temples. Well into middle years, she judged, but striking in appearance. His fair skin, made all the paler by rich brown robes so dark they appeared black, suggested he was from a faraway land, and his thin arms and long neck made him look birdlike.

"I am a true seer," he began, waving a hand with a theatrical flourish.

Or a good actor, Mainon thought. He had the voice and manner of a thespian. Did he really see Ilarion's demise? Could he in truth foresee the future?

"I work the caravan routes occasionally, not wanting to limit myself to any one city for an extended length of time. Ilarion would like to consider me one of his employees, but this is not the case. While I accept coins from the man—for my services—it is not a formal or permanent arrangement. I spend a fair amount of my days in Crullfeld ... and in a few nearby countries as well."

A silence settled between the two, Mainon studying Xeno's eyes. They didn't blink. He didn't look away. There was no nervous twitch, only a steady gaze, and she swore she saw herself mirrored in his pupils. She pulled in a deep breath, casting an enchantment at the same time, and scenting the magic about him.

"And I am a more powerful wielder of the eldritch energies than most in this city," he continued. "Certainly more practiced than those in Ilarion's steady employ. Stronger in the arcane arts than you. But no doubt you've just discovered all of that."

She cocked her head. There indeed was that much magic about him.

"Are you still skeptical of me, Mainon?"

She released a breath she'd been holding and turned to look out the window. "I am always skeptical of seers."

"Safer that way," he said. "But safer for Ilarion that he is not so skeptical and believes my vision. Had he not believed me, he would not have hired you. Had he not hired you, there would be no wedding, only a funeral."

"You might actually be genuine." There was hesitation in her voice. He didn't reply.

"So I will take this threat against Ilarion very seriously."

"Safer that way for him." Xeno stood and brushed at the folds in his robe until the garment hung straight. "As I said, my spells revealed that you are the best. This evening I will show you my vision that led to your hiring. First, I trust you'll want to more closely explore the grounds. I understand that you've been to the city before, but never so high up on the hill."

ONE DAY TO go until the wedding, and the kitchen buzzed with hushed conversations from a dozen men and women working to prepare complicated pastries that were being kept chilled by a wizard in Ilarion's employ. Castles made of sugar, swans sculpted of various confections, lilac-tinted pie crusts that would hold ... what? Berries? Chocolate? Something deadly for the groom?

Mainon's sense of smell was acute and her eyes keen, but she did not pick up anything amiss. Spell after spell revealed nothing poisonous ... nothing poisonous at this particular moment in time. Did Ilarion have tasters who would first be sampling everything on the wedding plate? Of course, she told herself. Still, poison remained a possibility; it was a method she would have considered were the contract to kill him hers.

The laundry was next, an oppressive, hot, stone room below ground where the steam swirled as thick as fog on an early-morning river bank. Here only women toiled, hair plastered to the sides of their heads and sweat stains deep in their garments. From time to time a long-nosed man came in to observe and bark orders. Mainon found no trace of poison in the soap or water, nothing anywhere.

She spiraled up and out, discovering magical wards that nearly caught her, guards stationed in shadowy niches, paintings with false eyes where more guards peered through to watch those who traipsed the halls. In the courtyards beyond she found enchanted snares—nothing lethal, but all of them designed to catch and firmly hold a trespasser. A good assassin could get by them all, she noted. She had. And no doubt many of the wards would be rendered ineffective on the wedding day, Ilarion not wanting any guests to be offended.

A good assassin could get onto the grounds and into the manse, especially someone well dressed and appearing to have an invitation.

She strolled by neighboring manor houses, pressing herself against garden walls and listening to pieces of conversation when "Ilarion" or "Erleene" were mentioned.

"He marries not for love," someone said. "He marries only to add to his wealth."

"She is beautiful. I could spend the rest of my days living in the glow from her smile."

"Ilarion wants to own the very top of the bluff, to have no one perched above him. This wedding will guarantee that."

"There were local women he could have had his pick from, beauties all of them. And from good families, too."

"Our daughter ... he once considered her." Mainon made note of this particular residence. She would discover who lived here and if there was animosity between them and Ilarion. "Too close to his own age, our daughter. Not young enough."

"Ilarion will put on a display the likes of which this city has never seen. I've heard they've been preparing cakes for weeks."

"He'll not live to see his first child born. There's talk of an assassin." Mainon found more than one home where this rumor flowed.

A good assassin could indeed succeed, she decided as she picked her way back to Ilarion's manse. But it would take a very good assassin to get back out undetected. The assassin would have a masterful disguise, perhaps looking like one of the groom's close friends or guards, and would need a considerable amount of magical talent.

Mainon's mind churned with the possibilities of how she would approach it. Perhaps Xeno's "vision" would give her a clue.

"WELCOME, SKEPTICAL MAINON." Xeno gestured to a velvet-covered cushion in the center of a small room.

There were no pieces of traditional furniture, just cushions spread across thick rugs. The room was heavily draped and lit by lamps that hung from the walls at regular intervals. Oil residue streaks extending up the walls from the lamp bowls hinted that the drapes were rarely opened.

She sat cross-legged on the cushion he'd indicated, back straight and shoulders square. He took up a position opposite her on a cushion that was not so plush. One he sat on often and had mashed down over time? She noted his eyes were glossy, and she detected a trace of flowery tobacco scent on his robes. Xeno had been smoking a water pipe recently. Did he need them for his visions?

"I trust you completed a most thorough inspection of the grounds?"

She continued to study him and the surroundings. The room seemed out of place compared to the rest of those in the manse, dark and nothing outwardly valuable in it. She hadn't noticed the door to it on her first two passes through Ilarion's home. Perhaps it had been magically masked. She would have to take another walk through the residence, this with a more careful eye and enchantments at hand to discover if there were other such secret rooms where an assassin might find a secure hiding place.

Xeno said something else, but she missed the first several words, caught up in thoughts about the manse.

"I came here to see this vision of yours," she answered. She drummed her slender fingers against her arm, making no attempt to disguise her impatience.

"My time is limited, too. Shall we begin?" He closed his eyes and rested his elbows against his knees, arms outstretched and palms up, fingers splayed wide.

Theatrical, she judged, a true wielder of magic needed few gestures or special poses; she needed only her mind and an occasional bauble to augment her natural talents. She peered at him closer, finding all four rings on his right hand pulsing with a steady, but faint dweomer. There was a magical pendant around his neck, and something under his robe that she couldn't see.

His lips moved and he spoke an archaic language that sounded vaguely familiar. An incantation, certainly, and when he finished an image formed between them.

"Ilarion," Mainon said.

"As he will be dressed tomorrow on his wedding day."

"You've seen the cloak and shirt?" They were shot through with gold thread, the fabric a creamy silk that shimmered in a light that cut through swirling shadows and came from somewhere within the vision.

The seer shook his head. "His wedding garb is secret, only seen by himself and his closest attendants. I merely know this to be a piece of time plucked from tomorrow."

"Before the ceremony?"

He shrugged. "Yes, but how soon before I cannot say. This sort of magic is not so precise ... as I believe you've pointed out to Ilarion and myself before. Continue to watch, please."

Shadows deepened around Ilarion, whether from candles and lamps flickering or people moving around close, but out of range of the vision. Curtains fluttering? A cape billowing? Mainon strained to make it out, but instead locked onto Ilarion's face. His once handsome visage suddenly contorted in pain and his mouth opened. He screamed, but no sound came from the image. It was long, and she imagined shrill, his agony obviously intense. He twitched and dropped to his knees, writhing and contorting in ways his limbs weren't designed to move. Sweat beads blossomed on his skin and dampened his wedding garb. A moment later tiny blossoms of blood erupted on the creamy fabric, as if invisible darts had been thrown at him from all directions.

The gyrations continued for uncomfortable long minutes before Ilarion stopped breathing. A line of black blood spilled from his mouth.

A quick death, she favored dispensing. More dignity in it for her and her target. But this assassin? There was malice involved. This assassin didn't just want Ilarion dead, but to suffer mightily.

Mainon stared at her client's face, frozen in torture. A shudder danced down her spine, chasing away the last of her skepticism in Xeno's arcane skills.

"And Erleene?"

Xeno drew his lips into a thin line. "I've had no visions of her. I believe she is safe from the assassin's wrath. She is the eldest of five girls, so killing her would not prevent the houses from merging. Ilarion would simply choose the next daughter in line, then the next. The marriage is for power, milady." His breath whistled out between his teeth. "But slaying my friend Ilarion ends the potential merger. Ilarion is an only child. Can you stop this? Prevent my vision from becoming real? Can you save my friend?"

"That is what I have been hired to do." She rose from the cushion and padded toward the door.

"Then hopefully his coin is being well spent."

Where would Ilarion be when the attack would come? When? Her repeated questioning of Xeno yielded no more information. He'd said if he could provide that information, Ilarion wouldn't have needed to employ her.

"And ... milady ... please find something more appropriate to wear for the ceremony tomorrow."

She glanced down at her ash gray robes and left Xeno's hidden room.

An hour later, she pinned one of Ilarion's guards to the floor outside the kitchen. He was wiry and squirmed beneath her, legs bucking and sending her off him and against the wall. Mainon's head struck hard and she bit down on her bottom lip to keep her focus. Then she leaped at him again, drawing a knife from a sheath on her calf and going for his throat.

He'd done nothing suspicious, said nothing to alert her that something was amiss. But she'd seen him two days past at the inn where she dined on the delicious pike, and again yesterday during her tour of the grounds. She spotted him moments ago after making another pass through the laundry when she searched for the garments she saw Ilarion wearing in the seer's vision. And she saw him heartbeats past outside the kitchen. He could not be in two places at the same time, and she doubted he was a twin. He'd used magic to borrow a regular guard's visage. A quick incantation confirmed that he wore a spell to mask his appearance—similar to the one she wore to color her hair and give her a scar.

The man was graceful as a cat, and stronger than his lithe frame hinted. He rolled to the side and jumped to his feet as she came at him again. A knife flashed from the folds of his tabard and met hers in a deft parry. For an instant his face blurred, as if he had trouble both maintaining his illusory image and fighting her. She didn't worry that he might have an associate sneaking up behind her; assassins with very few exceptions worked alone.

"Who paid you?" she hissed, knowing full well that if he was good at his trade, he wouldn't answer.

His reply was a gob of spittle aimed at her face. She blinked, and in that instant he lunged at her, dropping in a crouch and slashing up with his knife. The blade looked wet. Poison, she suspected, as she spun out of its path and managed to come up to the man's side.

He was fast, definitely skilled, she judged. Not her equal, but close. They danced in the hall outside the kitchen, the fight making little noise—the swish of his tabard and cloak and her silk robe, the soft clank of their knives meeting. But suddenly a crash intruded, the sound drawing his eyes away from Mainon for just an instant. A woman had emerged from the kitchen. She'd been carrying a tray heavy with crystal goblets. Startled, she'd dropped the tray and the resulting crash gave Mainon the edge she needed.

Mainon pivoted away from the assassin and slipped up behind him, rammed her knife into his back, the blade sliding between ribs and finding his lungs. He dropped to his knees as the kitchen woman screamed.

"Stay back!" Mainon warned as a trio of workers emerged from the kitchen, all of them gasping and pointing, one flailing at the air with a big wooden spoon. The assassin was dying, but remained a threat.

He tried to suck in a breath, but instead made a gurgling, wheezing sound. The woman with the spoon screamed when blood bubbled from his lips. In a last measure of defiance, he swung his knife wildly, catching Mainon's robe. She twisted the fabric and tugged the blade out of his grasp, then stabbed him in the throat with it. The woman who had dropped the goblets fell in a swoon.

Within moments, the sound of rhythmic footsteps filled the hall as real guards arrived. Mainon retrieved her knife and wiped the blade on the dead assassin's cloak. His face was much different now, thickly lined around the eyes, as if he'd often squinted into the sun, his hair thin like a wispy cobweb. She found a pouch of empty vials on him and discretely pocketed it, along with a ring that had the tingle of magic to it—her prize from the encounter. Then she edged away as more curious workers gathered.

Mainon had smelled something about the assassin—coriander, nutmeg, and other spices. He'd been in the kitchen, and that's where she went now. She focused her magic through her senses, fingers playing along the outside of the vials as she went, thumb rubbing against one like it was a worry stone.

"There and there and there." Poison in one of the wedding cakes, in the swan-shaped confection, and in a pastry boat that was taking shape. She found four more deadly delicacies before she pronounced the rest of the food safe. Poison was a method she would have considered to kill Ilarion, though she would not have used such a virulent, slow-acting one as this assassin had employed. Where had he acquired it? Who paid him to do it? Though she'd been in the city a few times before, she didn't know enough of its shadowy places to ferret out those answers quickly.

"Mainon." Xeno had entered so silently she hadn't heard him.

She whirled and pointed to the tainted treats.

"Indeed, my friend hired the best in you, milady. The vision of Ilarion dying before his wedding? I can no longer conjure it." He released a deep breath, and the lines on his face relaxed. "The threat is passed. My thanks to you. My friend will survive and enjoy his wedding."

Mainon, however, knew she would not consider herself successful until after Ilarion was married and the houses legally joined.

ERLEENE WAS BEAUTIFUL. Tall and thin, with a heart-shaped

face ringed in golden curls, she was escorted across the grounds on the arm of her father. Her dress was pale yellow, the shade of the sun dappling on a still pond, and it glistened in artful patterns where tiny gems and seed pearls had been sewn. Flowers were woven in her hair; more flowers circled her wrists and waist.

The late afternoon ceremony was in the principal garden, and the weather cooperated. Mainon perched herself on a balcony where she could overlook everything. She didn't want to take the chance that on the ground she might miss some nefarious activity in the press of guests and attendants. Athletic, she could leap to the ground without hesitation should trouble arise.

"I shouldn't worry," she whispered. She'd inspected the grounds twice, the manse until her feet ached. Xeno and she cast spells that would make it almost impossible for someone to magically disguise themselves as the assassin had outside the kitchen. She'd even dropped her own guise and wore an appropriately stunning gown—though not one so voluminous it would slow her movements.

But she worried nonetheless. She was being paid too well not to worry.

Music filled the courtyard as Ilarion arrived at the altar. Mainon continued to watch the crowd, not allowing herself to enjoy the pageantry, though both her client and his seer had encouraged her to. And then before she realized it, the wedding was over. A cheer erupted, crashing toward her like a wave. The guests—she estimated three hundred—followed Ilarion and Erleene inside. Music filtered out of a window below her, followed by the clink of glasses, gentle laughter, and the murmur of well-wishers. The scents of roasted meat and spiced vegetables drifted out and made her mouth water. Mainon had never cared for weddings, but she always enjoyed a good wedding feast.

One final meal at this fine, fine residence, and then she would gladly head home.

The festivities lasted well into the evening, the guests consuming more food and drink than she thought possible. Couples, some of whom had overindulged, tottered on the dance floor and stepped on each others' robes and skirts.

Later, Mainon, who had also overindulged, stood before Ilarion and Erleene, Xeno hovering behind the couple and beaming.

"I bid you farewell," Mainon said, nodding to her client. "And I wish you both a good, long life together." She said nothing else, guessing that Ilarion still had not mentioned the threat of an assassin to his bride.

"And I give you my gratitude." Ilarion bowed deeply, his smile reaching his eyes. "Safe journey home." He paused and gave her a wink. "You'll find something in the stable with your horse." Softer: "What we agreed upon…and a little more." Then Ilarion turned to face his wife. "And now let us retire to our chamber, my sweet. The night is not through with us yet."

Mainon wove her way between a portly man and his even portlier wife who were trying to keep up to music that had just turned lively. Once outside, she breathed deep, taking all the flowery scents of the garden far into her lungs, the fragrances more preferable to the warring perfumes of the guests.

She'd nearly reached the stable when she spun and ran back to the manse. She hadn't been able to enjoy any of the day, not the meal or the music or the expensive wine. Something had been festering at the back of her mind, something she couldn't place and something that wouldn't go away. She'd been turning all of the possibilities over and over.

The threat passed.

The threat passed?

She'd caught the assassin with his poison outside the kitchen yesterday.

The poisoned food discarded.

The ceremony finished and the houses joined.

The seer's vision quashed.

The seer.

The threat passed?

She'd come to know his many expressions, and the one he displayed several minutes ago was new to her. He was beaming, his face practically glowing, and his eyes were on Erleene. Xeno gazed at the young girl with deep affection. *Covetously so.*

Mainon cursed herself for not remaining skeptical about oracular magic and the seer himself and urged herself faster still.

She dashed through the main hall, narrowly avoiding a throng of guests who were leaving, and once past the dining room she vaulted over a maid scrubbing at something that had been spilled on an ornate carpet. She took the stairs three at a time, skirt hiked up above her knees and dagger sheaths on her legs showing.

Within a handful of heartbeats she was outside Ilarion's bedchamber door. A moment more and she was in, eyes adjusting to the darkness. Only a single candle burned by the bed.

"Xeno!" She shouted the seer's name to get the attention of Ilarion and his bride. "Xeno, show yourself!"

Shadows shifted near the bed, then a curtain a few feet away fluttered in a slight breeze. The shadows drifted closer to her.

"What outrage!" Ilarion said. He'd been in the process of taking off his exquisite cream-colored garment, the one in the seer's vision. "What is the—"

The shadows reminded her of what she'd seen around Ilarion in that vision.

"Xeno!"

"How did you know?" the shadows asked.

Before she could answer, the shadows swirled around her and took her breath. She scented the poison, like had been in the empty vials and on the assassin's knife, the same virulent stuff that promised a long, horrible death. She kicked out, connecting with something solid in the shadowy mass, the impact chasing away the shadow-spell Xeno had been maintaining.

"Xeno!" This time it was Ilarion who cried the seer's name. "Traitor!"

"The real assassin," Mainon said when she regained her breath. She pressed her attack, hands and feet furiously pummeling the seer. She had to keep him from casting another spell, as she feared he was indeed more skilled with magic than she. Her attacks were not so masterful as usual, they were desperate, almost maniacal, but it worked to achieve her purpose.

He was not her match physically, and she wore him down before turning his own dagger upon him and driving it in his chest. Mainon looked away as the scene in the seer's vision played out in the meager candlelight ... only with Xeno, not Ilarion, the victim of the horrid, slow-acting poison.

"I don't understand." Ilarion hovered over his young bride, smoothing at her face. The girl was pale, her lips quivering, and her eyes wide with terror—and filled with something else.

Loss, Mainon knew. She shook her head and glanced back at the quivering Xeno. For the briefest of moments Mainon considered slitting the seer's throat to end his suffering. Her fingers tightened around her dagger. She could...she should—

Then all thoughts of mercy fled as Mainon felt the hot, fiery sensation of a blade thrust in her back and swiftly and painfully removed.

Whirling and dropping to a crouch, she saw Erleene step back, holding a thorn knife dripping with blood, its curving and scalloped edges intended to inflict serious damage going in and worse coming out.

The agony centered in Mainon's back had a pulse to it, and she felt her clothes grow warm and sticky with her blood. Erleene smiled slyly and shifted so she could keep watch on Mainon and Ilarion.

"What? What is the meaning?" Ilarion shouted. Out of bed, he put his back up against a wall, glancing fearfully between the two women.

"Xeno and your bride, they hatched the plan to have you assassinated," Mainon said. A wave of weakness crashed through her and she concentrated to stay on her feet. "It would be expected, really, someone trying to prevent your houses from joining and from you becoming more powerful."

"By hiring you," Erleene spat, "and by you catching an assassin yesterday, my beloved Xeno could convince you any threat was passed." She swept in and lashed out, revealing she had a reasonable skill with the weapon.

But she was not as skilled as the assassin. Mainon gathered her magic and focused it on her wound. She possessed no healing enchantments, but she could mask at least some of the hurt. In that same instant she twisted and avoided Erleene's lunge, twisted again and got behind her, slashed down to hamstring the bride.

Erleene screamed in pain and outrage, fell to her knees and waved the knife in front of her in an effort to keep Mainon at bay. But the assassin continued her assault; she had to be quick, before the blood loss felled her. She whirled and came up on Erleene's side and drove the dagger forward, aiming for the bride's arm and striking her near the wrist, the force of the blow sending the blade in bone deep and lodging it there. A shriller scream and Erleene's fingers opened and the thorn knife clattered to the floor. Mainon swept up the knife and backed toward Ilarion as she caught her breath.

"Quite the wife you have," Mainon hissed.

The noble stared blankly, his face pale, eyes wide with surprise, sweat thick on his forehead. "I…I thought the threat had vanished," he said weakly. "By the gods, I was blind. The real threat was Xeno and Erleene. They wanted me dead *after* the ceremony."

"When we'd think the threat had been dealt with," Mainon said. She was feeling stronger, likely because the magic was tamping down more of the pain. She needed the aid of a healer—very soon, and she knew of one in the city below.

"Help me, husband," Erleene said. She tried to stand, but instead collapsed onto her side. "Help, please. You're wrong. I meant you no harm."

Ilarion shook his head. "She would inherit all my holdings, making her house unrivaled in power. And she would still have…*him*." He looked at Mainon. "So I hire you again, assassin. Finish my wife while she is down. An easy kill." His lip curled. "I will not be married to someone who wants me dead."

Erleene sobbed. "No! Please…"

Mainon looked from Ilarion to Erleene. The young woman should be able to recover from her wounds given time. Then she glanced at Xeno, his body still twitched in agony from the lethal poison, albeit barely. The would-be killer took his last gasp and stilled.

"My obligation to you is over," Mainon said. "You hired me to kill one assassin, and only one. As for your wife, I think you can manage the task yourself."

It was time for her to leave while she still could.

Mainon tucked the thorn knife in her belt, padded to the sobbing Erleene, who looked up with wet, fearful eyes. She stepped on the bride's hand for leverage and pulled her dagger free. Erleene screamed and wept.

"An easy kill," Mainon said. She certainly would welcome more gold from the noble for doing the simple task herself. But in all the years Mainon had worked as an assassin, she'd never made a man a widower; she had a personal code. "Too easy."

She slipped from the chamber and down the stairs, still losing blood, feeling the warm stickiness against her back growing. Crossing the grounds was laborious, despite all traces of her pain gone it did nothing to diminish her weakness. Climbing onto her horse—and securing the bag of gold from the noble—was onerous. Mainon fought to stay conscious as she led her mount into the city and toward the harbor.

A healer lived there, one who was not terribly expensive.

One who had helped her a few times before.

Mainon would regale the healer with a tale of the wedding.

She had never cared for them, too much fuss, too many people, though the feasts were typically good. From her vantage she could look back and see the manor, its lantern lights aflicker.

"'Til death do they part," she said, and looked toward the sea.

SEEKING THE SHADOW

Joseph R. Lallo

I N A SMALL and dark tavern in a forgotten corner of a kingdom once called Vulcrest, two men in heavy fur coats were drowning their frustrations in cheap ale. The tavern was lit mostly by scattered holes in the poorly thatched roof. From a hearth near the center of the room, a smoky fire provided meager warmth while roasting the remains of a wild pig, provided by one of the morning's patrons.

"Another!" growled one of the men, slamming his empty tankard on the table. He was a burly young man with a wooly brown beard and a face misshapen by his wont for fighting.

"For me, as well," said his drinking companion, an older and even more inebriated man in a rattier coat.

As the two men were the only patrons at the moment, the lull in activity had motivated the innkeeper to retire to a private room for the afternoon in preparation for the busier evening hours. That left only a mousy young barmaid to take orders and collect payment, a task for which she lacked the proper force of will to perform with

any degree of success. The two men had been taking full advantage of the arrangement.

"I… I'm sorry, but that's your sixth, Carlisle," said the barmaid. She was addressing the younger man, but her eyes were held low to avoid looking at him directly. "And Cassius, that's your eighth. Your tabs are both days old and awfully large. The keeper says I shouldn't give you any more until your bill is settled."

Each man gave the maid a hard look, which she still refused to meet.

"Now Belle," the older man began, "you would deny my good friend and your best customer the much needed salve of strong drink in this dark time of his?"

"You haven't paid in days, and the keeper… well, I can't—"

She was interrupted by a thump on the warped front door, finally heaved open after three attempts. A stranger strode inside and stamped the snow from his boots. He was tall and thin, dressed in finely tailored leather and fur more suited for a royal court than a nameless tavern. His skin was flawless and pale, neither baked by the sun nor marred by battle or blemish. He removed his fur hat to shake free its crust of snow and revealed short blond hair that seemed almost white in the dim light of the tavern. Despite the fact that the pair of drunken patrons and the barmaid turned distrustfully toward him, he didn't seem bothered in the least. The newcomer took a seat at an empty table, shrugging free a heavy pack. It struck the ground with the rattle of metal.

"Good afternoon, young lady," he said with a respectful bow of his head. "Might I trouble you for some brandy?"

"I'm afraid we don't have any brandy left, sir."

"Red wine?"

"Yes, sir."

He flipped her a silver coin. "A bottle please." He then turned to the two patrons. "Good afternoon, gentlemen. You were having a conversation. Don't let me interrupt."

"You aren't from around here," grumbled Carlisle. There was a quality to his voice that suggested he hadn't uttered a single word in the last few years without gruffness.

"Astutely observed, good sir," the newcomer said.

"Why are you here?" Carlisle said.

"I am a bit parched and badly chilled from my travels."

"But why are you *here*?" Carlisle repeated, a threat in his tone.

"I am a thirsty traveler. This is a tavern. Do I need a better reason?"

"Are you a trader?" Cassius asked.

"That I am not."

"Well, you don't look like a soldier."

"Another astute observation." The stranger turned to Belle, who perched on a stool, attempting to retrieve the requested bottle of wine. "Quite the savvy patronage you've got at this establishment, young lady."

Carlisle stood and rested his hand on the grip of a cudgel hanging at his belt, the end of it carved to reveal some kind of beastly creature. "You planning on joining the Alliance Army then? In the middle of training, maybe?"

"I'd wager a fair amount that I'm better trained than half of the soldiers at the front."

"If you're all that well trained and such, then why aren't you out there fighting?" growled Carlisle.

"Because, as you suggest, I am not from around here."

"Where are you from that you can't serve your time in the army?" Cassius asked.

"The mountains."

"This is Vulcrest. We're all from the mountains," Carlisle said, marching up to the man and pounding his cudgel on the table. *"Where are you—?"*

"You know something?" the stranger interjected, standing to meet Carlisle eye to eye. "I was warned when I came this way that I would not be well received. It is thus a welcome surprise to find the locals showing so keen an interest in their fellow man. I find it heartening to see two complete strangers make so thorough an effort to become familiar with the personal history of a simple visitor. So heartening, in fact, that I feel comforted enough—no, more than that, I feel *obliged*—to ask you each a few questions such that we might each know one another as proper friends do."

"I don't—" Cassius blurted.

"Rumor has it the estate just outside town lost its owner last night."

"You know about that?" Carlisle said. The statement came as enough of a surprise to briefly push aside his violent intentions.

"It is why I came here, sir."

"To this village?"

"To this tavern. When I asked some townsfolk who might know more about the killing, they suggested there was a drunken lout in this very tavern who was formerly employed by the victim. Would that be you, or is it your friend here?"

Carlisle started to raise his cudgel again, but Cassius stopped him with a hand to the shoulder.

"You're treading dangerous ground, stranger," Cassius said. "Look at you. Prime of life. Claiming to be well trained. You ain't in the army, and you ain't never *been* in the army. We're at war, stranger. We need every warm body we can get to take his turn at the front line to keep those Tresson devils at bay. We each took our turn. Barely made it back and got the scars to show. No one makes it back looking the way they did when they left. You don't look like you so much as busted a lip in your life. Only way that happens for a man like you is if you deserted, dodged, or bought your way out. In any case, you're no kind of man at all." He pulled out his own cudgel. "I'd say it's our solemn duty to make an example of you."

The stranger didn't look frightened. If anything he looked disappointed. "You are planning to make an example of me… with *that* misshapen piece of *wood?*" he asked, vague disgust in his tone as he indicated Cassius's weapon.

"It don't need to be pretty to cave *your* pretty little skull in."

"Violence…" The outsider shook his head. "I have no specific objection to violence. It is regrettable, but it has its place. If you *must* spill blood though, don't you owe it to yourself and to the target to do so with dignity? Use a tool that pays honor to the fallen. A tool like this, for example."

The stranger drew a unique weapon from within his coat—the action performed with startling speed—brandishing a serpentine blade as long as his forearm. The gleam of metal and blur of motion were enough to convince his would-be attackers to retreat a few steps. For a moment no one moved. Even Belle, wine and tankard in hand, was frozen in place in the doorway of the storeroom.

"Gorgeous, isn't it?" the stranger said, turning the blade to catch the light of the fire. "Look at the cutting edge. Asymmetrical. Curving back and forth in ever more delicate sweeps until it reaches its point. This is a dagger designed by people who knew the value and sanctity of a life, so much so that it first served its masters in rituals and ceremonies." He sliced through the air twice, advancing as he did until the weapon was mere inches from their faces. They took a few more steps back until a stout support beam blocked their retreat.

"Look at the runes," the stranger continued. "This is an ancient invocation to the gods, requesting mercy and bounty in exchange for the blood that would flow. Now, look at the curves. Thirteen of them, diminishing toward a point sharper than a serpent's tooth. Unquestionably beautiful, and yet the shape has value in function as well as form. Each curve slices anew, like a separate weapon. Each forward strike bites six times, each back strike bites seven. Each thrust carves thirteen separate slices into the belly of its target. Brilliant..."

"Now look at the hilt." He flicked the dagger toward them and each man dove aside. It twirled through the air and bit effortlessly into the beam, sinking a third of its length into the iron-hard wood. The drunks, now a good deal more sober, looked to the blade. "Made to resemble a coiled asp, its fangs needle sharp and curved toward the blade's tip. It is the one wholly artistic flourish, meant simply to intimidate." He glanced back and forth between them. "Effective, don't you think? Because if not"—he opened his coat to reveal the hilts of six similarly elaborate daggers and knives—"I've got many more fine examples."

In the stillness that followed, a stifled breath drew the stranger's eyes toward the storeroom. Belle still stood there with a bottle of wine and a clay tankard, her eyes wide and her hands shaking.

"You can put it on the table, young lady," he said. "And don't worry. I think the posturing has been put aside for now."

"You weren't lying about the training," breathed Carlisle, shakily returning his cudgel to his belt.

"I seldom lie. It is rarely necessary." He took a seat. Belle had set down the wine bottle, but after a casual inspection of the tankard had proved unsatisfactory she industriously swabbed at its interior with a rag.

"Who *are* you, sir?" Cassius asked. He returned his own weapon and lowered himself into a seat.

"I am many different things at many different times, good sir.

Today I am a hunter, and my prey is a mysterious creature. A creature of the shadows." He smiled. "A shadow himself, if the rumors are true. They call him The Red Shadow."

There was a gasp and the shattering of hardened clay. Belle stood rigidly, the rag still in her hand and the remnants of the tankard at her feet.

The stranger sighed. "Three men brandish weapons and the mug stays in your hand. Three little words, The Red Shadow, and it falls to the floor. It speaks volumes of his reputation."

"You think The Red Shadow was responsible for Sotur's death?"

"Sotur would be the local baron?"

"Yes."

"Then I have reason to suspect it. He was wealthy, from what little I've heard he was not overly popular, and now he is dead. Most importantly, no one I've spoken to has the slightest idea how it could have happened. I've been following The Shadow for years. He tends to leave things in such a state."

"The Red Shadow," Carlisle said. He stared blankly at the wall before him, rubbing at his stubbly throat as though genuinely surprised to find there was no slit. "I was guarding Sotur last night. I... The Red Shadow... he's... he killed a dire wolf. He killed a massive wolf the size of a horse, and he did it with his bare hands. Tore the thing's head off. Stained its fur with its own blood. Made the skull into a helmet."

"I know the stories. They would have me believe he is this supernatural thing, this demon that walks the world taking the lives of the corrupt."

"The Red Shadow has killed lords. He's killed other assassins," Cassius said. "No one has seen more than a flicker of the monster. He killed the second advisor to the king during a feast. *During a feast!* The man was smearing butter on his bread one moment and was slumped in his chair the next. He never even left the table."

"That's nothing. He killed Lord Marten the very first time the old man stepped into his new keep. He killed him while his own guards were showing him his own security measures," Carlisle said.

"As I've said, I know the stories."

"What makes you think you can find him when the Alliance's best men can't?"

"I don't have a high opinion of the Alliance's best men, but I also have an item that should allow me to follow him if I get close enough."

"You don't *follow* a thing like him! You *hide* from a thing like him," said Carlisle.

"This isn't the first time I've heard these words, gentlemen. And may I say that it never ceases to amaze me that the same people who would gleefully beat me to pulp for even seeming to abandon my army would caution me endlessly about seeking out a known murderer."

"You mustn't pursue The Red Shadow," Cassius said.

"Why would you try to stop me? Has this man not been a scourge of the Northern Alliance for decades?"

"*Death* has been a scourge for centuries. If you are going to hunt one of the two, death is the safer bet," Carlisle said.

"I'm not convinced there's a difference," Cassius added.

"The Red Shadow is a monster on the prowl. If you hunt it, you won't kill it. You'll just get its attention. Then it feeds on you instead of whatever it had its eye on. I don't want to be anywhere near the fool who would do such a thing," Carlisle explained.

"Be that as it may, I've got business with The Red Shadow that must be settled. There is a grave injustice that must be corrected, and I will not rest until I've done so."

"Then do it far from here. I've seen a slit neck before. Makes a hell of a mess, and my coat's stained enough," Cassius said.

"First I must find him, and as I've said, it is for that reason that I have come to this charming little establishment." The stranger paced to his seat, where Belle had returned with a fresh tankard and filled it from his bottle. She sorted through coins from her apron and counted out the change from his purchase. "Thank you. No, please. Keep the remainder. The service has been superb."

"What do you want from us?" Cassius asked.

Their visitor sipped his wine, wincing a bit at the flavor. "Information." He turned to Carlisle. "You say you were Sotur's personal guard last night?"

"I was. Everyone knows that. It was supposed to be Cassius here but the louse was passed out drunk. Look, why should I help you?"

The stranger reached into his coat and removed a satchel, which he upended onto the table. Two dozen silver coins clattered on the wooden surface. When the bag was empty, he tossed it down as well. "The usual reasons."

Carlisle eyed the small fortune on the table, his willpower visibly buckling. "I... even if I wanted to tell you something, I don't know anything. I didn't see anyone. I wasn't even there when the man died."

"Did you find him when the deed was done?"

"Yeah."

"Describe it."

"He was dead."

The stranger's expression hardened. "Care to elaborate?"

"What else is there? He was dead. Bled out all over the floor."

"What did the wound look like?"

"He had a bloody slit where his neck ought to be."

"Was it a clean wound?"

"I just said it was bloody. Does that sound clean to you?"

His benefactor sighed. "I can see I'll need to take a more direct role in the investigation. Do you know where the body is being kept?"

"In the baron's estate's infirmary."

"Has he been prepared for burial?"

"I don't think so."

"Take me there."

"How do you plan on getting inside?"

"If your susceptibility to bribery is indicative of the rest of the baron's staff, I don't foresee any difficulty."

Carlisle sat for a few moments, staring at the silver again. "I can't do this. I've got debts to pay and mouths to feed, but you are asking me to help you do something that might put my name in the mind of the bloodiest assassin in the history of the Northern Alliance. I'm not foolish enough to do that."

"Very well." The stranger turned to Cassius. "Are you?"

"Damn right I am," Cassius said.

"Cassius Whitmoor, you idiot! The Shadow will kill this lunatic for hunting him down, and he'll kill *you* for helping to find him."

"Maybe he'll kill *you*, Car. After all, *you* were the one on duty."

Carlisle lurched forward and attempted to grapple with Cassius. Having been denied a chance at violence once already, both men were eager for a second chance to let off some steam. For better or worse, they were still feeling the effects of the afternoon's libations and weren't the most graceful or effective combatants.

The stranger separated them and raised his voice. "Gentlemen, please! The Red Shadow won't give either of you louts a second glance."

"And why is that?" Carlisle growled.

"Because he is an assassin. Assassins kill *important* people, and they get paid handsomely to do it. Killing a drunken and ineffective guard and his still more drunken and ineffective cohort would be beneath him." He snatched his thrown dagger from the beam and gestured with it. "The common folk are safe as babes from the blade that kills kings."

"And you imagine you are safe for the same reason?" Carlisle asked. "You aren't concerned about the blade because you aren't a king?"

"On the contrary. The blade is of great concern to me, and I aim to be worthy of its bite, so long as its bite is worthy of me." He gave his weapon a final appreciative glance before slipping it into its sheath beneath his coat.

"You tie the language in knots when you talk, you know that?" Cassius said.

"I aim for artistry in my every endeavor. But enough delay." He finished his wine and corked the bottle, stowing it in an outer pocket of his pack. "If you mean to earn your silver, my good man Whitmoor, we'll need to be on our way quickly." He swept the mound of silver into two equal piles with a deft slice of his hand, pocketing the first. "Take your payment. You'll get the rest when I'm satisfied you've earned it."

"Gladly," Cassius said, messily clawing at the coins.

"Wait! What about me? I answered your questions!" Carlisle said, his eyes locked on the bribe that could have been his as it fell into his drinking partner's pocket.

"Here," the stranger said, snatching a coin from the table and tossing it to Carlisle.

"One silver? You must be giving Cass at least twenty!"

"Actions are so much more valuable than words, good sir. That's a lesson worth its weight in gold. Now if you will excuse me, I wouldn't want to keep a baron waiting."

———✦———

THE REST OF the late baron's family had fled the grounds on the night of his death for fear of sharing his fate, leaving the servants to watch over the sprawling residence and its former owner. It took three meager bribes to shift the loyalties of the staff enough to earn the stranger a private audience with their fallen master. Cassius led the way to a darkened room deep inside the late baron's estate and raised a torch. The infirmary was a frigid room with stone walls lined with cluttered shelves. It was discernable from the armory only in that the tools for drawing blood were accompanied by bowls to catch it. At the far end of the room was a slab, and resting in peace upon it was the former baron, respectfully concealed beneath a stained linen shroud.

"Odd that a baron would have an infirmary in his estate."

"Aw, the old codger said he wanted his estate built like a keep, made sure they put in a quarters for a squad of solders and an infirmary and suchlike," Cassius explained. "Guess he wanted to feel safe from invaders. Half a kingdom between him and the nearest border wasn't good enough. He even had a halfway decent healer, up until they made him send her down to the front. The butcher who runs the place now only knows how to pull teeth and cut off fingers and toes. Probably keeps 'em in one of these jars here..."

"Sound thinking. You would be surprised what one can do with a tooth and the right incantations."

"I wouldn't know anything about that stuff. All I know is when I die I'm going to make sure they keep a fire going wherever they lay me out," Cassius muttered, pulling his coat tighter. "Gonna spend a long time in the cold ground. The least you can do for a man is keep him from freezing before you put him in."

"It's just as well they didn't. With any luck the cold has kept the corpse fresh."

The curious stranger approached the body and turned down the sheet. The baron was a bloated and unpleasant man in life, and he was more so in death. He had the face and figure of a man who had never missed a meal; not fat, but with an overall pudginess that portrayed a life of ease. His beard was scraggly and gray, except for where it was stained brown by the dried blood of his murder. The stranger adjusted his gloves and gingerly lifted the end of the beard to reveal the wound that had claimed him.

"Bring the light closer," he instructed, leaning nearer to the slice.

As the flickering yellow light fell upon it, the strange newcomer almost seemed to admire the horrid slice across the late baron's neck.

"Oh yes. This is certainly the work of a fine blade and a steady hand. Look at the edge. It isn't ragged or torn in the least." He separated the cold-stiffened flesh on either side of the cut. "Straight to the bone in a single slice. There's no sign that the blade met anywhere but its mark. Where did they find him? In his bed?"

"Slumped on his balcony, I think."

"Dragged there perhaps? Was there a trail of blood, or merely a pool?"

"No trail. The servants made enough of a stink about cleaning it up where it was. If there was a trail, we'd still be hearing about it."

"Mmm." He pulled the shroud back farther to reveal the man's hands. "Spotless… no scrapes, no bruises. This man didn't have the chance to struggle. This was definitely the work of The Shadow." He restored the shroud and turned to Cassius. "Tell me about the baron."

"What's to tell?"

"I haven't noticed any mourners."

"I'm more surprised there aren't folks dancing in the streets. He squeezed his subjects dry, paid his servants and guards in copper, and squandered his money on damn fool things like his estate or mounds of jewels to keep that trophy of a wife interested."

"Did he have any sons?"

"None who survived the war. Just a wife and a daughter."

"Brothers?"

"Two."

"Younger, I assume. Otherwise one of *them* would have been the baron."

"That's right."

"And they are both alive?"

"Last I heard."

"Tell me about them."

"The middle brother is just as bad as him, only he doesn't have the title and didn't get the inheritance. His old man didn't leave him anything but the private hunting ground up north. He's practically a hermit, lives off the land and keeps his debtors off his back by having his brother accuse folk of poaching—whether or not they were nearby—then fining them."

"And the youngest brother?"

"As I recall, he didn't get land *or* money. But he's the richest of the lot, thanks to him starting an armory and supplying weapons and armor for the war effort. Rumor has it he's got his fingers in the black market, too."

"Have the brothers been informed of his passing?"

"How should I know? I'm just a guard. The steward would be the one to do that."

"Well then, where is the steward?"

"I think he had a meeting with the youngest. I expect they'll get to planning the burial and such when he gets back tomorrow."

The stranger paused to consider the facts, then reached into his coat to gather the second half of Cassius's silver coins. "Quickly, where is this hunting ground?"

"If you've got a fast horse and the weather's not too rough, just follow the road due north for a while."

"A while?"

"I forget how far. It's the only fenced-in piece of forest you'll see up that way anyway."

"Here is the remainder of your payment," he said, rushing for the door.

"Why the rush?"

"Because if the middle brother isn't dead yet, he will be soon. The youngest hired The Red Shadow to clear the way to the title and the estate."

He rushed out the door, heading for the outside. Cassius followed, trying to keep up.

"How do you figure?" he called after the stranger.

"I'm not a simpleton, that's how!"

"Are you going to try to save the middle brother?"

"He's already dead, or as good as, but if I move fast enough I just may reach him while The Shadow is still nearby!"

Cassius, not in the best of health, fell behind as his benefactor rushed through the estate to the stables and set about preparing his horse for travel. The stranger was mounting the steed when Cassius reached the door, thoroughly out of breath.

"Wait!" he gasped. "I don't even know your name!"

The stranger heaved himself into the saddle and spurred the horse out of the stable, calling back behind him, "That's just as well. It wouldn't have done you any good."

Cassius stood in the doorway and watched the bizarre outsider ride into the distance.

"Meh," he grunted. "Name doesn't matter anyway. If he's after The Shadow, by this time tomorrow he'll be dead."

———•———

THE VAGUE DIRECTIONS Cassius provided turned out to be

accurate, if not precise. "A while" revealed itself to be half a day, bringing the stranger to the fenced stretch of woods well after sunset. Most of the trip had been through snow-covered plains, with the occasional farm invariably growing cabbage or potatoes. Due to hearty types of each being the only crops that would grow beyond the southern border region of the Northern Alliance, most of the population lived on little else. This was doubly true in areas with poor hunting, which described most of the north—that the Sotur clan had claimed the one patch of forest for miles dense enough for decent hunting indicated just how little they cared for their fellow people.

The fence around the property wasn't very imposing, being merely a row of evergreen branches and trunks driven at wide intervals into the ground, most still bearing their needles. They served as a marker and little else. What kept people from crossing through and taking advantage of the hunting ground was the penalty imposed by its owner if they were caught.

The stranger paid the marked boundary little heed. Dense clouds blotted out the moon and stars, as was frequently the case in the Alliance lands, leaving the forest shrouded in an almost impenetrable darkness.

"A moonless night… not the ideal time to be searching for a shadow," he uttered, his voice low.

His equipment included a lantern and a few more exotic methods for creating light, but at the moment the benefits of being able to see weren't nearly enough to outweigh the consequences of being seen. He moved forward through the inky woods as surely as he could manage. Unfortunately it soon became clear he wouldn't be able to rely upon the horse. The forest grew steadily thicker as he approached its center, and within minutes the low branches and high shrubs blocked the way too much for the steed to penetrate. He dismounted and drew a shorter and simpler blade than the one he'd used to intimidate the guards. Such a weapon left him better able to put his final remaining advantage to use.

He dug into a well-protected pocket beneath two layers of clothes until his gloved fingers snagged, with some difficulty, a fine silver chain. When his grip was secure he tugged it into the open. A small leather satchel swung free from his pocket. He loosened his fingers and let the weight of the satchel draw the chain through them until it hung at its full length. It swung lightly, and when he whispered a few awkwardly phrased arcane words it swung a bit more. He closed his eyes and focused on articulating each unnatural syllable properly, though his untrained tongue tripped over them twice before the spell was cast in earnest; when it did the satchel tugged against the chain, angling out to the woods ahead.

"He's here." The man wrapped the chain around his fist and charged as quickly and quietly as he could in the direction it led.

Stealth was not an option. It was too dark to see more than a few steps ahead, leaving him at the mercy of every loose branch and boot-grabbing bush. Worse, the forest was silent, magnifying the noise of his own breathing and the crunch of his footsteps. There wasn't the chitter of a squirrel or the chirp of a bird. The woodland creatures were in hiding, all too aware of the danger lurking in the darkness. There was a predator in the woods.

Finally he reached a clearing and stopped short. A body lay face up on the ground. In the weak light the pool of blood looked black against the white snow, and the kill was so fresh steam still rose from the slit in his throat.

"Damn it," hissed the stranger.

He scanned the clearing. There were footprints, but they all seemed to belong to the dead man. None of the trees around him had dropped any of their snow, hinting that no one had hidden among their branches. The body was still warm and yet the trail was cold. He lowered his satchel and began the incantation.

The first word still hung in the air when a blow to his back sent him sprawling. His blade went one direction; the satchel went the other. He tried to scramble forward, but a weight dropped on his back and held him to the ground. The leather fingers of a gloved hand clutched his chin and pulled his head back. The stinging cold edge of a blade touched his throat. He gasped for breath but dared not struggle, lest he do the killer's work for him.

He sensed a presence beside his ear.

"You are alone," came a harsh whisper.

"Yes," the restrained man wheezed, his chest and mouth constricted.

"You did not follow my tracks. I did not leave any."

"No tracks."

"You did not follow the victim's tracks, because you came from the wrong side."

"Yes."

"You could not follow a scent, the wind is at your back."

"I didn't."

The next words were spoken with a force and harshness that simply wasn't human. "Tell me how you found me."

"If you kill me now, you'll never know."

"Neither will anyone else."

He swallowed. "You're holding a black blade to my throat. It isn't metal, it is stone. It was made for you by a gifted weaponsmith with the help of a fairy. You've used it for nearly sixty years and it still hasn't dulled. I know what you are."

The blade began to slide; blood ran down the man's neck.

"Five years ago you left a place called Entwell for the second time. I know these things because I was there. My name is Desmeres Lumineblade. My father is the man who made that sword."

The blade stopped. "Why did you come here?"

"I came because you and I have business together, even if you don't know it. Let me speak. We both know if you don't like what you hear, there's nothing I can do to stop you from killing me."

His heart pounded in his ears. Warm blood dripped in fat drops on the snow. The weight lifted from his back and the blade pulled away. Desmeres moved slowly and deliberately, climbing to his feet and spreading his hands to his side to avoid provoking any rash decisions from the assassin.

"Speak," The Red Shadow said.

"May I retrieve a bandage to tend to my—?"

A bandage landed beside him, tossed from behind.

"Speak." This time the voice came from a different position.

Desmeres fetched the bandage and applied it. When it was in place, he turned. The assassin had backed into the darkness of the trees around the clearing. His presence was felt more than seen. There wasn't even the telltale gleam of his eyes.

"I didn't have much use for you when you were in Entwell. I knew you were the first to go and return, but I was still honing my craft. I make weapons, like my father before me. But a year after you left I got into an argument with him. I became irate that one of my weapons, one of my best, was in the hands of a green apprentice. Father believes that the purpose of crafting a weapon is to make a fighter as formidable as he or she can be. He said my weapon was elevating the apprentice to more than he was. I believe that a fighter and a weapon are two halves of the same whole. Perfection can only be achieved when the greatest weapon is in the hand of the greatest warrior. By holding my weapon, that apprentice was spitting in the face of greatness, preventing my sword from finding the hand that would do it justice. And though my father's sword is an undeniable masterpiece, in your hand it cheapens you. I've learned much since it was made. I can and have made better. My weapons belong in your hand and yours alone."

"You came this far, risked your life, to give me a weapon?"

"This weapon, and the next one, and the next one. You are the finest warrior the world has ever produced. Through you, my weapons can finally achieve their rightful place."

"You would help an assassin in his deeds."

"Let me make this clear. Your skill with weaponry is the only trait that concerns me. The rest is irrelevant. I will do whatever is needed. This is my purpose. Surely you can understand how important it is to serve one's purpose?"

The Shadow remained silent.

"I can do things for you. Things you and I both know you can't do yourself because of what you are."

There came a sound, something less than the swish of fabric, and from the darkness emerged a form. It looked to be a human, until Desmeres' gaze lingered upon the shadow within the hood. There was a pointed muzzle, the glint of whiskers, and the gleam of animal eyes. It was not the face of a human. This "man" of whom the whole of the north lived in fear was no man at all. He was a beast called a *malthrope*, with more in common with a fox than a human.

"Killed a wolf and wore its bloodstained skull as a helmet. You started that rumor, didn't you? Whispered it in someone's ear from the darkness. You have become the most feared figure in Vulcrest, and you've done it with your hands tied, because anyone who so much as sees your face, even without knowing your crimes, will kill you on the spot. You are a monster at a glance. I am not. I can speak to humans, and elves, and dwarves. I can mix with society. Meet face to face. I can *be* your face to the world, if you require. Whatever it takes to put my weapons in your hands. If either of us settled for anything less it would be a crime."

The assassin released a seething hiss, then snapped back to his main concern. "Enough about that. Tell me how you found me."

"Anyone can follow the crumbs. The mark of an assassin is unmistakable, but you aren't the only one. I found three before I saw a wound that might have come from my father's blade. From there I traced your path, found where you lingered."

"I know you were following me. I know you've come close before. *Tell me how you found me.*"

"The last few steps came from that satchel on the ground. I brought it from Entwell. Inside are a few precious strands of your hair, a few flakes of dried blood from an old bandage, and a pinch of soil from where you slept. Coupled with an incantation the gray wizard taught me, it draws itself toward you. Without it, I'd never have found you. Destroy it and neither I nor anyone else ever will again."

The Shadow stood silent once more. Desmeres knew the time for talk was nearly through, the killer's mind nearly made up.

"I don't know what you believe in, but I know you believe in something. You aren't an assassin for the thrill of the kill. The men and women who have fallen by your blade are, without exception, corrupt and deceitful. You are selecting people who deserve to die. Perhaps you wish to punish the wicked, perhaps you simply wish to ease your conscience. I don't know. What I do know is that if what you are working toward is truly important you are obligated to take every advantage offered. Anything less and you are turning your back on it. *Let me help you.*"

"... You would ask me to trust you?"

"You would be a fool to trust me, and I would be a fool to trust you. But I'm more than willing to live what remains of my life with a knife to my throat. I don't even care if it finds its way to my back." He pointed to his fallen weapon. "As long as it is one of mine."

The assassin took two fluid paces toward Desmeres. They stood face-to-beastly-face, Desmeres's eyes locked on the predatory gleam beneath the assassin's hood. With a flicker of motion, The Red Shadow held one of the daggers formerly concealed beneath Desmeres's jacket.

"If I decide I have use for you, you'll see me again. If not"—the assassin held up the stolen blade—"you'll get your wish."

With those final words, The Red Shadow stepped aside, and in a blur of motion was gone. Desmeres adjusted the bloodstained bandage and breathed a long, slow breath. His eyes turned to the ground. In departing, The Red Shadow had snatched up the satchel and the fallen blade.

Desmeres smiled.

"And so begins the legacy..."

THE
LONESOME DARK

Anthony Lowe

THERE WAS A storm beating at the windows, and Evaline Cartwright wondered if one death would be enough to stop it.

"Not sure why you even bothered telling me if I never had a choice in the matter." John Wilbur paced the length of his bedroom, sweat building on his forehead. Even in the flickering candlelight, Evaline could see the man's eyes paying special attention to the exits. "You've got no right, merc."

"No, you see, that's where you're wrong," Evaline replied, easing herself down onto the bed. "I've got every right."

"You heard what the mayor said!"

"That doesn't matter, John. None of that matters." She removed her wide brim hat and set it upside down on the blanket chest. "I'm telling you because I'd like for things to be different. I'm letting you say goodbye."

"You heard the mayor! It was self-*fucking*-defense!"

"None of that *matters*," she repeated much more firmly this time. "Not to me, anyway."

Mr. Wilbur looked at the door again. His face was bright red and his eyes were bloodshot. "He was trespassing on my land. I have every right to protect my property and my family. He could've been a wicker."

Evaline had to laugh. Finally, she could speak her mind. "For what reason would a wicker *ever* have to come this far north? Longrove's a nice town, but it's not that nice." She cleared her throat. "'Sides, most of the plants they use for their rituals can't grow here. And a wicker without some singroot to channel auras is just an average nothing with bad tattoos and worse teeth."

"I..." Wilbur's resolve was receding into grim acceptance. His hands started trembling. "He could've been..."

"What's really funny about this whole thing is the Sharath are actually a very passive bunch. If you'd ever bothered to know one before killing 'em, you'd know that. They've taken it up the aft from us for so long, they've adopted an odd policy of indifference they're all sworn to follow. After all, their First Life begins in the spirit world, right?"

She pulled back her duster, revealing a six-slug revolver and battered sword. "But once you clip off a 'rath's clan bracelet, their way to the spirit world is lost, and they're forced to wander endless roads forever. And that's a lot worse than murder in their eyes, John. Even still, they might have given you a pass, but I'm not."

"Do you *hear* yourself?" he pleaded. "Spirit worlds and endless roads. You're gonna kill me over heretical 'rathian bullshit like that?"

"Yeah... Well, no. I'm gonna kill you because I had to haul that young Sharath's body all the way into the ass-end of Westfarleigh because of you. On top of that, you clipped off his clan bracelet, probably because you're a simpleton and thought it looked like gold. Bolt cutters are the only way to remove them, you know, and I saw the little slice you made. Like you were actually thinking of hacking his hand off to get at it.

"You crossed the line between murder and desecration—and you inconvenienced me greatly—so now I'm gonna kill you, John Wilbur."

"Fuck you."

Evaline stood and Wilbur took a step back. "You're on my time now," she said. "I'm giving you a chance to say goodbye to your family. If you don't wanna do that, I will gladly leave your headless corpse in this room for your kids to find." She ran a finger along the hilt of her sword. "And won't that be a cherished memory?"

———·———

THE SHARATH BURIAL rituals last for seven days, and the Fires of Tan'shar continue to burn until the next full moon, when they are finally snuffed out. It's only then that the journey of the departed concludes, their spirit peaceably birthed into the First Life and the presence of their ancestors.

Evaline covered the young Sharath's body with a dirty tarpaulin, watching as the collective torchlight of the small crowd played across its surface, giving the illusion that the dead had not yet passed on—and noticing the complete lack of a clan bracelet, that was almost certainly the truth. There would be no birth into the First Life for this boy, no ancestors to greet him. Only long roads and diseased forms conjured from fading memories.

She met the eyes of the Wilbur family, took note of their complete lack of remorse, and then pressed away through the barley to meet with the mayor and his wife.

The two were huddled around a lantern, their backs to the scene. The mayor was quietly dictating something while his wife, still dressed in her bath robe, carefully copied the words down onto a piece of parchment.

Evaline thought it odd that the couple would know to bring a stationery set out here to the outskirts. As if they'd known they would be writing an apology to the nearest Sharath commonage.

She sighed, quietly amending herself. Of course they'd known.

"The city of Longrove offers its heartfelt condolences," the mayor continued, "and a pledge to provide monetary reimbursement as well as any goods that will be required for the burial services." He took a moment to ponder any further words, but just ended up shaking his head. "Sincerely, Johnathan Meeker. Mayor of Longrove."

"Very good," Mrs. Meeker replied. "I think it turned out nicely, dear."

"Really? I feel like something could've been added at the end, you know? Don't want it to sound too official."

"Don't want it to sound too personal, neither. You know how they get."

"True, very true." The mayor took up the parchment and rolled it up. "Terrance Dankin comes down from Mariposa with a new story about the commonage every season. It's a wonder we have any treaties still standing."

He handed the letter to Evaline, along with a small pouch of what would be silver coins. Evaline knew the drill. "Get going tonight if you can," said the mayor. "It'll be better for everyone if you were on their roads before the week's end."

"Everyone," Evaline echoed, fixing the mayor with a stare.

The mayor nodded in the direction of the body. "Save for the departed, of course. Goes without saying."

"What are you going to do about them?"

"Receiving the body should be enough. I've never known them to push for anything more than that."

"I meant the Wilburs," she said, motioning to the family. "Am I carting John off to the lawkeeper?"

"Oh my, no." The mayor snickered a bit. "It's an open and shut case of self-defense, my dear girl. No need to wake old Daniels, though he'd tell you the same thing I'm telling you now. The grief will be enough for the Wilburs, I think."

Evaline felt the coin in her hand, but it just wasn't enough to keep her from speaking. "The 'rath had no weapons."

The mayor tilted an ear towards her. "Excuse me?"

"I said the 'rath had no weapons on him, Meeker."

He shook his head. "I don't plan on arguing this point with you tonight, Miss Cartwright. What's done is done. Please get the body to the nearest Sharath commonage before one of their rangers comes looking for it. Will you do this for me?"

A number of arguments breathed and died at Evaline's lips, all of which would've gotten her in the kind of trouble that would make living in Longrove a chore, possibly even dangerous. The Wilburs were friends of the mayor, and that was that. But she wondered how long that excuse would stay her hand.

"I suppose you wouldn't like the 'raths to know about the Wilburs," she said.

"That goes without saying," he replied, pointing to the letter. "That says he was killed in a fight with a thief, and that'll be the truth from here on out. The details don't matter. Correct?"

Evaline forced a smile. "The very words I live by, Mr. Mayor."

"Excellent. Good travels to you, Miss Cartwright."

Evaline turned without another word and made for her horse, a small wagon already attached. She led it over to the body. "You mind?" she asked Mr. Wilbur. He nodded and helped her carry the covered body into the wagon. He didn't set his end down gently. "You said you didn't know he was a Sharath?"

"That's right," Mr. Wilbur replied. "He was using that stone as a lantern. Thought he was a wicker."

"You get many wickers on your land, Mr. Wilbur?"

"You ain't supposed to let 'em speak. Everyone knows that. Took my chances for my family's sake."

Evaline nodded, but in truth she didn't believe a word the man was saying. A lone wicker this far north made no sense. "I suppose so."

Mr. Wilbur didn't say anything for a few long moments, but he didn't look the least bit nervous. He had no reason to be, after all. "That's all there is to it." He turned and led his family back to their home. The Meekers had already gone, as well, leaving Evaline alone with the body.

"Some night, huh?" she said to the dead Sharath. A reply seemed to come in the form of a cold wind passing through the barley. She pretended she hadn't noticed and mounted her horse. A rough ride to the commonage was ahead of her, but she knew the way by heart these days.

"WHAT'S THE GOING rate of a man's life, huh?" Wilbur was in tears now, his hand resting on the doorknob but unwilling to turn it. "How much did they pay you to do this to me?"

Evaline looked him in the eye. "What kind of money could buy a show like this?" She pointed to the door. "Go."

A moment of hesitation passed, but the man finally turned the knob and pulled the door open. Firelight spilled out, and almost immediately there came a pair of shouts. *"Daddy!"* His two little girls sprinted over and threw their arms around him. Wilbur pulled them both into a tight embrace, and he cried into their necks.

"It's okay," he told them, kissing their cheeks. "It's all going to be okay."

Evaline scoffed. "Don't lie to them."

Diane Wilbur rose from the couch just then, furious. "You let him go and get the hell out of our house!" she demanded, standing at arm's length from Evaline. "You have no right!"

Evaline shook her head. She hated repeating herself. "You see, that's where you're wrong." She tapped the grip of her revolver and Mrs. Wilbur stepped back. Then Evaline nudged Mr. Wilbur on the shoulder. "Hurry it up, John."

"For gods' sake, woman!"

"You better believe it." Evaline pulled the revolver from its holster, the mithral runes inlaid across its barrel and cylinder catching the light. "Tell them!"

Wilbur looked back over his shoulder, his eyes wide, lips quivering. Helpless. "Kids," he said, taking their hands in his. "Your father has to go away now."

"Where?" his youngest asked, tears flowing.

Wilbur's voice broke when he said, "I just have to go. Your mother will explain when you're older." He brought them in for one last embrace. "I love you both so much."

THE WHISKEY WAS always cheaper at the hangings in Little Horn. Most were too distraught to notice how much the stuff had been watered down, but they would keep on buying throughout the night to "ease their poor humors." It was a frustrating racket, but obviously a worthwhile one to the right seller.

"They don't use them hoods no more," said the bartender. "Sheriff reckons the fear in the bastards' eyes'll be enough to *dissuade* the youth from committin' to a life of, ah…unclean consciences." He cleaned his spectacles, flicking his eyes in the direction of the nearby window for a moment. "Ask me, I say hearin' their necks snap like a peach switch is enough to *dissuade* the youth from any and all potential indecencies."

Evaline held up two fingers, uninterested. "Double shot of whiskey."

The bartender set a glass atop the hardwood bar and was about to fill it when Evaline caught his arm.

"Nothing from Weathernell."

"Shoot." He scoffed and slid the bottle back on the shelf behind him. "Annexation's goin' through any day now. You got a grudge?"

"I've got standards."

"That's funny." He picked out another bottle—this one distilled in Marathon—and poured. It was the safe choice. "Couldn't help but notice the contents of the wagon tied to the back of your nag when you rode in."

Evaline looked up from her glass. "Couldn't help but notice the kids about to swing from a short rope across the street."

The bartender took the comment in stride. "Dissuasion at work, mercenary."

"They're young enough a day in the fields would've done the job."

"Better to nip it in the bud. So the sheriff says." He sniffed. "Kids ain't that young. Old enough to aim for the head."

Evaline shrugged. "Yeah, well…" She drained her whiskey and slid the empty glass across the bar. Practically a double shot of water. "I suppose if common sense was contagious, I'd be out of a job."

"It would be a shame. Maybe if you didn't get somethin' out of your profession."

"Some days I think I do." She slapped two silver bits on the bar. "Thanks for the drink."

"Sure. Happy trails."

She pushed her way out of the saloon, but now the crowd at the gallows had expanded up to the boardwalks. It would take some doing to get back to where her horse was tied up.

Hopefully no one had messed with the Sharath's body. Some people, like that Terrance Dankin fellow Mayor Meeker was so fond of, liked to collect 'rath ears for necklaces. There were places deep in the Highlands where hillfolk paid decent bounties per ear. To some, the severed pointed ears were exotic, to others, a sign of progress being made.

The crowd's chatter died down when Evaline got halfway across the street. One of the three boys about to be hanged was talking.

"I can only plead and pray that my trespasses will be forgiven by you all. Maybe... Maybe not today or tomorrow. But I think I, ah...I think I learnt a valuable lesson while looking at those bars. It weren't right to steal. It weren't right to shoot at those folks. Gods know, I never pondered killing a man before, not even just before it happened. It just...I can't...I reckon that's just the way it happened."

Evaline looked to the gallows and accidentally made eye contact with the boy speaking. He didn't even seem old enough to grow a beard.

"To my mother and my brother and my sister, I hope you do not think ill of me. I made a mistake to unforgivable ends, and I will pay for it in full. With my death...." The tears he'd stifled came forward. He stuttered and fought to catch his breath. "With my death, oh gods, I hope you see the error of my actions and neglect to follow me down this wicked path." He wept. "For a rope around your neck will be all it shall provide you."

The sheriff upon the gallows motioned to the second boy.

"Mama! Please make them let me go! I didn't shoot no one, please! I just wanna go home!" When the boy said nothing else the sheriff deemed of substance, he tapped the third boy on the shoulder.

"I'm sorry for what I done. My auntie said someone with a torch threw a brick through her window three days back. If you are in the crowd, please leave her be. I'll be gone for your grievance shortly."

The citizens of Little Horn were practically petrified, their mouths agape, eyes unblinking if they were looking at all. Evaline was finding it hard to push through to her horse. She could see the wagon, where the young Sharath boy's corpse was wrapped in that filthy tarpaulin. There really was no looking away for her, was there?

The lever slammed home. The boys cried out. There came a quick snap like a broken peach switch, and one of the boys kicked and choked against his noose until his tongue swelled and his face went purple.

———✦———

"ALL RIGHT, THAT'S enough." Evaline grabbed Wilbur by the hair and began dragging him towards the front door. The man cried out, grabbed at her arm and tried to pull her down to the ground with him. In the scuffle, Mrs. Wilbur rushed Evaline with a fire poker in her hand, screaming at the top of her lungs.

Time seemed to stop when Evaline leveled her revolver and pulled back the hammer. Everyone froze in place, though the kids pushed themselves further back into the corner, unable to keep from crying.

"Don't," said Evaline, and she whispered some word of power that caused the mithral runes on her revolver to glow a deep, unnatural blue. "This is not going to end well, regardless of what you do with that poker. But if you want your kids to grow up with at least one parent, your best course of action is to let me take him and cope on your own time."

The same look of grim acceptance Evaline had seen on Mr. Wilbur found its way onto his wife's face. Mrs. Wilbur gritted her teeth and let the fire poker slip from her fingers. "You can't leave my children without a father," Mrs. Wilbur said. She moved to comfort her daughters. "What did we ever do to you?"

"You pissed me off, for one." Evaline wrapped an arm around Wilbur's neck and got him to his feet. "You also thought killing a boy would go unpunished, which offends me greatly. Usually, I'm content to look the other way and let people like you take your clean consciences into another sunrise, but I'm convinced—absolutely convinced—what you did was supposed to nudge me off the middle way."

Mrs. Wilbur managed a laugh, but the rage never left her eyes. "That's what this is all about? That trespassing fucking thing? It carried sorcerous objects onto our land. John had kids to protect!"

"Thing? You killed a young man."

"That weren't a man!" one of Wilbur's daughters screamed.

Evaline stared at the girl, dumbfounded. "Huh…?"

———◆———

AFTER TWO DAYS on the road, Evaline woke to a steady stream of rain water soaking through her blanket. It hadn't been the worst idea to lay up in an abandoned miner's shack, but it certainly felt that way now. She was still weary, from the ride and a number of other things, but the sun was out so finishing up her trip to the commonage was the preference over trying to sleep in soggy linens on a cold morning.

Looking up through what had once been the shack's roof, she saw nothing but gray clouds. A fine way to close out her journey.

She gathered up her effects and tracked down her horse, which had taken shelter beneath a thick oak tree, and led it back to the wagon. She had to scare away a couple of vultures from the Sharath's body. They had picked through the tarpaulin overnight, and now a few bloodied strands of the boy's entrails were dangling out, pulled through the fabric.

Evaline mounted the horse and guided it back down the hill to the main road. The sight of the Sharath's mutilated corpse didn't quite hit her full-on until she was a few miles from the shack. The rain was pouring down harder than ever, soaking through every layer of clothing she wore, pulling blood from the corpse's open wound until the tarpaulin was stained with a rust-colored blot.

Lightning flashed behind the pines, and as the thunder rolled through Evaline cried out a torrent of expletives in every possible combination she could make. By the time the sky went silent, she was out of breath, nearly out of patience or any form of calm. The only thing on her mind was that self-satisfied look on Mr. Wilbur's face when he realized he'd be getting away with murder.

It was all she could do to keep from taking a shot at the image, if only to relieve her aggression.

"Ho, there!" A man walked out onto the road with a repeating rifle held over his head. "We'd like words with you, friendo!"

This far into Westfarleigh, with only scattered cabins and homesteads between her and the commonage, she wasn't about to stop for anyone brandishing a gun. But when she kept riding, the man gestured and four more of his similarly-armed buddies lined up on the road, blocking her path.

Short escarpments on either side of the road prevented her from going around, and an unwillingness to backtrack all the way to Little Horn kept her from retreating. So she brought her horse to a stop a few yards away from the men and their repeaters, and waited.

"Thanks for stoppin'," the leader said with a tip of his hat. "Name's Isa, by the by—and we mean only to trouble you with a proposition of mutual beneficity."

Evaline leaned back on her horse, placed a gloved hand on her thigh only inches away from her revolver. "You're troubling me with more than just a proposition at the moment, Isa. I have someplace to be."

"We are well supposed of this, lady, and will not stay you any longer than necessary." Isa threw a glance at his crew and took a measured step towards Evaline. "An acquaintance of ours privied us to the whereabouts of a woman who might be haulin' a cart of 'rath corpses back to their camp for burial. We do not wish you to quit this venture, but we would like to make you a coin offer here and now."

He pulled a pouch from his pocket and happily shook it so the coins inside could be heard. "Twenty silver for each ear, lady. More if'n they still have them fancy bracelets clingin' to their wrists."

Evaline's eyes narrowed. "I find it flattering that you're so 'well supposed' of my whereabouts, but I'm only transporting one Sharath corpse—"

"Forty silver, it is then!"

"—and he is not for sale."

Isa laughed loudly into the rain. His friends didn't so much as grin. "You would not pass up forty silver without cause. Hell, if'n you're worried 'bout decent burials and dignity and such, cast away those thoughts. The 'raths are not concerned with the stateliness of their dead. A missin' ear, or preferably two, would go unawares."

"Not if they show up without a clan bracelet."

"Which is why we would pay you extra for your troubles."

Evaline shrugged. "I'm gonna have to decline. The 'rath's ears aren't for sale."

Isa snickered, but the false mirth was draining away at a dramatic rate. "You don't understand, lady." He took a step back. "We are not exactly payin' you for the ears." He shook the bag again. "We are payin' you so we don't have to kill you, and take the ears anyway. Your life—that's what we are dealin' for."

"That's not for sale either." Evaline pulled her revolver, whispering a word of power as she took aim. The runes of her weapon glowed a bright blue, and the bullet that left the gun's barrel carried with it a similar hue. Isa took the bullet to the shoulder before he could get a shot off.

"Fucking—!" Isa went to fire his repeater, but the bullet in his shoulder started channeling arcane. Blue light poured out of his wound and worked its way through his veins. In a matter of seconds, the air around him flash froze. Falling droplets condensed into crystals, webbed out until Isa was little more than a human-shaped ice statue, trapped between bars of frozen rain.

By then, the others had started to open fire, but Isa's body was acting as a decent shield while Evaline dismounted. Her boots struck the muddy road just as Isa exploded into a mass of crimson frost and bone. She whispered another word and her revolver went red. A blind shot at her attackers' feet boiled the pooling water, sending up a cloud of hot steam and wisps of transient flame.

The group scattered, crying out in pain when their exposed flesh came back cooked. Evaline took long strides towards her attackers, emptying her remaining four rounds at their chests. Each connecting shot threw a bright red light out of their mouths, and concluded by channeling enough arcane to conjure fires worthy of a forge behind their ribs.

Their torsos erupted, one after another, throwing embers and burnt entrails across the road and down the escarpment. One of the men flailed, still clinging to life after being blown in half. Evaline, still seeing red in her vision, unsheathed her sword and brought it down upon the hillsman's forehead, splitting it cleanly to the bridge of his nose.

Evaline didn't give herself time to think, to take in the macabre scene she'd created. She quickly about-faced and remounted her horse, and drove it forward over blood and splintered bone.

WILBUR FELL TO his knees and gripped Evaline's duster with both hands. "Just give me a chance!" he begged. "They have to be paying you something. I can double it! Triple it! Mayor Meeker must have told you while he was here. The two of us go way back. He'll surely crack the treasury if it means saving my life. Damn you, ask him!"

Evaline shook her head. "I won't be doing that."

"We have savings! We have this land! We can get you the money!"

"Mayor Meeker paid me to take the kid's body back to the commonage. The 'rath sage paid me again, and you're trying to pay me to leave. What does that say about me, huh? What does that say about my morals if they can be redirected like a bitch on a leash? There has to be something immovable here, and this is gonna be it."

Evaline chuckled and pulled Wilbur further into the barley. There was no moon and the storm was still building heavy overhead, but she thought she could still pick out the spot where Wilbur had killed the Sharath boy. "No sea captain could sail his ship by my moral compass, gods know. But we'll change that together, John. You and me."

She planted a swift kick on Wilbur's back and the man tumbled over. Wilbur attempted to crawl away, but hearing the hammer being pulled back on the revolver was enough to dissuade him from going any further.

"There are worse ways to die, friendo," she said.

Wilbur sat back on his haunches, looked up to watch the storm clouds roil and threaten to burst. "I suppose you'd know," he exhaled.

"Oh, yes, I would most definitely know."

"Just make it quick."

"Tell me how you killed the 'rath."

Wilbur looked over. "What?"

"All cultures have their deviants. The Sharath included, but I don't think the one you killed fell into that bin. He had no weapons, and few 'raths desire human wealth enough to give over to thievery. So why did he get so close to your house, huh?"

"I don't know what you're talking about…"

"What did you offer the boy that prompted him to pass through your land? Food? Shelter?"

"He was using that enchanted stone as a lantern. I thought he was a wicker."

"You've said that. Now tell me the truth."

"What's the *point*?" Wilbur shouted. "You're just gonna kill me anyway."

"That boy isn't even worth the truth?"

"Wasn't worth *anything*, you bastard of a whore." He spat on the ground. "Isa didn't come back with a pair of ears, did he?"

Evaline gasped, and very nearly pulled the trigger right then and there.

———•———

THE FIRES WERE lit, like they'd known a body was showing up today. Evaline pulled the wagon deep into the commonage, and a crowd gathered every step of the way. Sharath ladies and men walked alongside the wagon, weeping and placing flowers around the tarpaulin-covered body. Near the sage's home, the bark and branches of the trees were warped into curving fractal patterns by their use of the arcane. The crowd began to sing a subdued melody.

The sage did not have much to say while the body was taken to be cleaned. She nodded at Evaline and said "Thank you" in a tone that sounded genuine, but tired.

Evaline waited patiently. She unsaddled her horse and brushed it down while it drank thirstily from a water trough. Then she took a seat on a bench beneath an elm and pulled the empty casings from her revolver. If she'd been at all concerned for her safety, she would've reloaded at some point. She wondered why she hadn't.

With the gun loaded, she ended up falling asleep on the bench, and dreamed of a barley field aflame until the sage woke her with a gentle touch on the shoulder.

"Thank you for waiting," said the sage. "That was very polite of you."

Evaline waved her off. "Not a problem."

The sage smiled warmly. "I can't imagine respecting our rituals was a stipulation of your contract," she said, "so I must reiterate my thanks."

"Respect shouldn't be that hard to come by."

"Agreed," the Sharath remarked sadly. She took a seat next to Evaline, tucking her hair behind pointed ears. "Can you tell me what you were dreaming about just now?"

Evaline snickered. "I've heard some of you were diviners." She pulled a wrinkled cigarette from her duster pocket and tried to strike a match. Her hands were unsteady. "I don't know if I like people knowing what I'm thinking."

The sage pointed to the cigarette. "May I?" Receiving a confused nod, she pinched the tip of the cigarette between her fingers. The paper smoldered at her touch, and the smell of old tobacco filled the space between them.

Evaline exhaled smoke through her nose. "Thanks."

The sage grinned. "I can't see what's in your mind, Evaline. Just the steam coming off a kettle, so to speak."

"Oh."

"Will you tell me your dream?"

"I, ah…" Evaline took a long drag off her cigarette, spat out a flake of tobacco. "Just not very happy about how that young boy died."

"Yes." The sage clasped her hands together. "He did not depart well. And without his nel'shar, he will wander."

"Is there anything I can do?"

"Honor the memories of the dead. Cherished thoughts are a beacon for the wanderers, and if they know where they have been loved, they will know where they are going." She peered up through the elm's branches. "That is what I believe, anyway."

"I would like to give the boy justice. That's how I'll honor him."

"That is not necessary. Or wise."

"But I know who his killer is."

"And if the boy was standing with us right now, he would be telling you the same thing I am telling you now: a life for a life is not justice, it is not balance—it is vengeance."

Evaline snorted. "Where I'm from, they're the same thing."

The sage didn't seem to care for that answer, but she scooted closer to Evaline. "The place where the dead boy wanders, we call it the lonesome dark. He will walk between the shadowed forms of things he once knew, always finding himself just shy of contentment.

"Such is the road through vengeance, Evaline. The dead will not find satisfaction through more death. Nor will you. It's a kind of fulfillment that will elude you for all time."

"Yeah, well..." Evaline snuffed out the cigarette on the ground. "Never know until you try." She stood and produced the letter from Mayor Meeker. "From the mayor of Longrove."

The sage didn't reach for it. "Is it anything of substance?"

"No."

"Then I do not think reading it will be necessary." She rose and took Evaline by the sleeve. "Before you go, I'd like to know how much you were paid to bring the boy's body to us."

Evaline didn't see any point in dodging the question. "Fifteen silver."

The sage reached into a pocket on her robe and retrieved a coin pouch. She tossed it to Evaline. "You're a mercenary, yes? In that case, I have a job for you."

Evaline looked at the pouch with marked hesitation. She'd never gotten an offer from a Sharath before. "What kind of job?"

"Thirty silver coins," the sage said. "To spare a murderer's life."

———•———

"AFTER EVERYTHING," EVALINE said, opening the cylinder of her revolver. "After everything you did, the Sharath sage wanted me to spare your life. She put thirty silver in my hand just to let you go about your concerns."

Wilbur opened his eyes. "Why...? Well, aren't you? Aren't you gonna listen to them?"

"Thought about it all the way back out here. Thought maybe it was best to just let this slide, you know? Why add to it?"

"Add to what?"

She pulled a round from the cylinder— "The lonesome dark." —and tossed it away into the barley. "That boy doesn't need company like you."

"Then let me go!"

"I was gonna," she said through a laugh. "I was gonna drag you out here and stick this gun between your teeth just to put the fear in your eyes. The fear that 'rath boy surely must've felt when you were about to kill him. And then I was gonna let you go."

She leaned over, stared him down. "But now, come to find out, you sent Isa and those highwaymen to kill me. With the silver I was carrying, plus what you'd make from the 'rath ears and the bracelet, you were gonna do well for one night's work. I'll let you off with a warning for that boy, like I promised."

Evaline peered at the storm clouds through her revolver's one empty chamber, then gave the cylinder a good spin and slammed it home. "But this thing between you and me, we're gonna settle up right now."

And then she was upon him, driving a knee into his chest and sticking the barrel of the revolver deep enough into his throat that he gagged. "One shot against five, Wilbur! Those are the odds you gave me!" She pulled back the hammer with a feral grin. "Good luck!"

Wilbur screamed. Evaline pulled the trigger.

A hollow click came back at her, and she gasped. Nothing happened.

Wilbur, seeing he had beaten the odds, started laughing. Even with the barrel of a gun at his throat, he celebrated.

She pulled the trigger again—spraying blood and chunks of brain and skull across the field. Blood layering upon the blood of the slain Sharath. In the distance, Wilbur's family cried out.

Evaline stumbled back, watching Wilbur's body convulse and spit crimson. It took him far too long to die. She went to stow her weapon but missed the holster the first time. Thunder rolled, and though she quietly pleaded for rain to wash away the scene, it didn't come.

She walked a trail through the barley with some haste, leaving the Wilbur farm behind, and felt her way back home through pitch blackness. Someday, she would have to return the coins she was given for the job she had just failed.

Someday—if she could only find her way back.

FRIENDSHIP

Laura Resnick

THE WATERY WALLS of Kiloran's palace undulated smoothly around Najdan as he entered his master's lair. Hidden deep beneath the surface of Lake Kandahar, the waterlord's dwelling was imposing, luxurious, and maintained by sorcery. If Kiloran chose, he could loosen his control on any of the airy underwater rooms, allowing the icy lake to swallow them up—and drown whoever happened to be there. Entering Kiloran's home was a matter of trust if you were one of the assassins sworn to his service—and a matter of desperation if you were a supplicant seeking his help.

Upon finding Kiloran comfortably seated in conversation with a well-dressed young stranger, the assassin crossed his fists in front of his chest and bowed his head in formal greeting.

"*Siran*," said Najdan. *Master.* "I came as soon as I received your message."

"Najdan." The old waterlord, who was stout, coldly intelligent, and formidable, smiled and gestured for the assassin to join him and his

young guest. "Allow me to introduce you to *Toren* Varilon."

The title didn't surprise Najdan. The young man's expensive attire combined with the arrogance of his attitude, apparent even at first glance, had led Najdan to guess he was one of the *toreni*—the landed aristocrats of Sileria.

"I am honored by the introduction, *toren*," Najdan said politely.

The young man looked him over as if he were a Kintish courtesan, then said to Kiloran, sounding pleased, "Oh, this is excellent! He looks exactly the way I imagined an assassin would."

Najdan raised one brow and looked at Kiloran, whose face remained impassive as Varilon rose from his seat to walk in a circle around Najdan.

"The black tunic and leggings, the red woven sash... The unkempt hair of a *shallah*—he *is* a *shallah*, isn't he?"

"Yes," said Kiloran. He caught Najdan's eye, and the assassin could see that the old waterlord was amused.

"Of course," Varilon said with a nod. "He would have to be a *shallah*. Just look at the scars on his palms—from swearing bloodvows, yes? And that brutish face!" When Najdan gave him a cold glance, the *toren* fell back a step—then clapped his hands. "Marvelous!"

The *shallaheen*, Sileria's mountain peasants, were the poorest and most numerous of the island nation's disparate people. Although the assassins of the Honored Society came from all walks of Silerian life, the grinding poverty of the mountains drove many *shallaheen*, in particular, into this dangerous but lucrative vocation.

From the day he swore his loyalty in blood to a waterlord, an assassin's life belonged to his master and to the Honored Society. But since family ties were strong in the mountains, a wise waterlord nonetheless respected those bonds. When ordering Najdan to exact tribute, ensure obedience to the Society's will, or kill men, all of which the assassin did efficiently and ruthlessly, Kiloran had never required him to do so with his own clan. Then again, Najdan's clan was small, poor, meek, and submitted readily to the Society's will in exchange for Kiloran's favor.

"You are a magnificent specimen," the *toren* said to him. "I couldn't be more pleased."

"I am delighted to please your guest, *siran*," Najdan said to his master. "Have you summoned me merely to be admired? Or is there work for me to do?"

Kiloran's lips twitched. "Now that you mention it, there is some work."

"I need someone killed," Varilon said baldly.

"Anyone in particular?" Najdan asked.

"An *Outlooker*," the *toren* said, clearly intending to make an impression.

He made one. Najdan looked sharply at Kiloran—and was surprised to see that this was not news to the waterlord. *"Siran?"*

Kiloran nodded, his expression serious. "You heard correctly. An Outlooker."

"I don't understand."

"You don't need to understand," the *toren* said dismissively. "You just need to kill him."

Najdan said nothing, awaiting an explanation. Because there must surely be one.

The Outlookers were the occupying force of Valdania, the conquering mainland empire which had ruled Sileria for two centuries. The Valdani were powerful and greedy, the Outlookers were callous and brutal, and their emperor had outlawed the Honored Society and Silerian water magic. But Dar, the destroyer goddess who dwelled inside the snow-capped volcano of Mount Darshon, had ensured that Her home was not an easy one for foreign conquerors to control. Outlawing something was one thing, but enforcing the law in Sileria's mountainous terrain was quite another. And so the Honored Society, though heavily inconvenienced by the Valdani, continued to function much as it had for centuries, through successive waves of conquest and foreign rule.

But it was a delicate balance, one that relied on exercising good judgment and maintaining traditional boundaries. And one of those boundaries was that the Honored Society did not assassinate Valdani.

The slaying of an Outlooker would motivate the Valdani to work much harder at enforcing their will in the mountains and pursuing their emperor's goal of destroying the Society.

"The dry season was short this year," Kiloran said to Najdan. "And the rains have been good."

This seemed a feeble explanation for the extraordinarily foolish act that Kiloran apparently expected him to carry out.

No matter which mainland power held the coastal cities of Sileria's lowlands, the Society had always dominated the mountains by controlling Sileria's water supply. Through their power and magic, the waterlords created thirst and drought among the disobedient and those would who not pay tribute, and their might was enhanced by the practical skills of their assassins. The Society rewarded its loyal and submissive friends with a generous water supply—and by not inflicting terror and violence on them.

Sileria's annual dry season was the Society's most powerful and profitable time. Although always feared and respected, they were less easily able to impose their will in a year like this one, when the rains had come early and were still falling. Currently, almost everyone in Sileria had enough water, whether the waterlords willed it or not.

Even in a good year, the Society had to resort to other means of exacting tribute after the dry season ended, such as abduction, ransom, and killing. The blood extracted during the rainy season was how the Society continued to exert its authority and influence.

And in a bad year, as this one was, they must be bold and innovative to ensure their own well-being.

Nonetheless... assassinating an Outlooker was foolhardy, not bold. The consequences could be costly and severe.

Yet Najdan could tell from Kiloran's expression that his master had already decided they would do it.

Kiloran said to him, "*Toren* Varilon has a difficult problem to solve. Recognizing the enormity of the favor he asks, he has offered us a generous gift, along with his sincere and lasting friendship."

Naturally, there would be coin involved; not even this young fool would come empty-handed to Kandahar to ask Kiloran to kill an Outlooker. But influence mattered more in the mountains than money did. For Kiloran to grant such an audacious request, the friendship Varilon offered him in exchange must be extremely valuable. Najdan wondered why. What made this pompous *toren's* loyalty worth taking such a risk?

"In addition to the bountiful rains," Kiloran continued, "we've had other misfortunes this year, have we not?"

They exchanged a look of acknowledgment.

"Yes, *siran*. We have."

The Honored Society was far more disciplined than the *shallaheen*, who were prone to constant clan wars and bloodfeuds, but the waterlords were allies rather than friends. And not always even allies, in fact.

For reasons that Kiloran had never shared with Najdan, and about which Najdan knew better than to ask, Kiloran had been locked for some years in a bitter, distracting, and occasionally destructive feud with

Baran, a half-mad and wholly unscrupulous waterlord who inhabited a notoriously damp, abandoned ruin surrounded by a deadly, ensorcelled moat. Although much younger than Kiloran and insanely reckless, Baran was very talented and his power was growing. He had recently succeeded in taking over some of Kiloran's territory. This put Kiloran—and therefore Najdan—in a dangerous position, since it undoubtedly suggested to the other waterlords that Kiloran's strength might be waning, and these were not men to ignore an opportunity. Najdan knew that Kiloran had devoted much thought and attention lately to the problem of reasserting his predominance—and crushing Baran.

"Difficult times call for daring solutions," said Kiloran. "I have given due thought to the *toren's* situation, and I believe his desire to form a deep and lasting friendship with us represents an opportunity that makes his request one we should honor."

Najdan again wondered what qualities or advantages the silly young man possessed that were not apparent at this meeting.

"An opportunity," Kiloran repeated.

And Najdan, who knew that he served a shrewd man, as well as the greatest waterlord in Sileria, said, "As always, *siran,* you know best, and I obey."

"I felt certain I could count on you."

"I am honored by your faith in me, *siran.*"

"There is one thing..."

"Yes?"

"This business should be accomplished discreetly."

Najdan nodded. "I will find out where the Outlooker sleeps and do the work by night."

"Even more discreetly than that." When Najdan just looked at him blankly, Kiloran said, "It should never be known that a Society assassin was involved."

"Ah." Najdan nodded. "I am to disguise myself?"

The red and black colors of an assassin represented honor and ensured respect; but they also made him noticeable and clearly identified his allegiance to the Society. Kiloran hoped to escape consequences by obscuring the identity of the Outlooker's slayer. Najdan did not relish masquerading as an ordinary *shallah*, but he could see the sense in it.

"Yes. I'm sorry to say that you must also leave your *shir* here. If anyone were to see it in connection with this work..." Kiloran shook his head. "That would be bad for us."

"I understand, *siran.*" With some regret, Najdan removed his *shir* from his sash and gave it to Kiloran for safekeeping until his return.

"Oh, I've never seen a *shir* before." Varilon glanced at Kiloran for permission. "May I?"

Kiloran gestured to Najdan, indicating that it belonged to him.

The wavy-edged dagger was an enchanted weapon created for him by Kiloran, fashioned from water by the wizard's cold magic. It was thing of beauty, as well as deadly. Even a minor cut from a *shir* took a long time to heal, and a wound inflicted by the unnaturally cold blade could seldom be staunched or healed. Yet, having been made for him by his master, the blade could not harm Najdan, and so it could be carried next to his skin, concealed and unsheathed, always ready for combat.

Najdan shrugged, which Varilon interpreted as acquiescence, and the *toren* picked up the dagger—then instantly exclaimed in pain and dropped it.

Having expected this, Najdan retrieved the weapon from the crystalline floor of Kiloran's enchanted water palace and placed it on the small table at his master's side. "Has no one ever told you that others cannot touch an assassin's *shir?*"

One of the reasons that every assassin of the Society valued his own deadly *shir* so highly was that no other could use it—or even touch it without pain.

"Yes, but I forgot," Varilon said stupidly. *"Ow."* He studied his hand, which he held awkwardly in front of him. "That thing is so cold it burns."

"Your hand may pain you for several days," Kiloran said, "but it will pass."

Evidently knowing better than to criticize the most powerful waterlord in Sileria, Varilon said petulantly to Najdan, "You might have warned me."

Najdan ignored the *toren* and kept his gaze on his *shir.* He could kill—and *had* killed—without it, of course. But he valued the weapon and used it well, so he would have preferred to take it with him. However, Kiloran was right. A *shir* was too easily recognized as the weapon of a Society assassin. And since each waterlord created *shir* in his own distinctive style, Najdan's dagger could, in particular, expose Kiloran's involvement in the slaying.

"I'll keep it safe for you," Kiloran said.

"I know." Najdan nodded, then asked, "Where shall I find the Outlooker in question?"

"I'll take you to him," said Varilon. "I know where he gambles and drinks."

"That should be sufficient," Najdan said.

Outlookers were hated in Sileria, but attacks on them were rare. So an off-duty one leaving a tavern in the dark, after an evening of gambling and drinking, should be vulnerable and unwary.

Kiloran said to Najdan, "I place this task completely in your hands."

"I will complete it quickly and quietly," Najdan vowed.

"I am confident that you will." Kiloran turned to regard their guest and said formally, "May our friendship endure all tests and never disappoint either of us, *Toren* Varilon."

It was both a promise and a warning, but Najdan didn't think the young man realized that.

———•———

AFTER SEVERAL DAYS of wet, muddy travel, they reached Britar, a town that lay between the mountains and the lowlands. The Valdani fortress there accommodated a large contingent of Outlookers, and Varilon announced that his family had a modest estate nearby. The *toren* stayed in the family villa there, while Najdan was given quarters in an empty tenant cottage.

As agreed, that evening Najdan waited for Varilon outside the villa. When the *toren* emerged from his home, Najdan accompanied him on foot to the town, dressed in the humble clothes of a *shallah* and posing as a servant.

"How are your accommodations?" Varilon asked as they made their way to the tavern where they expected to find their quarry.

"Fine, thank you, *toren*."

In fact, the cottage was damp, drafty, infested with insects, and dirty, but Najdan was not prone to complaining, and he had come here to kill an Outlooker, not to enjoy his temporary quarters.

Varilon snorted and said, "All of the cottages on the estate are in a sad condition, I'm afraid. The place is rather neglected."

Najdan had noticed this. The estate was not large, the villa clearly needed repairs, and the land was not well tended. It seemed surprising that Varilon's friendship (and gold) had been enough to convince Kiloran to get involved in killing an Outlooker.

"But it's such a minor estate," Varilon continued, "my father says that it's not worth the money or attention it would require for improvements. So he won't help me."

"Ah, your family has other holdings."

"Oh, of course," Varilon said. "And my father regards this place as more of a burden for me than a *holding*. I inherited it last year from a relative on my mother's side. Having my own estate seemed appealing for a while, but now I don't know... Maybe I'll follow my father's advice, much as it galls me to say so, and sell it to some fat Valdan who wants a country home."

"Your family does not live here," Najdan surmised.

The *toren* snorted again. "Dar, no!"

That would certainly make it much easier, he realized, for Varilon to act without their blessing—which seemed likely, since what landed family would want their son mixed up in the slaying of an Outlooker?

"My father has *never* been here, and even if he visited, he'd flee the place after just one night!" Varilon added, "Not that he could come here, anyhow. He's old and ill. Can't travel anymore. And he's used to luxury and everything being just *so*. He'd despise this place if he actually saw it." He sighed. "If I'm honest, I really *should* sell it."

"Then sell it," Najdan said, closing the subject. Or so he thought.

"But one gets attached and has reasons for staying..." Varilon was pensive for a moment, then his mood changed and he said angrily, "What a fool I was!"

Najdan resisted the urge to agree; regardless of what Varilon was thinking about now, he was a fool without question.

"By Dar, I *will* sell," the young man vowed. "When this is done, I'll put all this behind me, and—and—and I'll *laugh* about it!"

"May it be so," Najdan said politely. "And there are worse things than returning to a life of luxury, after all."

"Hmmm. Living with my family again," Varilon said without enthusiasm. "Back at Shevrar."

"Where?" he asked alertly.

"Shevrar. My family home. It's an estate in—"

"I know where it is," Najdan said. "It belongs to your family?"

"Yes."

"Ah." After a moment he asked, "You are the eldest son?"

"The *only* son. My parents had seven girls before they got me."

"Hmm."

And now Najdan understood why this young fool's friendship was worth so much to Kiloran. Shevrar, an old estate so large that even a *shallah* assassin knew its name, was in territory controlled by Baran.

It seemed unlikely that the father knew what the son was involved in, and perhaps he would never know. But, according to his son, he was old and ill. And Kiloran was patient. So rather than dismissing the youngster, he was cultivating the heir. When Varilon inherited Shevrar, he would be in debt to Kiloran. And the waterlord would use that friendship with the biggest landowner in Baran's territory to his advantage.

An opportunity, the *siran* had said. Now Najdan understood. Killing the Outlooker was worth a lot to his master.

So it was reassuring to find the man so easily that evening.

He and Varilon reached town, and as they approached the tavern Najdan could see it was frequented by Outlookers from the nearby fortress. He and the *toren* went inside, chose a table, and surveyed the crowd. Before long, exactly as Varilon had predicted, their man arrived, accompanied by several comrades, all of them wearing the gray uniform of the Outlookers. Their quarry ordered a large mug of ale and settled down to some enthusiastic and noisy gambling.

He was a handsome young man, about Varilon's age, and obviously popular among his companions. He laughed a good deal, both at himself and at others, and seemed good-natured about losing his money to better players.

Unfortunately, as a popular and sociable fellow, he was unlikely to leave the tavern alone when he returned to the Valdani fortress. And Najdan would much rather not kill *several* Outlookers; that would make discretion very difficult and the consequences of tonight's work more complicated.

On the other hand, this Outlooker was a thirsty lad and drinking a great deal of ale. Perhaps that would suffice. Before long, he'd go outside to relieve himself in the dark. With any luck, he'd do that alone.

Najdan turned to Varilon, intending to suggest they leave quietly and wait outside, but the expression on the young *toren's* face silenced him. It held such intensity of feeling that he was startled. It had not occurred to him to wonder before now why Varilon wanted this Outlooker killed. Najdan's duty was to perform the work for Kiloran, not to pry into the motives of others. But now, seeing that uncharacteristically powerful expression on this vapid youngster's face, he was curious.

It was not his concern, though, so he dismissed this thought and quietly instructed Varilon to leave the tavern with him. The *toren* flinched slightly when he spoke, as if having forgotten Najdan's presence. As if having forgotten everything but the young man he was staring at so fiercely.

"What?"

"Let's wait outside," Najdan repeated.

"Huh? Oh... yes." Varilon nodded. "Yes, of course." But instead of rising, he looked again at the Outlooker.

"Quietly. And lower your eyes," Najdan said tersely.

Varilon ignored this and continued staring as they stood. As Najdan feared, the Outlooker felt that intense gaze, looked around to see what was intruding on his senses, and locked eyes with Varilon. The smile fled from his face, and he stared back at the *toren*.

Najdan had only a moment to wonder what had led to deadly animosity between these two fresh-faced young men—a gambling debt? a woman? a blood insult?—before the Outlooker, to his surprise, lowered his gaze and turned his back.

That was good. A confrontation or verbal exchange would have called too much attention to the business at hand. Najdan doubted Varilon could be relied on to say nothing about Kiloran if questioned about the Outlooker's death. Fortunately, though, as long as the *toren* didn't attract attention tonight, such a problem was unlikely to arise. The Valdani imposed heavy taxes on Silerian aristocrats, but they wouldn't actively seek trouble with an important old family by questioning their son in this matter, unless he gave them a very good reason for doing so.

Najdan took Varilon by the elbow and guided him to the door. "Outside."

They stepped out into the cool, damp night, well away from prying eyes or curious ears, and Najdan said, "I will wait for him to come out to relieve himself, lure him into the dark, and finish this. It will be best if the Outlookers think someone wanted his purse enough to kill him for it, so I will take that—though it may be empty by the time he comes outside."

"He shouldn't gamble. He's terrible at it." Varilon's voice was breathless and tight. "I keep telling... Never mind." A pause, then: "How will you do it?"

"I have a *yahr* with me." Valdani law prohibited Silerians from bearing arms, but many *shallaheen* carried the *yahr*, a flailing weapon. It looked like a couple of short, thick sticks connected by some rope.

Varilon drew in a sharp breath. "You're going to *beat* him to death?"

"Keep your voice down," Najdan instructed. "Now that I have seen him, you need not remain, *toren*. I will deal with this business while you return home."

"You want me to go? But I... I..."

"Tomorrow morning, before I leave to return to my master, I will come to the villa to inform you that your request has been fulfilled."

"My req—*Wait.* I need to—to think."

"Think on the way home, *toren.* You should leave now." Najdan put a hand on his shoulder to turn him in the right direction for the journey home.

"No, wait. This is happening so fast."

Fast? As far as Najdan was concerned, this was the culmination of a long, wet journey in tedious company, and it couldn't be over soon enough. "Believe me when I say these things are best done quickly."

"I suppose you know what you're talk—"

"Shh." Najdan slid into the shadows, dragging the *toren* with him, when a man came out of the tavern, chuckling cheerfully, and walked a little unsteadily in their direction.

"It's him," Varilon breathed.

It was so dark, Najdan didn't take this identification seriously.

Varilon took a step forward, as if intending to approach the other man. Najdan grabbed his arm and yanked him sharply back into place, which made the *toren* grunt in surprise.

The stranger approaching them heard this. Speaking Valdan, he said, "Who's that?"

Also speaking Valdan, which he knew well enough for this at least, Najdan replied, "It's me."

"*Damn,* it's dark out tonight. I can't even see the path!" The man stumbled, then laughed again. "Oops!" He sounded relaxed and a little drunk. He obviously thought he was approaching a fellow Outlooker, perhaps even a friend. "Where are you?"

Squinting through the dark, Najdan still couldn't tell if this was the man he wanted. He could feel Varilon's tension, but that was probably fear rather than recognition.

Trying to get a better look, Najdan shifted his weight slightly—and Varilon said, "Stop!"

"Huh?" said the man.

Varilon tore himself from Najdan's grasp and stumbled forward in the dark. Najdan heard the two men collide. Then he heard a gasp, some scuffling, and the Valdan said, "*Varilon?* What are you doing out—never mind. I'm going back inside."

"No!"

This was the man, all right. And now the *toren* was directly involved. Oh, well. Nothing to be done about it.

Finish it quickly.

"Varilon, *stop.* It's over."

"But I love you!"

Najdan withdrew his *yahr.*

"Quiet!" snapped the Outlooker. "What if someone hears you?"

"I don't care!"

"Let *go* of me."

Najdan leaped forward, his *yahr* making a soft whooshing sound as he swung it at the Outlooker's head.

"No!" Varilon cried as the man grunted and fell to his knees. "Stop!"

"*Quiet,*" Najdan ordered. So much for not attracting attention.

He struck the Outlooker again. The man fell to the ground and rolled onto his back, blood gushing from his broken nose as he groaned in disoriented pain.

"*Stop!*" Varilon flung himself between Najdan and the Outlooker, nearly getting hit by the swinging *yahr.* "Najdan, *no!*"

"Var..." The man lay gasping, blood flowing from his scalp. "V... V..."

"No, don't!" Varilon wailed as Najdan struck again. "I was wrong! I was *wrong.* Don't."

Najdan looked down at the unconscious, bloody young Outlooker, whose handsome face would be ruined even if he were spared now and managed to survive.

"Please, nooo! *Stop!*" Varilon begged.

But sparing the Valdan was no more Najdan's decision than coming here to kill him had been. With the death of an Outlooker on his head, *Toren* Varilon of Shevrar would be bound to Kiloran forever. It was what the waterlord wanted, and Najdan served his master—not a spurned lover who'd been too foolish to understand the difference between fantasizing about death and actually causing it.

Najdan struck twice more, finishing the job, then knelt and took the Valdan's purse. They had not yet been discovered, so perhaps the killing would, after all, be taken for a violent robbery.

And he knew now that Varilon would not be suspected, as long as they could get away from here quickly. Because both the *toren* and the Outlooker would have been very secretive about what was between them. Najdan minded his own business, but there were those in Sileria who'd kill two men over a thing like that—and even a fool like Varilon certainly knew it.

He dragged the weeping *toren* away from the corpse and into the dark before anyone else from the tavern came outside. He kept his pace fast, hauling the sobbing and disoriented young man with him. They traveled some distance from the body, and were shielded by the night, when Varilon yanked out of his grasp and turned on him.

"I told you to stop! How could you?" he cried. "What did you *do?*"

"I did what you asked," Najdan said. "This was the favor you purchased with your friendship."

"My friendship?" Varilon spat. "Do you think I'll be *friends* with—"

"Yes, I do," he said. "This deed was your choice, not ours. That you chose unwisely is your burden, not mine and not my master's. The bargain is made, and we have honored it. So will you. Because even *you* must know the consequences of betraying Kiloran."

"I don't want friends like *you*," Varilon said bitterly.

"Nonetheless, you have us now," said Najdan. "And you would do well to remember that in Sileria, a man's friends are always more dangerous than his enemies. Farewell, *toren*."

Najdan turned and left Varilon alone in the dark. He decided not to return to the cottage on the estate, in case the *toren*, in a fit of ill-advised vengeance, reported his deed to the Outlookers. With that possibility in mind, he thought it also best to be as far away from here as possible by dawn. This night had not gone smoothly, and there might be some complications ahead; but he thought that, overall, the waterlord would not be displeased with his work, and so Najdan got his bearings and, taking care not to be seen, headed north, in the general direction of home.

JANCY'S JUSTICE

Kenny Soward

J ANCY TIPPED HER serving tray as she wove through the crowd. Four dented, pewter cups filled with Laureen Pimpleton's best watered down swill leaned dangerously over the heads of her drunken patrons. A single spilled drop could ignite a wall-shattering brawl, and Laureen knew it.

"Walk straight and keep your tray up, Jancy, or you'll be eating outside with the dogs tonight!" The squat, black-haired proprietress belted out from behind the chipped oaken bar where she scrubbed dirty cups in a barrel of sudsy water.

Jancy smiled and gave the tray an extra twist as she spun between Rex Knuckleminder and Friar Beltonis. Her lithe form swam in her skirts. Her feet danced. Yet, she was never in danger of spilling anything; in fact, she'd never spilled a drop throughout her employment at the Broken Dog Tavern, never in the ever-crowded great room, and *never* in front of (or on) the patrons, many of whom were Half Town regulars with their toothy grins and sly hands, others just passing through on their way to Pelore or Vrath.

Illustration by ORION ZANGARA ▸

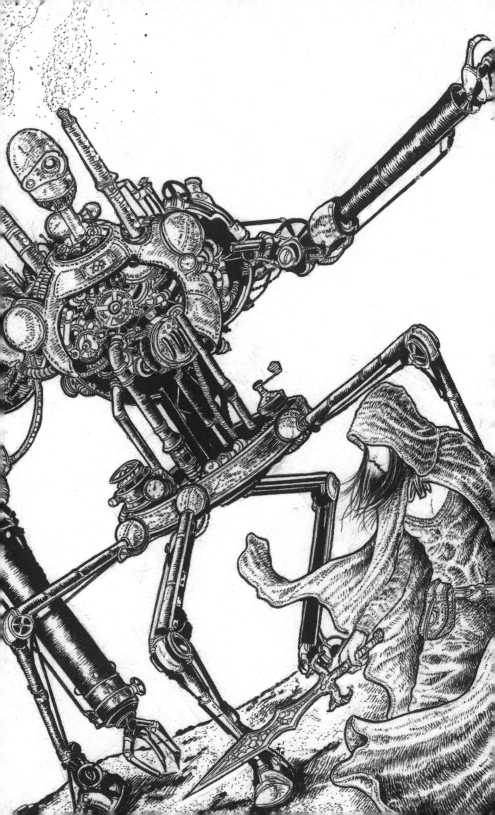

But let Laureen think I'm some clumsy, yellow-haired twit. That's me. Just your average serving wench.

Despite Laureen's bawling (a noise these patrons were used to), everyone's attention focused on the traveling bard, Hopper. The gangly fellow sat splay-legged on the lip of the stone hearth, and his long fingers trilled delicately across the strings of his worn, wooden harp. Words sprung from the man's buck-toothed mouth in golden tones at odds with his bucolic persona, and his ridiculous feathered cap seemed to dance upon his head. The crowd was rapt. Even rowdy Billben Hardhand's jaw hung open as Hopper's tale unraveled. A somber yarn about the arrival of the gnomish race from far across the Dawnbreak Ocean, had them enthralled.

"Exiles," Hopper crooned, "from some faraway land, the race of sharp-brained folk arrived on Sullenor's west coast, wet and bedraggled, in wood ships banded with steel and brass and copper, driven by tremendous steam engines, autonomous paddles beating mercilessly at the ocean waves. Wherever gnomes settled, the sky above swarmed with a flotilla of aeroships buzzing like giant wasps—*bzzzzzz*. Armored plates covered wooden hulls, kept aloft by clusters of brawny, air-filled teats, sails driven by conjured gusts—"

"You talkin' about teats? Ain't seen any in *my* bed!" Rodge the drunken glass worker shouted (a fixture at the Broken Dog Tavern) and fell forward into his ale.

"Go home, Rodge," someone yelled. "We want to hear Hopper's tale, not stories about your teatless bed!"

Laughter rippled through the crowd, and then Hopper continued: "In this time there was but a thousand gnomes left in the *entire* world. And just as fast as they made land, they were turned away by the humans of Teszereth, and so they drove south down the coast to the shores of what would one day become the Pelorian capital; there, the gnomes found their respite, however brief. They gathered themselves, salvaging and modifying their ships and engines, sinking the rest, and then ventured inland, seeking a place to burrow, some place deep and dark and well-protected. An aerostat scout led them on one final trudge through the Cogspine Mountains to its highest peak, Kubalesh, named so by the thick-headed barbarians who dwelled there." Hopper growled that last part like a severely malnourished bear—(the bard was so damn scrawny). "Not for long though, because the gnomes were ruthless and cunning in their desperation, and their hands were soon steeped in blood."

Rodge's head rose. "Gnome bastards," he complained, then hiccupped. "How big do you think their gnomewoman's *teats* are?" Spittle flew from his mouth as he made a smallish gesture with his thumb and index finger.

"More than what you're getting!" That might have been Rex.

The crowd bent and swayed with raucous laughter. Even Jancy cracked a smile. Like clockwork, nearly every night, Rodge would start his mouth up and the others would tear him down.

"Now SHUT UP before I smash your face in!" And that was *definitely* Rex.

"Deep within the mountain," Hopper proceeded yet again, "like a great stony helm above their gnomish heads, they dug. The city they forged there in those cavernous halls was called Thrasperville.

"With their safety ensured, the gnomish Mayor was re-established, and the King and Queen from the old world, who had lived in the shadows for two dozen years to protect their gnomish line, were to be re-seated in the glorious new throne room made from the parts of broken machines, a new foundation built on iron and steam and steel, cogs and gears, and bone-numbing voracity.

"The gnomes had survived…"

Rodge clapped weakly and nearly rolled off his seat. Someone shoved him straight again.

"...yet, too much time had passed, and the Thrasperville gnomes were too distant from their original home in the old world. Many did not feel bound by the old ways; it was a different time, and their recent hardships had carved out a new type of gnome. Rebellious *cogweavers* and powerful *thaumaturges* made their claims to power. Old royal families, far removed from their lofty places, thought to regain their lost glory.

"One such gnomestress, a *machineweaver* called Vilka, sought the gnomish crown for her family, the Stillbrights. She marched into the throne room surrounded by a small army of whirring automatons and threatened to take the crown by force.

"It was a sad moment for gnomes," Hopper's voice had turned melancholy and droll. "One of the few times when greed surpassed the curiosity of invention." He strummed a mournful chord for emphasis.

"Jancy!" came a cry from the kitchen. Five seconds passed, and then again, "Jancy!"

Damn, Laureen!

Jancy reluctantly got back to work just as the story was getting good. She knew better than to ignore the proprietress twice. She resumed serving mutton and carrot stew, and more ale, while receiving a few well-placed slaps on the backside because she was too enthralled listening to Hopper to dodge them. Finally, turning her hip to avoid yet another grabby hand, she gave up on the story and focused on finishing her job and dodging deviant patrons.

That evening, when the patrons had all gone home (either on their own two feet, or dragged out by their less drunken friends), she found Hopper at the hearth with a flagon of wine for company. She usually found him there after a performance, except on overly rowdy nights, in which case he made a hasty exit, but tonight he'd left them thoughtful and melancholy, and they'd gone quietly home to their ale-spun dreams. His demeanor, shoulders slumped and eyes filled with weariness, conveyed how much energy he'd expended during his storytelling.

He put on a buck-toothed grin at her approach. "Hello, luv. I was just gathering myself for a good, long sleep."

"What room are you in?"

"Oh...can't stay here, dear. I'll be out in the stable with my pony."

"You outdid yourself tonight. The drink is on me. For that matter, let me get your room and board for the night."

Hopper's thin red face lit up, his smile large and even a bit frightening in the low tavern light. Then he sobered, cocking his head. "What's the catch?"

"Finish the story."

"Already done, dearie. Finished 'bout an hour ago."

"No...for *me*. I didn't get to hear it all."

His head sunk, and his eyes studied her from a lower angle. Jancy could tell he'd been taken for a fool before, and probably paid dearly for it, too. "So's you're sayin' if I finish, you'll buy this flagon....the *wineskin* the flagon was poured from, *and* you'll have me put upstairs where it's warm?"

"That's the deal."

The bard sighed, nodded, and re-arranged his expression. It was a miraculous transformation, one Jancy had seen several times before. His chest puffed up before her eyes as all traces of weariness slipped away, as if he was sucking life from the fire, the candles, and even the lingering smells of mutton and fried potatoes, and feeding off it. He worked his jaw around and puckered his lips. Twisted them. Squeezed his eyes shut. Then loosened everything into a visage of happy contentment, complete with a big, dumb grin plastered on his face, buck teeth still as gargantuan as mill stones, but far less pronounced.

"Yes, dearie," he said, his voice markedly higher, happier, and a touch mischievous. "I saw you whisked away by your duties 'bout the time I was telling what Vilka did after bursting into the throne room with her steel soldiers."

"Yes! That's it. What happened next?" Jancy said, as she pulled a chair over and sat facing the bard.

"Well," Hopper began, edging forward, "she demanded her crown, that's what she did. She demanded half the metal in the mountain and her choice of suitors to start her bloodline fresh and new and full; yes, that was what she wanted the most. A *child*...wooooeeeeeooooo...a child." Hopper sung that last part in a lilting falsetto that made the hairs on the back of Jancy's neck stand on end. He picked up his harp and launched into the tale's finale.

"The high-ranking gnomes in attendance called their swordsmen to them, realizing their sure doom should they remain divided. They banded together and shouted down Vilka and her claims; wizards and tradesman alike joined the fray.

"But Vilka did not back down, ruthless and cunning as she was. She ordered her stiff-legged, clankity-clank automatons forward. They marched to a song of spinning cogs and glowing eyes, steel hides deflecting all brave blades.

"And rather than christening the great hall with laughter, the place rang with steel and cries of horror as the already bedraggled colony suffered even more horrible deaths. Fathers and sons, young gnomes and even gnomelings just come of age perished in the desperate fighting.

"The throne room was bathed in blood and oil."

Jancy felt a little sick at the thought. "Oh no. I don't like this Vilka gnomestress at all. Not one little bit."

"As well you shouldn't," Hopper continued, standing now, his arms open wide in oratorical ecstasy. He fairly shouted, "Vilka has forever been the thorn for Thrasperville gnomes, stuck in their side, even to this day."

"Quiet down in there!" Laureen shouted from the kitchen.

"Never mind her," Jancy said. "Go on. *Please.*"

"Just when it seemed Vilka would win her throne by bloody battle, a young gnome named Frank Grundzest carted in a mighty magnetic stone they'd used to lift machines across great chasms on their path through the mountains. With a few quick words and the flick of a lever, he removed the spell that bound the stone's power and loosed its magnetic effect upon the throne room.

"The defenders encircling the throne gaped in awe as the automatons ground to a halt, toppling backwards at the mercy of the stone's pull!"

"Oh, but what about the gnomes? Their *armor?*"

"Fortunately for them, most of the gnomes in attendance wore leathers and tradesman's garb, yet the pull from the magnetic stone stole the weapons right out of their hands and yanked any loose metal from the walls and ceiling in a deadly rain. The center of the throne room was a heap of twisted, twitching metal, and a floor greased with the blood of their kin.

"With the motorized clatterers incapacitated, the gnomes went after Vilka. But she was impossible to kill. Once she saw the battle lost, she simply vanished."

"That's strange." Jancy bit her lip. "But I'll bet everyone was quite pleased with that."

Hopper shook his head vigorously. "Not so, dearie. You see, Vilka the Damaged, as she later came to be known, had absconded with the royal child."

Jancy's stomach twisted. "She took their *child?*"

Hopper nodded. "Thrasperville's scryers caught up with her soon enough. A hundred furious gnomes plunged down through the Cogspires in pursuit, stopping before a deep valley that twisted through a flock of knobby hills. A dozen went in, never to return. A dozen more, with the same result. Of the last dozen, one returned, crawling up the barren hillside to his kin. His lips raced with incoherent babbling, his eyes bulging with distant terror. He died in their arms, against the wishes of the company cleric, whose gods seemed to have abandoned them in the face of the evil sorceress, Vilka.

"Full of rage and sorrow, what remained of the Thrasperville gnomes left the valley and returned to their new home under the mountain, more haunted now than ever before.

"That's terribly unfair." Jancy was disappointed the story had taken such a melancholy turn. She was even more upset about the fate of the stolen child, the little prince or princeling who might have had a wonderful life and ruled the gnomish subjects with a fair and just hand.

"That's not all, lass. No. Upon hearing news that her child had not been retrieved, the Queen threw herself from a high peak."

Tears welled up in Jancy's eyes and spilled down her cheeks (the first thing she'd ever spilled at the Broken Dog).

"What's wrong, lass? You look like you just lost a friend to a river dragon."

Jancy wasn't entirely surprised to find herself furious and heartbroken. She often got this way whenever she experienced some sort of mindless injustice, especially when it came to children. Only most of the time there was something she could do about it...and she often did. It was the '*itch* to move,' she called it, a feeling that she needed to act, to be in sudden motion, sudden *emotion*.

She sputtered. "It was a wonderful tale, Hopper. Really. I'm just sad for the child, is all. Taken from its mother and carried away by some complete stranger. Poor thing was probably dead before dawn."

"That's a thing, isn't it?" Hopper giggled. "You might think Vilka and the child passed away, victims of time and the natural order of death. Never mind magic elixirs and youth-altering spells..."

Jancy cocked her head, shifted in her chair. She started to speak, stopped, started again. "She's not still alive, is she?" Jancy was incredulous, but curious too. "That was hundreds of years ago. Even with magic, there'd be no way anyone could stay alive *that* long, could they?"

Hopper grew suddenly quiet, a mere whisper of the personality that been ringing through the tavern for the past half hour. He leaned forward, his wormy lips twisting. "I know she's alive, because I've *seen* her, luv. I've sang for her... in her tower at the foot of the Cogspire Mountains."

"Hopper..." Jancy threatened him with a look. She was in no mood to play.

"Aye, she is alive." He gulped. "And she still has the child. I've heard its cries. I've heard it *wailing*..."

———————

JANCY STALKED SWIFT and low across the night-blackened field of thigh-high razor grass with a knot in her stomach and a nervous sheen of sweat covering her skin. She held a shadow stick in front of her, its trailing plumes of *non-dark* flame and smoke shielding her, she hoped, from scrying eyes. The Pelorian vendor had guaranteed the crude stick's worth, and Jancy had accepted his word with all the coin she had left.

If the shadow stick failed, there would be no getting her money back.

Looming south, the Cogspire Mountains. Not the largest or most far-ranging she'd ever seen, but as spiny and prickly as they came;

dangerous and close, stone protrusions covering the odd-shaped hills and valleys like a pox, gnarled fingers of rock through which strange currents of wind sang. The ostentatious lowing of beasts—*giants?*—vibrating through the star-speckled sky.

Standing somewhere in all that tremendous power; Vilka's tower.

Jancy had gotten herself into some precarious spots before, but this one was looking worse by the minute. *You knew that, though. Didn't you? You heard Hopper's story. But, the child!*

Yes, indeed, the child. This *specific* child, who, if Hopper's story could be believed, remained trapped in some sort of sorcerous time bubble, never having felt its true mother's touch, never able to grow up, never to grow old.

How, then, do you justify yourself this time, Jancy? It was true. She had no mental category for this particular jaunt. Usually, it was "if I can just make this one child's life better, it will be worth the danger," or "I may die doing what I'm about to do, but this family won't be bothered by collectors anymore," or "putting my blade through that wretch's throat will be the best thing that ever happened to them. He was their father, yes, but with a father like that, who needs enemies?"

A bad life for a good life. A chance to make the world a better place when the *'establishment'* failed—a far too common occurrence for Jancy's liking. Her methods seemed like a solid approach. And, in a strange way, it was as if every life she freed from the yoke of injustice seeded for her a little family of her own. They may never remember her, of course. She was just a shadow, some flicker of movement passing through their lives in the blink of an eye, cutting out all the bad things like...like...well, like, any *good* mother would do.

But this child. *This child.* Isn't it long past helping? Wouldn't it be a deranged soul by now, whatever mental and spiritual growth it may have attained in a normal home now stunted by magic and the selfish wishes of a cruel sorceress? Jancy had no real appreciation for wielded magic. Too wild to control, it corrupted even the wisest of wizards.

What does magical imprisonment do to a child so exposed over the course of hundreds of years?

Still, she had to see, had to be sure, even though Death's attention was turning her way once more; even as she stalked the landscape and carefully picked her way south into the teeth of the unknown, Jancy found herself grinning. It was not an unfamiliar thing. It was the itch.

The *itch* to move.

———•———

JANCY HAD HATED breaking Hopper's trust—especially with the business end of her dagger—but she minced nothing when it came to things like this. From the pointed end of her blade, she'd wrung the directions from the bard. He'd been reluctant at first, fearing Vilka's wrath for his indiscretion, but when given a choice between dying now and dying later, Hopper had wisely chosen to extend his life a little while longer. She hoped the bard would forgive her as he rested comfortably on the stuffed wool mattress in the cushiest room in the Broken Dog.

Probably thought of it as his last good night's sleep.

In any case, her course was set.

The dilapidated dock was right where he said it would be, next to the slow-rolling mountain river. Smelled like moss and mold and old wood. The thing was so rickety she was surprised it still stood. *But that's what you want someone to think, isn't it, Vilka? This is where Hopper would be expected. But not me.*

Jancy followed the lazy river upstream several miles to a small lake surrounded by sloping rock walls on three sides. A waterfall gushed an icy cascade over a weak lip of rock across the way, drenching leafy branches that sprouted from seams and cracks.

Jancy crouched behind a clutch of brush and two moping trees and gazed at her surrounds. Another dock perched at the lake's edge with a wide, flat-bottomed boat moored to it. It was amazing, this secret, this clandestine operation at the northern edge of the Cogspire Mountains, just a hundred miles from the original crime. Aside from Hopper, Jancy wondered who else visited Vilka in her remote tower? Who else knew this criminal remained alive? Surely, someone in Thrasperville? Maybe they did, and there was nothing they could do about it. She had to believe, if they knew, they would have finished her if they could.

Jancy shuddered. This was no ale-swilling brute of a parent, or even an uncommon thug. This was an evil older than she could imagine. Vilka was a thick rod of might... a master witch... who'd laid low a small army of trained gnomish fighters and mages.

I'm a fool. What can I hope to do that they could not?

Jancy clutched the hilt of the dagger at her side, her teeth grinding as she imagined the poor *wailing* child kept prisoner in that tower. She could turn around now knowing this was likely too much for her to chew. Good chance she'd die; who could she help then? But another part of her said this was the perfect time to stand true, to leap from the edge of the precipice and fly, kicking, at the face of doubt. To prove her justice reached far... even for someone as heinous as Vilka. But even then what would it prove if she could pull off what so many others could not?

That I'm quicker, that's what.

Her clear emerald eyes scanned the hills and rises, cliff edges bathed in star light and the glow of a fat, somber moon. The wind was up, shifting branches and carrying leaves across the surreal landscape, stirring up the scents of musty fall.

She didn't *feel* watched, yet the air rang with tension. Or maybe *she* was the tension. Yes, that must be it. *Quicker.*

Jancy found the path, a track of dirt wide enough for a horse, and followed it around the lake and up into the rolling hills, steeper, deeper, toward the heart of her mad obsession. She moved swiftly, resting only to grab a bite of food and to stretch like a cat. As she jogged along, courage and doubt competed inside of her, fighting for control, twisting her stomach into nervous knots. At the head of a long, stone path flanked by obsidian posts, she stopped, eyed the subtle etchings—*wards*—presented on the smooth surfaces.

"I think not," she chimed, softly.

Shadow stick held high, Jancy leaped off the path and into a lightly forested area, hoping it would shield her from watchful eyes. She made pace with her steady breathing, hypnotic, as she fed off the chill air. Ahead, through gaps in the claw-fingered branches of trees, she spied a spire of darkness rising from a distant hill. A thrill ran through her, and dread, too; Hopper had spoken true, and the reality of Vilka's legend struck her in the face like ice water, a sobering reminder that this was no ordinary foe. Doubt edged up again, but she forced it down. Her legs propelled her onward, strong and fleet, undeterred by her mind's wavering confidence. She pushed the pace, sticking to gullies and wooded areas where she could, rebellious against common sense, until sweat beaded her brow. She'd exhaust herself reaching the tower if she must, but she'd not be a coward. Sure enough, the effort of tackling the rugged terrain soaked up the nervous tension like a sponge soaking up water.

Soon she was beyond worry, beyond fear. A bit worn out but soul-fired. For a long time, her feet on the ground and her quickened breathing were the only sounds, but then came something else. A series of hums and metallic screeches, interspersed with loud clangs that echoed through the hills, growing louder as the tower loomed larger. The echo of *machinery*.

Jancy approached a low wall at the base of a gently sloping rise. Dilapidated and in ill-repair, missing whole sections in places. The black, mossy stone marked the edge of Vilka's fortress. At the top, rose a curtain wall and a gate made of the same stone.

Vilka's main tower was a beast of an edifice, a thick and imposing hunk of rock and steel... moving and glinting mechanics in the sheer moonlight.

What kind of place is this? More importantly, Jancy, what's your plan?

She skirted the edge of the wall, looking sharp. If she went up the hill, they'd surely see her. *They? Who?* It didn't matter who. She felt the scryer's roving eyes, felt *other* eyes, too. But then she came to a place where the short wall had crumbled inward, followed by a thick patch of brush and grass intruding up the hill and well into the outer courtyard. The wall was only twenty or thirty yards distant at that strategic point.

Without another thought, Jancy charged silently through the brush, keeping low, then sprinted across the open ground to the wall, slammed her back against the slimy stone, and listened for signs she'd been detected.

Too quick.

She took the shadow stick in her mouth. Its *non-fire* burned her nose and eyes like a smoldering soot as she proceeded to search for purchase up the wall. Her thin fingers found cracks, her toes crevices, and then she was scaling... the inhuman or *unhuman* part of her taking over, an instinctive skill she'd had since she could remember.

At the top, Jancy slipped over and crouched on the battlement, eyes searching. Within the inner yard, she spied a squat tower, its veined, domed ceiling, like translucent skin pulled taut over a brazier, pulsed with a pale, sickly glow. She sprinted down the battlements toward the gate and then angled toward the tower. Leaped... soared... her eyes half-lidded in the gusting wind... until she met the wall. Her fingers gripped the lip of a protruding window sill, her feet knocking gently against the stone below.

She listened for a moment, pulled herself up, and spied inside. The scryer at his work bench, head buried in a contraption made of metal framework and lenses, a scrying stone suspended from wires beneath it. The pale, worm-skinned gnome used handles to maneuver the contraption over a map of the surrounding lands.

Didn't see me, did you?

Jancy crept into the room, drawing one of her twin blades from her hip. Her heart thudded in her chest, her eyes narrowed in focus, her breathing all but silent. She hung close to the wall. Circling... circling...

The gnome jerked up from his divinations and slung a splatter of molten energy where Jancy *used* to be; the scalding magic struck the wall in a sizzling spray. But Jancy had already spun away, appearing in a quiet rush of air to stand beside the surprised wizard. He gasped and fell backward, knocking the contraption from the scrying table, clasping at the blood bubbling hole in his neck.

Jancy wiped her blade on his dingy robe and crept down the spiraling steps of the tower into a single large room. The scryer's living quarters, sparse and bookish, accoutered with the tarnished remnants of some bygone era. She spied the door to the inner courtyard and made for it, hoping the scryer's death had gone unnoticed by the tower's occupants.

Midway into the chamber, she stopped. What was that scuttling? What was that squeak? Her eyes scanned the dark corners, ears strained. There was nothing else alive in the room, she was sure of it.

But then came a thin, quiet *clink*, a slow hiss of steam, and Jancy looked up.

Two spider-like automatons clung to the ceiling, their bulging brass eyes fixed on her. She dove away as they dropped, a cacophony of ear-shattering noise, wiggling torsos flipping, legs flailing as they scrambled to bring her down.

Realizing she couldn't make it to the door before they were on her, Jancy turned and faced the snapping, hissing machines. They were a mass of legs, pincers, and claws, each with a stinger-tipped tail. A burnt oil smell rode blasts of hot steam, nearly choking her. Fast but crude things, stupid and ungainly, they pinched, snagged, and pummeled Jancy before she was able to hold her ground with a flurry of desperate parries, both daggers flashing in sparks against the patchwork appendages.

Most nimble fighters would *never* have chosen daggers so heavy or long, each blade the length of her forearm, yet Jancy found she loved the weight of her weapons in her hands. They were balance and counter-balance, sharp as sin, and when they met their mark, they could punch right through even plate armor, much to more than one armored assailant's surprise.

She leapt above a darting stinger and landed atop one of the wiggling, dog-sized things, burying a blade into a crevice between the head and thorax, pinning it to the ground. Rolled away just as the other crashed through, tearing into its brother in haphazard confusion. Jancy circled, waiting for a proper opening between the snapping, jittering forms.

Breathe. Wait for the itch...

And there was the opening she needed. Jancy reached out and snagged the thing's tail at the base of the stinger, heaved the squealing thing off the pile. Its brass eyes rolled around to find her. It twisted, biting, slicing with an assortment of deadly implements affixed to flexible segmented appendages. Jancy deflected two buzzing saws and buried her remaining blade into its head assembly—ping, ping, *crunch!*—parting the metal plate and cutting through cogs and gears and cables.

The thing crashed limp to the floor, although some internal mechanisms continued to whirr and click in broken confusion.

Jancy sighed. A dull pain in her side screamed. Something warm and wet soaked her shirt. She looked down, although she already knew; the sliver of a hooked leg had buried itself into her flesh.

Damn.

It came out easily enough, had only penetrated a couple of inches, thankfully. Superficial, but it hurt like hell. She dressed the wound with a poultice of herbs and a patch of *sticky leaf* from her light pack. She'd not wanted to waste time doing it, but the bleeding had to be mitigated before she moved on.

Moving to the door, she took a peek into the inner courtyard. Clear, as far as she could tell. Nothing but the sing-song of mechanics coming from the tower, and a slight vibration beneath her feet. Had that been there before? The strange, shifting edifice rose up before her, massive at its base, hardly tapering at all toward the top; three-hundred feet of stone and steel with pinwheels and cogs set flush into the wall or rising and descending through slits. Her curious eyes roamed the moonlit construction, wondering at its marvel. She began to hear a cadence to the cacophony, a *shurrr, shurrr, clink, click, clink, click, thwack!* Over and over.

It must be some kind of war machine, something to thwart an army. Her mind drifted back to Hopper's tale, and she wondered how many Thrasperville gnomes had lost their lives assaulting Vilka's fortress. *Good thing I'm not an army.*

And then another sound made her pulse quicken; the unmistakable, warbling cry of a baby. The child's squall echoed down from the top of the tower, somehow louder than anything else, filling her head with agitation. In Jancy's mind, the child sounded unhappy. Urgent. Alone.

"Bitch," Jancy murmured through pursed lips. On an impulse she opened the door and sprinted across the courtyard. She'd already traced her path up the three-hundred foot tower, and it wouldn't take long for her to get to the top. Then she'd deal with Vilka.

She leapt to clutch one of the steel beams that made a frame at the base of the tower, but a firm hand grasped her foot and jerked her down. She met the ground with mind-numbing force, crushing the air from her lungs, and snapping her teeth together. Her vision went black. Her head rang. Even in her dazed state, having her senses knocked flat out of her, she knew. Something wanted to kill her.

Move... roll... crawl... up... up on your knees... up on your feet! It was all she could think to do until her brain righted itself. All the while, something heavy smashed the ground in pursuit. She tasted dirt and machine oil. Sounded like a giant bashing a tree trunk on the ground!

A moment more... and her vision crawled back; she was in the courtyard, yes.

The violent crashing stopped. She'd outdistanced it.

Another moment... and her head quit ringing; the baby's hiccupping wail cut through.

Jancy turned to meet the thing—a brute of a machine, all chest and piston-thick arms, greased parts flexing, glinting moonlight. It positioned itself between her and the tower with thumping footfalls.

"I could just run around you," she told it, striding forward. "I'm quicker."

The bulk sunk into a crouch. Something inside thrummed with growing intensity.

"But where's the fun in that?"

Jancy burst ahead in a blur of motion. She swung both blades left across her body, allowing their weight to throw her off balance and into a careening stagger. The stuttering, sibilant roar of the automaton burned her ears as it reached out a paw to snatch her up. Jancy's right foot planted itself, stiff-legged, breaking her momentum, reversing her body in a dizzying, slingshot spin. She lost sight of the machine for an instant... until it popped back into view. But by this time, the girl was committed, pitching forward headlong, blades held together, stiff-armed, above her head.

Her momentum carried her off her feet. For an instant, she was airborne. A feeling of weightless elation passed through her before her blades slammed home to the hilt: the joint at the machine's hip, a sliver of hope. A weak spot. Steam ruptured from a sliced pressure line, bathing her face in hot agony. Tiny metal fittings trickled downward out of the wound. Something snapped. The machine's leg buckled, then lifted, and Jancy saw a shred of opportunity. She planted her shoulder into its crotch, gathered her legs, and shoved. Her back screamed, muscles quivering with the effort. If the boys at the Broken Dog could see her now, they'd never take another swipe at her backside again. No, this wasn't something even a very large man would attempt, much less a waif of a girl. Not even a waif, but a *wisp*.

It was the *unhuman* in her.

She gritted and grinned as it pitched... backwards... in a fall that seemed to take an eternity. It shook the ground in a violent crash, arms flailing helplessly. Jancy spied a tiny window on the breast facing, leaking a soft, green light. She leaped atop it and plunged her blade through the glass. The machine stopped moving.

For her own curiosity, she pried open the faceplate with the tip of her blade, and found another gnome inside. Like his kin, that same cold, pale skin, and luminous green eyes that stared up at her, *past* her, at the twinkling sky.

Were these the gnomes who'd supported Vilka in the centuries-old fight for the gnomish throne? Had she blessed them with unusually long life, too? Jancy curled her lip at the gnome's pasty, dead skin. "Some price to pay…"

The wailing baby ripped her attention upward, and soon Jancy was scaling the wall of Vilka's tower.

THIS IS IT. This is the window.

Jancy had followed her ears to the right spot, or so she thought. Wouldn't know for sure until she pulled herself over the jutting, angled ledge to see what awaited her. And would that be Vilka? Yes, certainly. The shadow stick, lost. The scryer, dead. The fight in the yard. The sorceress could *not* have felt Jancy's presence.

So be it.

Jancy took one glance over her shoulder—the breathtaking view from this dizzying height as she clung to the sill's underside like a spider, fingers and thin leather climbing boots locked into the tiniest of crevices, arms and legs bent at rigid angles to keep her from plunging down, down—and took a deep breath of night air.

And then she pulled herself up and over the ledge to land lightly on a plush, animal skin rug. Light oozed from brass wall sconces holding clear domes of glass. A smell like old garments and machine oil tickled Jancy's nose. The room was wide, spanning the tower's full diameter. A set of stairs spiraled up along the wall, another set spiraled down.

Jancy was hardly an expert in valuable antiquities, but even her untrained eye could fathom the pricelessness of the artifacts displayed on the walls, bureaus, and tables all around the room. In a far niche stood a cluster of exotic, pale dolls, clockwork beauties with skin made of porcelain and brass plates, nearly seamless rivet work and clear, vibrant eyes that looked down or away; some right at her.

"Waaaaaa!"

Heart racing, senses piqued to screaming, Jancy darted to an ornate bed in the center of the room, slid across the golden quilt, and landed softly beside a gently rocking cradle. The child's prison swayed of its own volition, the *click, click, click* of mechanisms inside as the machine wheel turned and the rocker arm gently labored.

Jancy stood over it, looking down. She pursed her lips in disappointment. The baby wailed again and Jancy nodded to herself—*dumb, dumb, dumb, Jancy. You are so dumb. A fool, even, for coming here.*

She shook her head and reached inside to touch it, see if it was real. Its skin was cold and unyielding, tarnished, marred with faint, circular scratches from what must have been centuries of polishing. Eyes made of azure-tinted crystal shifted around, looking at nothing. Brass eyelids blinked with soft *claps.* Its hinged mouth flopped open, and that discordant cry came again. "Waaaa!"

"Damn it." *You should have known not to trust a bard's tale. Only half right, it was. He said he'd heard a child, but you never thought to ask him if he'd actually seen it. And you're a fool for not noticing it sooner, so blind...*

"I'm trying to discern what you are." The voice reached her from another part of the room; a child's voice bathed in callousness.

Jancy froze.

"A human? An elf? No, I think neither of those."

Unhuman. Jancy pulled her hands out of the cradle and turned.

The owner of the voice separated herself from the other dolls with slow, easy steps for one so small. She came to just above Jancy's waist but seemed taller. Must be her elegant posture; back straight, shoulders up and stiff, weight balanced perfectly on her hips.

"You're Vilka."

"I am." No hesitation. "But that still doesn't answer my question. What are *you?*" The sorceress lingered in the shadows at the edge of the light, playing.

"Don't you want to know my name?"

Vilka made a dismissive noise. "It hardly matters." She crossed to Jancy's right, passing behind a sitting chair, her pallid hands tracing gently across its back. The sorceress moved in and out of the shadows, exposing her features a little at a time. She wore a simple black gown, slippers on her feet, and bracelets that jangled as she moved. Hair the color of ink fell in tiny ringlets around her brow and down over her shoulders. A sharp jaw was set in something like anger, softened by glowing skin. A startlingly blue eye flashed in the light and then dimmed as the sorcerous found another pocket of darkness.

It was unnerving the way she moved, especially since Jancy had thought herself something of an enigma in that category. "What happened to the baby?"

"The baby? Oh, you mean my son, Nurthrik? He's been gone a very long time, both from this tower and from the face of Sullenor, too. Dead, I'm afraid. But he lived a very long life."

Jancy shook her head in confusion. "I don't understand. Hopper..." *Damn!* She hadn't meant to expose the bard. Well, no use in protecting him now. *That* squirrel was on the spit. "Hopper told me you took the child from the throne room in Thrasperville. That you *stole* him."

Vilka's chuckle was a wicked stab. The sorceress turned and crossed back the other way, toward the window, showing Jancy, quite plainly, the other side of her face. Jancy gasped, stepped back, stomach turning with revulsion. Vilka's face was... it was... skinless... no, plated. No, an assembly. Delicate rivets ran across her forehead, encircled her ear, and plunged beneath her chin. Her jaw was hinged with a finely-grooved bolt. A blue stone blazed from her lidless eye socket. Brass teeth clicked when she spoke, and her voice no longer feigned at kindness or even curiosity. It was cruel. "Is *that* what he said?"

"Yes, and he said you killed so many good gnomes. That you slaughtered them for no other reason than ambition."

"Well, yes. I did the stealing of the child, and the slaughtering. Well, some of it, anyway. But, as usual, the scribes and bards only have one side of the tale. The side that is the most compelling and cruel and pointedly *not* in my favor, no doubt." Vilka was standing not fifteen feet from Jancy, staring out the window. She sighed, cocked her head. "You do know there's always *two*... sides."

"Yes, of course." Jancy sought her itch, longed for it. But it was gone. She was frozen to the spot, unable to move. Barely able to breath. She gulped. "What's your side, then?"

"The truth!" Vilka's chin jutted in defiance. "Hopper painted the Thrasperville colony as the perfect picture of victory over great odds, yes? Pure of purpose?"

Jancy nodded.

"The last of our kind?"

Again, Jancy nodded.

"Hah! No, Thrasperville was founded by criminals and miscreants, necromongers and polymagicians, who fled across the sea to this insipid rock you call Sullenor. We were prisoners of the cogweavers in the old world. Entire generations of us, slaves. Entrapped so long no one remembered why we'd been imprisoned in the first place. So we broke free, killed hundreds of them, stole what we could, and trudged across the sea.

"Who knew that when we came here, we'd turn against one another?" Vilka shrugged. "Looking back, it shouldn't have come as a surprise, I suppose. We all had our egos, and our pride. We all wanted to rule in the new world with the others at our feet. What happened in the throne room at Thrasperville was nothing short of chaos. Bloodshed. Brother against sister. Father against son.

"My stealing that child got their attention. It bound them together. It gave them a common cause. You see, I *saved* that city. They came after me rather than destroy themselves."

"They couldn't defeat you."

"No, they couldn't. And my dear son, Nurthrik, grew up to be quite normal. A great cogweaver in his own right. A decent wizard, even. In fact, he got very bored of this tower and sought his fortune elsewhere, out there in the world." She waved her hand absently at the window. "Met some of our Thrasperville kin who were not happy with the current Mayor, or whatever they called it at the time, and struck out eastward to begin a new city. They called it Hightower, I believe."

Jancy's nerves began to calm as she sensed the truth in Vilka's story. Jancy knew the hearts of men, had witnessed their cruelty and malice firsthand, and she figured they weren't too far removed from the hearts of gnomes. She could picture the slaughter in the throne room; a combination of her and Hopper's tales, the truth lying somewhere in between the tellings. It didn't matter, though, because there was no child in danger. There was no *child*. Jancy had no reason to be here, no reason to trouble this gnomestress, strange as she may be, any longer.

"Why do you keep this?" Jancy nodded to the hulk of metal in the cradle.

A flash of sadness passed over the Vilka's face, a quick sprinkle of sorrow, and "because it reminds me of him. My son."

Someone else's son. But Jancy didn't press the point. "I'm sorry for coming here. I shouldn't have. I didn't know—"

"Yes, assumptions. They always get us into trouble, don't they? I find it ironic that a *baby stealer* came here to accuse me of the selfsame thing."

"I don't *steal* them."

"Oh? What would you call it, then? Did you come all this way because you thought it was hungry?"

"No!" Jancy bit her tongue. That itch wiggled inside her belly, that tease of premonition she always got when something was about to go horribly wrong. "I'll just be going, if you don't mind." Jancy started to slide across the bed, since Vilka was directly in her path if she wanted to go around it, but the sorceress stepped quickly and quietly toward the window, blocking the way out. Her gaze remained outside, though, leaving that awful side of her face for Jancy to consider.

"You won't take the stairs? Don't you trust me?"

Jancy stopped, put her feet back on the ground. "I don't even know you."

"That's right," Vilka's voice dripped venom. "And you broke into my home."

Jancy shifted nervously from one foot to the other. She'd already taken stock of every possible escape route, but the only sure exit was out the window, *through* the sorceress. "I... I apologize for that. My intentions were—."

Vilka faced Jancy, smiled, half honey, half horror. "Apology *not* accepted. You see, if I let everyone simply stroll in here, have a cup of tea, and then leave, I fear my reputation would suffer. I might even seem somehow *vulnerable* to those wobbleheads up in Thrasperville who, for the most part, have forgotten all about me."

Jancy's body became taut for a nervous moment and then relaxed into state of calm resignation. It would be a fight. She could feel it.

"Plus I have a collection to keep up." The sorceress gestured to a large tank behind Jancy, a massive block of glass so opaque that not even Jancy's superior eyes could pierce it. Now, though, it was crystalizing, clearing, so that she could see what was stored there...

Jancy gasped, unbelieving.

Heads.

In ornate glass jars.

Bloated things in some murky brine. Humans and elves, dwarves with their beards spun around at the bottoms, trolls in the bigger ones. But mostly gnomes. Old ones, to be sure; flesh sloughed and floating in that putrid slosh. Jancy felt their eyes on her. Accusing! They all knew what she'd been doing these past few years. *Fixing* those poor fathers and wretched mothers, killing, no, *murdering* anyone that didn't fit her sense of right and good. Whispers in Half Town's taverns spoke of a misguided vigilante. She knew then that hers would be the next head in a jar. And probably Hopper's soon after.

She returned Vilka's wicked stare, blue eyes against green, her fingers brushing the hilts of her knives.

And then Jancy got the itch to move...

ANGEL OF TEARS
·A TALE OF THE WORLD OF RUIN·

Erik Scott de Bie

The Outpost of Gardh
Winter 978, Sorcerus Annis

MIDNIGHT'S CHILL WIND swept up the gray snow into skirling ghosts that danced wildly in the deserted street, radiant in the moonlight and beautiful in the silence. At a distance, these specters seemed harmless, but only a fool or a corpse would believe it. Winter had come in earnest to the northland, and with it dense flurries of the burning rain from the gray skies. The snow sizzled against the tar-sealed oak buildings and seared exposed flesh, leaving red streaks that could take years to fade.

Pain in beauty—such is the World of Ruin.

The Victorious Hunter, Gardh's stout common hall, squatted beneath a corroded sign that depicted a leaping hart, an arrow thrust through its breast. Someone had drunkenly shot an actual arrow through the coat of arms, but the shaft had found the animal's rump rather than its heart. The sign twisted lazily in the cold breeze.

Within, a dozen wind-burned men and women in worn garments perched around stained tables cluttered with half-empty tankards and tureens of congealed stew. They had returned from a hard day's labor spent hacking at trees and tearing the frozen ground, all the while avoiding the blistering snowfall. A harried dark-haired woman of about twenty winters moved among them with practiced grace pouring ale, mead, and fresh bowls of wine. A crackling alchemical fire kept the chilling darkness at bay, its purple flames pungent enough to fill the room with the smell of metallic lavender.

A single man sat at a table in the center of the room, as he did every night when the sun fell and cold swept through Gardh. He had seen perhaps forty or so winters, but his posture made him seem much older. The weight of the season, of the town spiraling into ruin, of the decaying world itself—all of it seemed to rest on his shoulders. A forward-curved sword sheathed in a worn scabbard lay on the table within his reach, but he hardly seemed aware of its presence. He bore a single mark upon his face: a black inked teardrop below his left eye, which glittered faintly in the firelight.

The old man stared at his stew in its stale-hardened trencher, and the small loaf of the same bread sitting alongside it. He hesitated before eating, as he did every night, as if considering starvation as a preferred fate. Ultimately, he took up the bread and began mopping the stew into his mouth, and all assembled breathed a faint sigh of relief.

Little changed in Gardh, not since the mage-city Tar Vangr had abandoned the place to its fate years before. Life proceeded in the same dreary circle year after year.

Until the traveler came.

The thick oak door rattled open, admitting a gust of cold wind and setting the worn metal fittings to vibrating against the wood.

It produced a grating sound that filled the common room, drawing a chorus of glares that ranged from the irritated to the suspicious. A single figure crossed the threshold—slight and soft of step, with snowflakes sizzling on her gray cloak. Her features hid beneath a thick leather mask and tinted goggles to keep the snow from her face. She breathed hollowly through the sweaty cloth over her nose and mouth.

Despite the scrutiny of every gaze upon her, the woman stepped boldly a few paces inside and scanned the common hall for something in particular. When her eyes settled on the old man sitting in the middle of the room—the only one not watching her—she drew in a breath in both relief and unexpected anger. She strode to his side and stood across the table from him, arms crossed.

"Regel," she said, her voice muted through her leather mask.

"Serris." He kept his eyes fixed on his stew, eating slowly.

The traveler undid the cowl she had pulled tight against the scalding snow, releasing a fall of golden hair, and unbuckled the mask she'd worn against the cold. The heat of the common hall put a touch of color in Serris's sharp-featured face and made the livid red scar that cut from cheek to jawline glow brightly. Like unto that of the old man, she bore a teardrop mark of her own, inked in the same place. Serris had fierce gray eyes like the heart of a snowstorm, which seemed to absorb the firelight in the room. Only a fool or a madman would not recognize her wrath from a distance.

Regel gestured to the opposite seat without looking up. "Sit. Your road was long, I expect."

"Long enough." Liberated from her mask, Serris looked around at the patrons of the common hall, as if she had noticed for the first time that they existed, and dismissed them all. She sat, staring across at her master with cold focus. "Time to come back," she said. "The Circle of Tears needs you."

Regel gave a slight shrug, barely moving his shoulders.

Seeing his indifference made Serris bite her lip to restrain her anger. "I stood by you for years while you let this pain rot you from the inside, and for what?" She leaned forward and put her elbows on the table. "Are you any better? Is *this* any better?"

Regel shrugged once more. "I have a new master now," he said. "A purpose."

Serris narrowed her eyes. "And who must I kill to relieve you of it?"

She became aware of another presence and tensed for an attack that never came.

"Coin?" The dark-haired ale-bearer stood beside their table, her deep brown eyes focused on Serris. She held aloft a tray with a rough-bread trencher of stew, which quivered on the surface and smelled quite wonderful, as well as a steaming bowl warm with mulled wine.

"Of course." Serris fished out her purse and set two silver coins freshly minted with the mark of Tar Vangr on the table. "This enough?"

The woman looked down at the proffered silver with widening eyes, then swept them up with a flick of her wrist. "More than," she said as she set out the stew. "Rooms are all full."

"Food and a place by the fire. And these." Serris fumbled a weathered bit of paper out of her belt pouch and plunked down two more coins atop it. "Supplies for the road for my master and me."

The ale-bearer unfolded the paper and scrutinized it, then shook her head. She looked embarrassed. "I cannot read."

That made Serris smile despite herself. "I couldn't either," she said.

The woman returned the smile, and the expression made her face lovely. She smelled strongly of lilac rather than the dull, false lavender scent that filled the room. Serris found it refreshing.

"I'll give this to the quartermaster." Hastily, she tucked the note and the coins into her bodice. She glanced about the hall, visibly uneasy.

Serris caught the woman by the wrist. "What?"

"Naught. Only…" The woman looked down at Serris's hand on her wrist, cool fingers pressed against her veins, and Serris could feel the woman's heartbeat quicken at the unexpected intimacy. Years of hard work had roughened the woman's skin, and she felt strong. "Pass wary." She hurried away.

The ale-bearer had glanced twice at a group of men sitting a few paces distant, who had not taken their eyes from Serris since her arrival. Not that she blamed them—she was an outsider, and she saw no one else in the room with hair the color of fresh straw. Their gaze made Serris acutely aware of the scar that ran from her cheek down to her jaw, making her stand out even more. One of the men cast a greasy smile in Serris's direction and made a lewd gesture with his pipe. Shame rose up, but she throttled it down. Fear belonged to the old life she had left behind. Instead, she let her anxiety become anger.

Serris felt Regel stir across the table, but he merely went back to spooning his stew into his mouth with the regularity of an automaton. Serris sniffed at her own food and scowled. She hadn't eaten in more than a day, but she could not make herself do so now. Her stomach churned under the scrutiny.

Two of the men approached, as she had known they would. They wore hunting leathers etched with the mark of a fist clutching three arrows. *Local soldiers*, she thought. One of them took up a stance just to her right and behind, while the other slid his fleshy form onto the bench at her side. He had the face of a man firmly convinced of his own strength and charm but the eyes of a coward.

"Not invited," she said. "Leave."

"What's a matter, beautiful?" The local breathed sour wine and pipe smoke in her face. "Too long without a sword in your sheath?"

Smoothly, Serris retrieved her tankard and took a long pull, using the gesture to conceal the dagger she drew from her belt and clutched in one white-knuckled hand. The old blade had become well worn, but she kept it honed and polished. Two years before, Regel had given her the dagger—the first weapon she had ever possessed, and the only one she would ever need. "Do not touch me," she said.

Coward-Eyes ignored the warning. "You're a whore, right? I can smell it. Lots of men touched you." He traced the air just above her scar. "Looks like one missed. Mayhap I should try—"

Serris splashed the contents of her tankard into his face and jammed her dagger through his hand into the table. At first, the man's face scrunched in confusion, then opened in a flurry of agony. Blood welled around the fine steel, and the man screamed in shock and horror. Reflexively, he wrenched away, but the dagger held fast and his pain only worsened. With a certain fascination, Serris heard the rattle of bones and saw flesh sawing itself against the blade. She tried to pull the dagger free, but she'd nailed it into the table too firmly and it resisted.

The man behind Serris lunged and she felt him touch her shoulder.

Then Regel moved, almost too fast to see, and the air parted around the right side of Serris's face. The man who had grabbed for her staggered back, clutching at his hand. His fingers sailed through the air to plunk against the ceiling, then rained down onto the table around them. One struck Coward-Eyes in the face, and his screaming redoubled. Serris looked at one that had fallen near her, and marveled at its seared stump, which squeezed out not a single drop of blood.

Regel paused for a moment—half-standing, half-sitting—with his blue-bladed sword gleaming in his hands. Then he set the deadly blade on the table beside its scabbard and returned to his stew without a word. At this distance, Serris could feel the weapon, called *Frostburn*, like a shard of ice, hungrily drinking in the warmth of the fire and nearby bodies.

Serris looked at her initial assailant, whose hand had become a seeping fountain of blood and pus on the table. Wordlessly, she laid her second hand on the handle of her dagger and wrenched the blade free. Coward-Eyes staggered back, jostling another table and showering blood all over. He stumbled and cursed and fled, as did his maimed companion. She made sure to wipe her dagger in full view of the hall.

Conversations faltered into silence and all eyes fell on Serris, but she ignored them in favor of Regel. Her heart raced. She had seen it for just a moment—that same fire that had woke a walking dead girl and turned her to an angel.

"The Winterblood knew respect, once," Regel said. "All unravels..."

"All falls to ruin." Serris touched him on the wrist. "Come with me."

His icy eyes burned into hers. She saw anger there—rage against the injustice of his imprisonment—but he could not come with her. Not yet.

"You'll come with *us*," a voice said.

Two soldiers in ringmail emblazoned with the fistful of arrows sigil stood at her sides, both pointing casters that crackled with full thaumaturgical charges. Lightning raced along the bow of the weapon on her left, while the murderpiece on her right smoked with fire magic. Each soldier wore a leather hauberk etched with the same arms as the two who had assaulted Serris. Wrath scripted the contours of the soldiers' faces, and murder shone in their eyes. The woman was badly burned all along her face, and the man wore a crimson beard shot through with gray patches, like bones floating in blood.

Serris looked across at Regel, who focused again on his stew. He showed no sign of aiding her. She had no allies in this place. She stood and walked away, spine erect, between the two soldiers.

———

AS THE SOLDIERS led Serris up a creaking spiral staircase, growing hotter as they rose, she noted which boards made the most noise. Ultimately, they reached a balcony above the main area dimly lit with two smoking braziers that burned the same alchemical incense as below. The lavender aroma became a cloying morass at this height, and Serris felt swelteringly hot in her winter clothes, and she tried to ignore her discomfort by looking out over the heads of the patrons.

From this perspective, Serris saw so much more than she had from the entrance. Some patrons played at bone cards, and she could pick out those who cheated and hid cards behind their backs or up their sleeves. More than a few patrons subtly enjoyed each other with their hands below the table, and she saw a few ready weapons in case a situation turned violent. Had the soldiers not stopped her, Serris might have faced an entire hall of foes.

"Remarkable," a man said behind her. "The difference a small change in elevation makes."

The ruler of the Victorious Hunter stood from a throne-like seat that was the finest she'd seen outside Tar Vangr: a wide, padded throne of red leather and feather pillows. He wore threadbare robes that seemed nonetheless more extravagant than anything else worn in the common hall. He had graying raven hair and a network of riverbed-like wrinkles that made his unreadable eyes into pits of pitch. Serris saw immediately the man was no warrior, but in her experience that made him no less dangerous.

"I am Jeht, Defender of Gardh." He bowed. "Be welcome in my hall, Serris, Angel of Tears."

Serris met his courtesy with indifference. "You know me?"

He smiled. "Your master has told me often of you."

She understood. "Lord of Gardh, then."

His mouth curled into an expression halfway between bemusement and curiosity. He waved the soldiers to lower their weapons, which they did with only a touch of hesitation.

"Gardh has no ruler and never will," he said. "I am its protector. I deal with threats to its safety, as you have so eloquently proved yourself." He draped himself back into his throne. "Please. Sit."

He gestured to a cushioned divan positioned two paces away and lower than his own throne. Serris saw, in the flickering firelight, that others had clustered behind Jeht's seat: beautiful men and women, clad in silks and chains, the eldest no older than she. Serris recognized the desperation in their faces mingled with a growing resignation to their awful fate. She had lived with the same dying hope for years until Regel had saved her, and to see it now made her teeth stand on edge. She remained standing.

"You seem ill at ease, Serris," Jeht said. "You have not yet eaten of my food, yes? Please, accept my hospitality, so we can sit as friends rather than enemies."

He gestured one of his slaves to bring her a platter of sweet flatbread, and she took a piece. The ancient forms craved respect, after all. When she had tasted it, the soldiers relaxed their guard.

"You call my master one of your servants," Serris said. "I would persuade you to release him."

"A true opening thrust, one without hesitation or guile. This, I like." Jeht grinned. "He is of great value to me. If you compensate me for his loss, I will free him."

Serris had started to dislike his smiles. She would not bother to ask how Jeht controlled the greatest assassin Tar Vangr had ever known. She gritted her teeth. "Speak your price."

Jeht held out a hand to the male guard, who handed him a yellowed, much-read scroll. Serris noted the broken seal, which made her breath catch. She knew the fiery mark of Blood Ravalis. "This arrived two years ago, only days after the fall of the Winter King. It states that the conspirators who overthrew him had fled the city. It offers a description of your master and his fabulous sword, and—"

"Liar." Serris half-drew her dagger, prompting the soldiers to aim their casters at her. "Regel loved the Winter King. Had nothing to do with his murder. That was Ovelia the Bloodbreaker."

"As you say." Unconcerned with her, the so-called Defender of Gardh spread out the scroll. "In any case, the Ravalis offer a prescription prize for his return, or a lesser reward for that of his corpse. I suspect they would pay a prize for you as well."

"That a threat?" Serris glanced at the soldier to her left, whose fingers had gone white around the haft of her caster. The woman's blue eyes burned with a building rage, and Serris knew she awaited a single gesture to strike. She smiled up at her. "I could simply take him."

Jeht waved his hand to indicate the hall and its many grizzled occupants. "Over the last fifteen years, Gardh has accumulated a goodly number of hardened soldiers—outcasts, brigands, exiles disaffected with the rise of the Ravalis in Tar Vangr. None of them have read this scroll, but do you think they would treat with you any better than I? And while you may excel with a blade, do you truly believe you can slay every man or woman with a blade in this place? *Would* you?"

Serris saw the futility of her position. She understood the knife Jeht held over Regel, and now over her. She pointedly sheathed her dagger, and the soldiers relaxed. The tension eased in everyone but her. At the edge of her vision, she thought she saw someone watching from the stairs. She caught a flash of dark hair and eyes against a pale face.

"Now that we understand each other," Jeht said. "I shall think on what service you might provide me to discharge your master from my debt. In the meantime, you will eat and drink and sleep in this hall, my guests and under my protection. And tomorrow, we shall discuss the first of your tasks for me." He grinned that same infuriating grin. "I'm sure I can find a use for you, despite the scar."

Serris nodded, rose without a word, and headed down the stairs.

———•———

THE FOLK OF the hall had started to shuffle off, either lying down closer to the fire or braving the snow to return to their homes. A few found shadowed alcoves together, and Serris heard giggling and sharp intakes of breath that told her all she needed to know of their activities. She stood alone in the common hall, veritably trembling with rage, while Jeht's soldiers looked on, smirking at her. Serris found Regel still sitting in the center of the room and went to stand over him.

"You are a...*slave* to that man." The word came hard. She had been a slave until Regel had freed her. "How dare you?"

"What choice do I have?" Regel spoke softly. "I have a life here. I sleep in safety. I eat. I live."

"You *live*." Contempt dripped from her tongue. "Flee, more like. How long have you hid in this place, away from your path?" She closed her fists. "What of tomorrow? Or the next day? When we become his whores to do with as he pleases?"

"What is tomorrow?" Regel asked. "Or the next day? Or the next?"

The fiery, fearless man who had saved her from a wrathful lord seemed to have melted away. No longer did Regel see any path before him. Serris understood, in a way, after his entire world had dissolved beneath his feet. And yet, she could not help the rage that built within her to see him so helpless.

From her pocket, she drew forth a hunk of reddish rosewood, a piece of a dying tree in a very special garden back in Tar Vangr. As far as she knew, that tree numbered among the last of its kind in the World of Ruin, where centuries of conflict and the continual assault of the world's monsters had all but eradicated civilization. Firmly but with a touch of reverence, Serris set the hunk of wood on the table beside Regel's mostly empty trencher.

"You saved me once," she said as she turned to go. "Now it's my turn."

Regel stared at the wood for a long, long time. He picked up the chunk of rosewood and turned it over in his hand, exploring its contours. What he saw in its depths, none could say, but he certainly saw something. Then he palmed a small, sharp knife from his sleeve and began to carve.

———◆———

SERRIS WOKE LATER that night, though she could not immediately say why.

At a glance the hall stood empty of activity, its rough-hewn floor covered with huddled bodies in varied attitudes of sleep. The fire had burned down to purple-glowing embers, their lavender scent reduced to the odor of wilting flowers. She half-expected to find Regel beside her, but Jeht's favorite pet likely had his own chambers. Perhaps it was for the best. She had learned in their time together that he too slept only lightly, and his absence gave her the chance to deal with the threat alone.

Only when she saw the shadowed figure lurking behind a pillar nearby did Serris understand what had awakened her: the scent of lilac.

Serris drew her dagger subtly, then waited until the ale-bearer came upon her. When a tentative hand reached for her shoulder, Serris caught the woman by the wrist and put the dagger to her throat. She gazed up into her dark eyes, speaking without words. They exchanged a nod. Slowly, the women rose together and left the common hall, out into the snowy night.

The storm had passed, and moonlight illumined the empty street and the yard littered with corroded bits of metal, splintered lengths of wood, and other trash. It felt entirely too open, where anyone could see or hear them. The cold made Serris's exposed skin itch and she pulled the ale-bearer in close. She could feel the woman's body like a blazing beacon in the night and wanted all of it. The blade in her hand grounded her, though, and she resisted the urge. They could not tarry out here.

Serris forced the ale-bearer ahead of her and into the comparative warmth of the stable. The pitch-treated wood creaked around them, and snow made the roof groan. A dozen horses occupied the stalls, draped with blankets for warmth. The beasts seemed thin and weak compared to the one Serris had ridden to Gardh. At the end, her stallion whickered softly, luminous black eyes blinking sleepily at its mistress, then turned back to its rest. She recognized Regel's black stallion snoring nearby.

Serris pushed the ale-bearer ahead of her onto the loose hay and stood over her. "Why did you wake me?" She gestured with the dagger. "You trying to kill me?"

The woman watched her, unmoved by the gleaming blade. She rose to her full height. "If you thought that, you'd have killed me already," she said. "Do you have a name?"

"My master named me Serris, for the angel of vengeance."

"That is beautiful." She came forward and laid her hands on Serris's hips gently. Suggestively. "I've done nothing worthy of a name, but I aspire to do so one day."

"Answer." Serris pressed her dagger against the woman's neck. "What do you want?"

"I think you know."

Heedless of the blade, the ale-bearer leaned forward and kissed

Serris. Her lips were warm and soft despite the frigid air. Her hands massaged Serris's sore backside and slid along her taut muscles. In that touch, Serris felt the rage of so many futile months melting, and her body relaxed. She lowered the dagger and seized the woman's head to kiss her back. When the ale-bearer pulled her down into the straw, Serris followed gladly. She dropped the dagger onto the floor.

The woman had her bodice unlaced and her breast freed to the cool air before Serris came back to her senses. "Wait," she said. "Why seduce me?"

"You know that, too." The woman smiled with her full, sweet lips. "Or do you object?"

"No." Serris kissed her.

The woman wrapped her legs around Serris's waist and pulled her back to the ground. Their bodies coursed together for one shivering moment. Warm hands reached inside Serris's clothes, lighting her skin to tingling. Need burned in her core. It had been so *long*.

Through force of will, Serris pulled back, breaking their lips apart. "I know you want something," she said. "But why *me*? Why not my master? I am but a learner—he is far greater. Why have you never tried to win *him*?"

That gave the woman pause, and Serris could almost see her mind working to find an answer that would not offend. "He is...broken."

The ardor cooled in Serris, and she pulled away to sit back on her haunches. The dagger Regel had given her lay next to her left foot, but she made no move to reclaim it. She did not want to touch it.

"He watched the king he had served all his life die," Serris said. "He has lost everything."

The woman sat up behind her and wrapped her arms around her. Serris welcomed the warmth. "He has you," the woman said as she rubbed Serris's shoulders. "You can save him. Save all of us."

"He has spent years fleeing me." Serris shook her head.

To that, the woman had no answer. She turned Serris toward her and ran her fingers along the lines of her cheeks and jaw. Her touch made the cut on Serris's face stab sharply, and she looked away.

"You shouldn't hide it," the woman said. "You're beautiful despite it."

Serris drew in a breath, then blew it out slowly. "What would you have me do?"

The dim moonlight dancing in her dark eyes, the ale-bearer smiled and kissed Serris again.

———•———

LATER, AS THE moon dipped toward the distant horizon but dawn had not yet arrived, the storm returned in force, and the gale woke Semana as she lay entwined with the nameless, raven-haired woman in the stable. She thought, for a moment, that someone stood above her—perched upon one of the rafters like a carrion bird scrutinizing its next meal. She felt icy eyes watching her and thought the world had become just a touch colder. When she blinked to clear her gaze, her watcher had vanished.

As she drifted toward wakefulness, Serris burrowed closer into the woman to cling to the warm comfort of that moment as much as she could. Then she rose silently, affixed her clothing, and pushed out into the swirling storm, head down against the wind.

In the early hours before dawn, the Victorious Hunter seemed more like a death house than a common hall. All slumbered soundly, desperately clawing at the last bit of sleep their harsh world granted them. The nauseating reek of lavender had subsided somewhat as the fire burned low, and now Serris could smell sweat and unwashed flesh. The whole place stank.

Shortly, the cooks would rise to stoke the fire and commence the process of feeding Gardh, but Serris had an hour yet. She stole soundlessly among the sleeping bodies, a wraith made of winter wind and purpose. She climbed the stairs, making certain not to step on any of the boards that had creaked the first time. At the top of the stairs, Jeht's soldiers stirred sleepily and raised their weapons, but she held out her hands to signify peace.

"Need to see Lord Jeht," she said. "Alone."

The burned woman narrowed her eyes. "To what end?"

Slowly, Serris reached to the laces of her bodice and gave a tug, letting the garment slide loose to reveal a gentle expanse of bare flesh. She raised her chin and gave the guards a suggestive look.

"Ruin smiles upon Jeht," the male guard said under his breath.

The other guard scowled. "Your weapons."

Serris flinched away from her grasp, stepping into the male guard, but the female guard pulled her off before the man could touch her. She ran her hands along Serris's limbs and body, finding nothing but the fine dagger sheathed at her belt. The woman took the blade, then nodded.

Serris entered into Jeht's court above the common room. The ceiling creaked under the onslaught of the storm but held. The Defender of Gardh sat dozing upon his throne, while his slaves lay slumped about the room in various states of undress. Serris crept toward him, making no sound on her graceful feet, but his eyes opened all the same when she came within two paces.

"Ah," he said with a self-satisfied smile. He stretched, fully confident that she intended him no violence. "As I expected. You've come to bargain for your master."

"In a way."

Serris reached toward her laces, making Jeht's smile widen. When she reached inside her bodice, however, his brow furrowed. When she drew forth a small scroll, his expression grew utterly confused.

"What is—?" he asked, then his eyes went wide. "No."

"Yes."

Serris held out the item she had stolen from the guard at the stairs: the scroll promising the proscription prize for Regel's return. Casually, she cast it into the nearest brazier, and the old, dry paper caught within a heartbeat. Jeht rose, but Serris kicked him back into his seat and held him down with one foot. Black char swept across the scroll, and the long-ago broken wax bubbled and melted away.

"Do you...?" Jeht looked torn between confusion and fear. "Do you know what you've done?"

Serris stepped off him, interlaced her fingers, and cracked her knuckles. "Murdered you."

The soldiers appeared within a three-count, drawn to the commotion. They hissed challenges and pointed their casters at Serris, who had eyes only for Jeht. His various love-slaves had started to awaken, and they scrambled away from the throne.

A chill swept through the room, though Serris felt no breeze. The last remnants of warmth from the braziers vanished, consumed by something cold and ravenous. The burned soldier and the one with the patchwork beard shivered. The Defender of Gardh's face widened in rising horror and Serris knew he understood what she had brought to pass.

One of Jeht's slaves noticed first and uttered a tiny gasp of surprise. That drew Serris's gaze to the throne, and she saw him. Regel stood over Jeht, his curved sword like a sharpened icicle poised at the lord's throat. None had seen his approach, and none could move fast enough to stop him. And now that his shackles had broken—Jeht's last hold over him burned away—Regel Frostburn, once-shadow of the Winter

King, would call no man master any longer.

All fell to silence and stillness, but for Jeht's accelerating breathing, which turned to terrified sobs. He inched away from the sword, but its unearthly cold held him in thrall. A dark stain spread across the front of his robes and his eyes rolled back and forth madly in his head. Serris watched as Regel destroyed his once-captor without uttering a word or making a single move. With only a glare and the weight of his presence, Regel the Frostburn unmade the man to his very core.

"Squire," he said finally.

"Master?" Serris replied, her voice soft.

"Ready our horses." He drew the sword away from Jeht's throat and the man swooned on the throne. "We are done here."

"Not going to kill him?" Serris asked.

Regel looked at the two soldiers, who lowered their weapons and refused to meet his eye. When he passed them on his way to the stairs, they turned murderous eyes on their humbled leader.

As they walked away, Jeht pleaded for mercy that would not come, and his words became cries and then groans. Serris allowed herself a tiny smile of satisfaction.

They descended toward the common hall, which had come drowsily awake at the sounds from above. Confusion reigned, and a thousand murmured questions danced across the room like crackling flames. But one stood ready to answer those questions: the dark-haired woman of an age with Serris, who had laid down her trays and rose to the center of the throng. All turned to the ale-bearer, and she held the residents of the hall under her sway.

"Know that I have done this," she said. "Jeht has betrayed the confidence of Gardh and has lost the power he once held to hold you under his thrall. I take the name Phend, the ancient guardian, for I will be Gardh's new Defender."

At first, Serris did not understand, but then Regel answered her unspoken question.

"She is Jeht's daughter," he said.

The revelation stabbed Serris in the gut. She could almost feel a blade sawing through her innards, and she could imagine the dark eyes of the one who held it by the hilt.

They paused on the threshold of the Victorious Hunter. The storm had lessened and now hung over the horizon, brooding and rousing itself to new violence. The road to Tar Vangr stretched before them, and Serris knew they should go. But she could not—not yet.

"Hold!" The newly-named Phend appeared behind them, and Serris turned to her. The women stared at one another over the intervening pace, which felt like leagues.

"I owe you a debt," Phend said. "My father has lost the fear and respect of the people, and his power lies broken. You are the one who made that possible. I will not forget this." She reached out and traced the scar on Serris's face. "You are so beautiful—my flawed Angel."

Serris considered for a moment, then turned and left without a word. Phend bowed her head.

———◆———

THEY SADDLED THEIR horses in the stable, falling as of old into a companionable, efficient silence. Serris felt shame and sorrow rising, but she would not give it tears. She could still feel Phend's fingers tracing the gash along her cheek, burning hot with angry shame. When she thought Regel was not watching, she touched it lightly and almost wept.

Only when they sat stride their horses in Phend's main street did master look to the squire who had saved him and speak.

"Your scar is not a flaw," Regel said. "It is part of you. A strength."

Serris glanced over at him and their eyes met. "So is your pain," she said.

Regel considered a moment, then nodded. He put out his hand and Serris took it.

They rode away from Gardh under an uneasy sky.